The Last Casualty of the Great War

The Last Casualty of the GREAT WAR

A Novel

GREGORY M. GALVIN

THE LAST CASUALTY OF THE GREAT WAR
A NOVEL

iUniverse books may be ordered through booksellers or by contacting:

iUniverse LLC
1663 Liberty Drive
Bloomington, IN 47403
www.iuniverse.com
1-800-Authors (1-800-288-4677)

ISBN: 978-1-4917-4559-5 (sc)
ISBN: 978-1-4917-4560-1 (e)

Library of Congress Control Number: 2014916393

Printed in the United States of America.

iUniverse rev. date: 09/29/2014

This story is dedicated to my brother Casey.

ACKNOWLEDGMENTS

To Amy Murray for again being the first to read this story. She improved it greatly by freely sharing her thoughts.

To Christl Webster for helping with the German-language phrases.

To Michael Creese for granting permission to use an image of his original oil painting *Poppies in Flanders Field.*

To the National World War I Museum at Liberty Memorial in Kansas City, Missouri, for the privilege of volunteering at this world-class museum. The National World War I Museum is dedicated to bringing to life the stories of those involved in the war. This story could be just one of millions.

To my wife, Sandy, for so much.

MAPLETON VALLEY

JULY 23

One

What is it about this face of mine? John Alston thought to himself. He pursed his lips, narrowed his eyes, and cocked his head to the right as he regarded the man in front of him.

On the near side of fifty-two, John Alston considered himself the poster boy for physical failings of men of a certain age: thinning and receding hair that, in his case, used to be a brackish-blond but was now chalky gray; gray-blue eyes that needed stronger glasses and brighter bulbs each year; facial jowls that hung pendulously down, looking like those on a basset hound; and a paunch encroaching ever more into his own view of his feet. On occasions when he ran into a long-lost high-school chum surprised at how much he had changed, John would say with a chuckle, patting his belly and the top of his head at the same time, "It's just not fair; I'm thickening and thinning at the same time."

After shifting weight from one foot to the other and then clearing his throat, the man opposite him asked in an embarrassed tone, "You're not who I thought you were, are you?"

Mentally, John ticked off the number of times in the past three years alone someone had mistaken him for somebody else. And such mistakes had occurred not only in Mapleton Valley. Not long before, while on business for the day in Tulsa, his lunch server had asked while dropping off the check, "Are you hiring servers at your restaurant? I'd like to work there."

He had given her his special look—the one for just such occasions—that said, *I don't know what you're talking about.*

That had caused her to blush.

"I guess you're not who I thought you were, huh?" she said.

He had shaken his head. "No, I'm not even from here."

"I'm sorry. It's just that you look like the general manager at the bar and grill down the street. I'd love to work there; the crowd is bigger, and I hear the tips are better. Can I get you anything else?" she had asked, an awkward smile on her face.

Backing away, she had turned and quickly disappeared.

Watching her hasty retreat from over the top of his glasses, John had sensed she would not be back to make change for the twenty he had slipped into the check jacket. She had ended up with a nice tip.

John turned his attention back to the man in front of him. "No, I'm not who you think I am. I don't have any kids at Driscoll High School. I live in a different district, and mine have graduated to boot. Don't feel bad; it happens more times than you can imagine."

"It's just that—"

John held up a hand. "Let me tell you about one time—really an unbelievable story. You won't feel so self-conscious when I'm done. It's been almost ten years, maybe longer; I was having lunch with a coworker in the sandwich shop in the back of Gilded Steer Steakhouse. Do you know the place?"

"The one in the French Bottoms?" the man replied hesitantly. "I know of it, but I've never been there. I live and work out south and wouldn't think of venturing down there unless I had to."

"Yeah." John nodded. "The one in the French Bottoms. That's too bad about not going down there; it's an interesting part of town—great old buildings and lots of town history. Since you don't know the place, let me tell you the setup. You have to go round back and enter through a rickety old door; they keep the front door locked and the front part, the nice part, shut during lunch. Once inside, you'll find a queue snaking its way up to a cafeteria-style line where you grab one of those molded fiberglass serving trays; you've seen them, I'm sure. They're green or tan—or were at one time—and most of them are chipped or cracked. Stray fiberglass strands stick out in all directions like eyebrows," he said, motioning towards his own.

The man grinned in understanding.

"Anyway, you grab a tray and slide it along a stainless-steel rail in front of the food-service area. You can't see the food, because the glass panes are fogged up. The daily special is an open-face sandwich—either smoked turkey or roasted beef, fresh from the night before, both thinly sliced and piled thick on white bread. It's served with a heaping helping of mashed potatoes, and it's all drowned in gravy, brown or white—your choice. After you've paid, you go find a seat at long Formica-topped tables, set end to end—the kind you'd see in school or church cafeterias. The tabletops are chipped or have names, initials, and other stuff carved into them. Their edges are ragged, so if you're wearing a tie, make sure you tuck it into your shirt or else—a lesson I've learned and relearned several times. The chairs are folding metal. Some have cushions; most don't. When it's really crowded, which is most days, you've got to thread your way past those already sitting down; the ends having already been taken. You'll probably end up in the middle next to or across from somebody you've probably never seen before and aren't likely to see again, except there. If you're outgoing, it's a nice way to make a new acquaintance; if not, you're only put out for about thirty minutes."

John stopped; his eyes glazed over for a second, as if reflecting on something.

"Anyway, this coworker and I'd gotten there early enough to get an end. We'd just about finished, when an older woman—the age my mom would've been at the time—came up to our table. Without any warning whatsoever, she bent over from the waist and leaned in; she was no more than four or five inches away when she whispered just a bit too loud in a raspy voice, 'I can't believe you've come to town and haven't come to see me.'

"I looked first at her and then turned to the person sitting off to my left," John recounted, physically acting out his narrative, "thinking she must be talking to him. When that person showed no sign of recognition, I slowly turned back to her, not really sure who her statement was meant for.

"She was glaring at me. 'Ma'am, are you talking to me?' I asked innocently. I asked because I didn't know who she was; in fact, I'd never seen her before.

"'Who else would I be speaking to?' she answered by asking. You can imagine my surprise at that!" John bolted upright, acting out his astonishment.

"When I didn't answer, she continued, her voice a bit more agitated, 'Of course I'm talking to you.'

"'I don't know who you are, so why would you be talking to me, and why would I go see you?' I asked matter-of-factly. I turned and again looked at the person sitting next me. I shrugged my shoulders and scrunched up my face as if to say, *I have no idea what this is all about.*

"'Because I'm your mother!' she answered loudly. 'That's why!'"

John sighed, shaking his head slightly. He chuckled to himself.

"My response had made her straighten up and glare at me before answering. By this time, most people around us had stopped eating or talking and had turned toward us. Every face was staring at me. I replied much more forcefully, 'You're not my mother.'

"'Not your mother? I know it's been a while since we've seen each other, but how can you say that to my face?' Again, she leaned toward the people sitting next to me, as if to look around me, and added, 'How do you like that? I brought him into this world, devoted all my attention and energy to him, and gave him everything; he comes into town from Omaha and doesn't bother to visit his mother. Where did I go wrong?'

"'Lady,' I replied even more firmly, 'I'm telling you—you're not my mother. My mother is dead.'

"'So I'm dead to you. If that's not the worst thing anyone can say!' she replied.

"'No, ma'am; my real mom died almost twenty years ago.'" John stopped and swallowed hard. "She just wouldn't believe me, no matter how hard I explained. This went on until I finally pulled my driver's license out and let her see for herself."

"Did that satisfy her?" the man asked.

John answered, "Who knows. At first, she looked at it funny, probably thinking it was a fake ID like I had in high school to buy beer with. Ultimately, she just walked away, never apologized. Unbelievable! I could tell you other stories, but that's the most outrageous. So, you see, it's something that happens fairly regularly to me."

The man laughed halfheartedly and said, "Well, that makes me feel not so stupid. Sorry about the confusion, and thanks for the story."

As he shuffled away, John called out to him, "If you happen to go down there, don't go on Fridays; the crowd's crazy."

Without turning around, the man acknowledged that tidbit of information with a casual wave of his hand over a shoulder. John watched the man disappear into the milling crowd and then surveyed the large knot of people waiting just outside the entrance to the theater, near the Bavarian army field howitzer, for the next showing of the introductory film. Glancing at his watch, he realized the film was about to end.

John double-timed it to the theater, pulled open one of the double glass doors, and slid unobtrusively along the near wall. In the somber stillness that had settled over the audience, he watched the scrolling series of events, all within a week in late July 1914, that had led up to the commencement of hostilities of the Great War.

When the screen went dark and the theater lights came up, John stepped to the front and, motioning with his left arm, invited the crowd to make its way out into the museum. He led the crowd to the doorway and held open one of the glass doors. As the people streamed out, a few muttered thank-yous to him; he nodded slightly in appreciation and lipped "You're welcome" back.

After the last person exited, John approached the waiting pack and announced, "For those who haven't had a chance to see the introductory film, it will start in about two minutes."

He motioned to the doors behind him and then glided deeper into the museum, letting those who had yet to see the film know that it would be starting any moment.

He had some knowledge, possibly more than most, of the war and that era because of his grandfather's service in France, yet John had begun volunteering only about four years prior, after reading several histories of the Great War and the time period. Those volumes had made him aware of how limited his understanding was of the war, its causes, and its aftershocks. They too had piqued his interest in the wholesale slaughter on all fighting fronts during the war and wholesale changes on all home fronts after. In a month, he got in about ten hours at the museum. He would have considered putting more in if he had believed it would help him scare up more and better business contacts. As he already knew most of the important businesspeople involved, he didn't see the purpose of putting in any more time.

He made his way to the display of a nearly life-sized model trench, where a patron asked him its significance. He explained that similar prototypes had been built back home so that moms and dads could feel good about the conditions in which their Tommy, Pierre, or Heinrich lived, fought, and died for king, country, or kaiser, respectively. John always recommended that visitors peer into the German trench next to this one and compare it to the British and French ones a little farther down.

"You'll notice differences in the ways the trenches were constructed. Keep this in mind when studying them: the Germans built theirs the way they did because they never planned on leaving; the British and French built theirs their way because they never planned on staying. Yet hardly moving forward or backward for most of four years, the armies faced each other across no-man's-land from practically the very spot where they'd first started digging in September 1914. You'll see how the conditions in the trenches might've played a role in the French army mutinies in the spring of 1917."

As John was coming around the corner from that area, a tap on his shoulder made him stop. He turned and found himself looking squarely into the face of another man much like him: he was middle-aged, maybe a little older; had thinning hair and sagging jowls; and was also wearing glasses, though a different style. John was taken aback by this man's resemblance to himself, at least at first blush.

John smiled. "Yes, may I help you?"

The man leaned his head slightly to the left and then squinted at him. A moment later, in broken English tinged with a heavy German accent, he replied, "Excuse me. I thought you were someone else. I am sorry."

Oh boy, not another! And a foreigner at that! That'd be a first—two in one day, John thought to himself.

More slowly and more loudly than normal, John responded, "No problem. If you have any questions, please let me know."

The man bowed politely from the waist, turned, and walked off.

John continued toward a section entitled "All-Out War." Glancing off to his left at the chronology wall, he noticed a woman motioning to him.

As he approached, she commented, "I've been reading the events of May 1915. I thought we went to war because of the sinking of *Lusitania*, but according to this that occurred in 1915, and our declaration of war didn't happen until April 1917."

John explained the sequence of events from the sinking of the *Lusitania* up to the United States of America's declaration of war. She nodded, thanked him, and moved on to the next month.

Just as he headed off, another tap on the shoulder caused him to stop. He turned. A woman maybe ten to twelve years his senior was looking up into his face. She was petite in size; had flowing, long white hair past her shoulders, high cheekbones, and a strong jaw; and wore thick wire-rimmed glasses that magnified her steely blue eyes.

He smiled. "Yes, may I help you?"

She took a breath, as if on the verge of saying something, and then said nothing, standing quietly and looking fixedly at him.

"I'm sorry; could I help you?" he repeated.

She answered in English but also with a German accent. "You will please excuse me. I thought you were someone else. I apologize. It is just that you look like him."

John laughed nervously. Three times in a year was sometimes typical, but three times in a day?

"Who do I look like?" John inquired.

The woman replied, "My *bruder.*"

John asked, pointing over her shoulder at a person coming up behind, "Is *he* your bruder?"

The woman turned. Returning her steely gaze to John, she stated, "*Jah und nein*. He is my bruder but not the one who I thought you were."

"You have another bruder here?" John asked.

"Jah, my older one." She looked around John and pointed over his shoulder. "He is coming behind you."

"Okay," said John.

Exhaling loudly, he pushed his glasses up onto his forehead and turned slowly to see who was behind him. He gasped, startled by what he saw. Staring back at him, as if peering into a mirror, was an image of himself.

His breathing quickening almost to the point of hyperventilation, John stammered, "Wh-who are ... Who are you?"

The woman translated his question.

The man nodded in greeting, smiled, and answered, "*Guten Tag. Ich heiße* Johann."

John reached up with his right hand, flicked his glasses back down onto his nose, and then deliberately pushed them into place with his right index finger. Turning to the woman, he asked, "What did he say?"

Looking from her brother to the name badge on John's volunteer shirt, the woman responded, "He said hello und that his name is Johann. It is John in English, jah? Just like your name."

John swallowed hard. "Yes, it is. My last name is Alston. What's his?"

The woman smiled kindly, her eyes coming alive in the last few seconds. "Our family name is Neuberger."

John exhaled in relief. "So you are brothers and sister, right?"

"Jah, we are family. You have met my brother Johann," the woman remarked. Then, pointing at her other brother, she added, "This is Wilhelm, und I am Magdalena. It is our pleasure to meet you."

"Same here, I think," John answered, unsure if it really was a pleasure.

The four of them stood quietly together for a moment, none daring to speak next.

Ed, another volunteer, approached the group. He stopped next to John, regarded the others, and then garrulously said, "John, I never knew you had family; you never say anything about them. They must be from out of town. I'm glad they could come in for a visit. Are you going to introduce them to me?"

Wilhelm and Johann leaned toward their sister, Johann saying something in German. A moment later, after she had replied to them, they all chuckled. The two German men continued to talk back and forth between themselves.

John cleared his throat and laughed nervously. "They're from out of town all right." His eyes darted back and forth between Ed and the other three.

Ed, listening to the Germans' conversation, again looked at John, glanced at Johann, and then said, "I recognize some sounds. I took three years of German in high school and two in college, but that was long ago. I didn't understand a thing."

Magdalena said, smiling at Ed, "My brothers wanted to know what you said, so I told them. I am Magdalena. This is Wilhelm, und this is Johann. It is nice to meet you, Ed."

All three extended their right hands at the same time, and each in turn grasped Ed's hand and gave it a good tug.

John jumped in. "Obviously, Ed, we're not related; they're German."

"That may be, but it is freaky how much you and that one look alike," Ed answered, pointing directly at Johann. "Freaky," he repeated.

Magdalena translated Ed's remark, which had made John bite his lower lip—something he did when stressed or anxious.

Johann whispered to his sister. Wilhelm, leaning in at the same time, immediately shook his head as if in disagreement. Magdalena considered both her brothers.

"What did he say?" Ed asked loudly.

"That's not polite," John commented, nudging Ed with an elbow. "Some things are private. If it pertains to us, I'm sure Magdalena will tell us."

Expectantly, both men turned their gazes on her.

Magdalena smiled. "You have other visitors. We will finish our tour und not take up any more of your time today. Thank you." She bowed her head slightly and turned, motioning with her head for her brothers to follow.

John, not moving, watched them walk off. The three glanced periodically over a shoulder, as if wanting to keep him in sight. Magdalena smiled each time.

"Well, what do you make of that?" Ed inquired, shaking his head. "That's proof, if proof is needed, that each of us has a twin somewhere in the world. I can't think of a time I've ever seen so strong a resemblance, except for identical twins."

Regarding John, Ed asked, "You okay?"

"Yeah. What's really strange is that just minutes before I ran into them, someone else had mistaken me for somebody he knew; he told me I looked just like that person. I told him of a time when a lady had ... Never mind; it's not important. So you think that guy"—John motioned in the direction the three Germans had gone—"and I looking alike is not that surprising. Just another story for the future." His voice trailed off, and he laughed nervously.

John turned to go, stopped, and looked back. "Ed, did I hear her correctly? Did she say they wouldn't bother us anymore *today*? She said *today*, didn't she?"

Ed knitted his brow and rolled his eyes upward, as if mentally rewinding the conversation. "If she did, it didn't register. You sure you're okay?"

John nodded and said, "See you."

His last duty station that day, between 4:00 p.m. and 5:00 p.m., closing time for the museum, was at the glass bridge. Besides taking tickets, his responsibilities were to greet new visitors and thank departing ones for having visited. As usual at this time of day, the crowd had dwindled to a trickle. Whenever the exit doors opened, John made a point of asking departing visitors if they had any questions. Few people ever asked any. He always suggested they recommend to family, friends, and acquaintances a visit to the museum.

While waiting for security to come relieve him, John reflected on his day. He could not put his finger on why he was uneasy about the Germans; all he knew was that he was. *What a bizarre day. First, that guy thought I was someone else. Then the Germans show up. Ed was right; it was freaky how much Johann and I looked alike. That theory about everyone having a twin must be more than just a theory. On top of that, we share the same first name in different languages. Very strange! Doesn't matter; I'll never see them again.* He glanced around the entry hall, perhaps checking to make sure he could make that statement. *Wait until I tell the family. Since they rarely believe my stories, I doubt they'll believe this one.*

The guard approached the bridge desk. "I'll take it from here. If you'd just do a quick once-through and let me know about how many people are still inside. After that, you can head on out."

John nodded and strolled through the doors to his right, deciding to go backward through the galleries. He silently counted as he came across visitors.

Just before he was halfway through, he stopped in front of the oil painting that hung in the best location in the museum, a spot designed to catch the eye of visitors. It was a painting well known to him, one he had paid a great deal of attention to when he had started volunteering but had hardly looked at since. Like other artifacts of little interest to him in the museum collection, this one had become almost invisible to him.

The portrait was of the most famous local war hero of the Great War. The artist had painted it a couple of years after the hero's return, when the soldier had been in his midtwenties. Here was a person whom others should have been confusing him with, but John knew why no one did; he looked nothing like the subject, his grandfather on his father's side, Private Henry Alston.

The portraitist had perfectly captured his grandfather's likeness and character. The man in the portrait wore the uniform proudly and well and was an extremely handsome man, with a chiseled chin, high cheekbones, and broad and deep-set eyes. Shiny medals and bright multicolored ribbons hung brazenly from the left breast of his dress uniform, an orgy of decorations that grateful and victorious governments had generously bestowed, for valor in the face of a superior enemy force, in the euphoria following November 11, 1918.

In the portrait, Henry, sitting ramrod straight with his chest puffed out, his chin set, and his eyes narrowed, was looking directly at the observer. His left hand rested regally akimbo on his left hip, which he thrust slightly forward, further drawing the observer's eyes to his medals and ribbons. In his right hand, resting casually across his right thigh, a cigarette smoldered, the wisp of smoke mixing freely with the wisps of battle smoke in the painting's background. Over the portrait's right shoulder, a careful observer could just make out silhouettes of German soldiers, distinguishable by their *feldgrau* uniforms, their coal-scuttle helmets, and their arms raised in surrender. Leaning in closer, John silently counted the number of spectral background figures. John already knew the number from prior counting and recounting. Twenty was the number of German soldiers Henry had single-handedly captured, corralled, and brought in on the morning of November 11, 1918, just an hour before the armistice was to go into effect. The foes' few identifiable features were gaunt faces filled with fear and withered by lack of sleep and food. The majority had barely been teens; the others, the prematurely elderly, the veterans, had been no older than their midtwenties. The capture had been only a part of the Henry Alston hero story. The other parts had to do with what Henry had done behind enemy lines to save a French woman—a woman who'd become John's grandmother—from a German deserter's lust, ultimately returning two years after the war to finally bring her back to the States.

John's eyes traveled the short distance from the faces in the background to the young, stern facial features of his grandfather. For the umpteenth time, he studied them and, for the same umpteenth number of times, shook his head, in either amazement or disappointment, that they shared not a single physical trait. By his late twenties, when John's life did not resemble his grandfather's storied one, he had had to reconcile himself to the reality that his grandfather's intangibles also had not been passed on.

Shaking himself loose from his grandfather's gaze, John finished making his way through the museum.

"There are about a dozen still inside. Most have migrated over to the west side, but a few are still lingering in the east," John reported, coming out of the opposite set of doors.

The guard grunted in acknowledgment without looking up, too busy with his phone.

John made his way across the glass bridge. At the far end, he heard the guard call out, "Hey, do you ever have something in the back of your mind but can't put your finger on it?"

"Yeah, that happens on occasion. Why?" John responded.

"This thought has been in my mind for most of the day; seeing you, it just dawned on me what it was," the guard remarked. "Did you happen to have family in today? There was a guy in the museum that looked just like you."

John shook his head, choosing to let the remark go unanswered. "See you next time."

On his way out, his phone rang. It was his sister Donna. She was the older of his two sisters and just younger than him.

"Hello," he said, putting the phone to his ear. "How are you?"

"Fine. Where are you?" she asked curtly.

"You don't sound fine. I'm just about to leave the museum; I've been here all day. Why?"

"I'm at Dad's. He called me about three."

"Okay. What's up?"

"He called because he got a letter yesterday, which he didn't bother to open until today."

"Well, I guess that's pretty unusual to get a letter; how many of us get letters anymore? Why did he call you? Couldn't he find his glasses again?" John joked.

"No, he has his glasses; he hasn't lost them since I put them on that cord he can put around his neck. He called because he couldn't read it."

"Couldn't read it?" John could detect an air of concern in his sister's voice. "Is he okay? Did something happen—a slight stroke? Is that why he couldn't read it?"

"I was thinking the same thing, but his words weren't slurred, and he could answer my questions with no problems."

"Okay. What did you do? Go over to the house?"

"I immediately headed over. When I walked in, he handed the letter to me. He asked me to read it. I couldn't."

"You couldn't? Why?"

"It's not in English."

"What do you mean it's not in English? Are you sure it's addressed to the right person? I got a letter one day—"

"John, I don't have time for one of your stories, and besides, the letter's addressed to Francis Alston at his street address, with the correct city, state, and zip. The only thing that's out of place is the way his first name is spelled."

"How's it spelled?"

"With a *z* in place of the *c*," she replied.

John went momentarily quiet before commenting. "Sounds German. Is the letter in German?"

"Yes, I think so."

"That makes sense. Any words you recognize?"

"The last words in the letter, just above the signature, are *danke schoen*," she replied.

"You're sure?" he asked.

"Of course I'm sure. I recognized them from that old record jacket. You remember the one, John; I'm sure. How many times, when we were kids, did we have to listen to that stupid song by the same name when Dad would play it over and over on the hi-fi?" she asked, laughing.

"What's so funny?" John asked, irritated by her laughter.

"Have you forgotten you used to go around singing it? Don't you remember you got the words wrong? You thought the singer was saying 'donkey shin.' You couldn't understand why anyone would write a song about a donkey shin. Mom laughed so hard she had to run to the bathroom before she wet her pants. Don't tell me you've forgotten. When did you lose your sense of humor?"

John groaned and replied flatly, "According to you, I never had one, so I couldn't have lost it. By the way, that's real funny, Donna.

Thanks for reminding me; I'd no doubt suppressed all memories of it. You're right, though; Dad must've played that damned song several times every day for years."

"Can you swing by Dad's on your way home?" Donna asked.

"I can't, but—"

John went silent, thinking of the coincidence of his father receiving a letter in German on the same day three German visitors, including one who looked just like him, had shown up at the museum.

"But what?" Donna asked.

"Can I stop by your place in twenty minutes? You've got Grandma Jeanne's photo albums and journals, don't you?"

"Yeah, I've got them. I think I know where they are. Why do you ask?"

"Couldn't tell exactly why, but I'd like to pick them up and keep them for a few days," John said. "That okay?"

"That's fine. Give me forty minutes so I can get home and find them. You sure you can't tell me why you want them?"

"Honestly, I don't know for sure. Not yet. Give me overnight to think about it. In the meantime, how about tomorrow night for the letter? Can we meet at your place after dinner to discuss it? Invite Steven and Monique; they might want to be part of this."

"Okay, let's say eight at my place," she replied. "What should I tell Dad?"

"Tell him we're going to find someone who knows German and have it translated. Take the letter with you when you leave."

"Okay, I will. Anything else?"

John didn't respond, lost in thought of what this could mean—a letter in German to his father showing up on the same day as the appearance of a German man who looked just like him. At minimum, he'd unfortunately have to deal with his father regarding the letter; anything beyond that would depend on what was in the message. Worst case, if the letter and the German were somehow linked, the entire family might have to be involved, including his two estranged sons. If it got to that, maybe Donna knew how to get hold of them, since he didn't.

"John, you still there? Is there anything else?" his sister asked.

"Yes. Maybe. No. No, there's nothing else. Not at this time."

Two

How could such a big man fit into this? It's so small, John thought to himself as he held up his grandfather Pappi Henry's uniform tunic. He remembered thinking as a kid that his grandfather was huge. He'd seemed biggest when marching in the annual Armistice Day parade. From the curb, John would proudly wave as Pappi Henry marched up to him, his medals glinting in the sun and making a soft metallic, clinking sound. He'd stop, snap off a crisp military salute, and then, with a smile, pat his grandson on the cheek. Henry had always been at the front of the parade—that was, until that last year, when cancer had forced him to ride in a convertible. Larger than life—that was how he had seemed to John both in size and in standing.

Turning the tunic round, John noticed it was still in pretty good shape, considering it was going on ninety years old. There were a few small holes clearly visible in the area of the shoulder blades and upper sleeves, and the lower hem was fraying in places, but otherwise, it appeared to be in decent condition.

Hooking it onto his shirt collar, he reached out with his right hand and drew the left sleeve of the uniform up against his left arm. That brought a laugh, as the sleeve was about three inches too short. The last time he had tried it on—when he was probably about the same age his grandfather had been when he had gone to war, well before John had developed his paunch—it had been tight through the midsection and pinched him hard in the armpits. The ill-fitting uniform was just more proof, if he needed any, John was not like his grandfather.

Though he had been big by the standards of his day, Henry Alston had been shorter and stockier than John. According to the story, he was a natural leader of men. He was brave and loyal to a fault, thinking of others first. Wearing the uniform had apparently done nothing but magnify those traits, if the stories of his World War I adventures were to be trusted.

He unhooked the hanger and put the uniform back in its protective bag. John hung it up in the back of his closet. Reaching up, he pulled from the overhead shelf a large shoe box. He carried it to his bed, sat on the edge, and removed the lid. Rummaging through, John found what he was searching for. He pulled out one of four plastic baggies, each containing a well-worn and creamy-yellow newspaper article. After taking out the one he wanted, he carefully unfolded it and set about reading, for the first time in years, the account the *Mapleton Valley World Journal* had written of his grandfather's wartime exploits.

> Paris, November 18, 1918—The German army should be thankful the fighting ended when it did, considering the tenacity and ferocity of the American Expeditionary Forces arrayed against them. Since our doughboys arrived on the scene, the Huns have suffered one defeat after another and have been reeling. That they could pick themselves up after each bloodying and punch back is a testament to their courage and resolve, but they eventually had to acknowledge that they were not going to best us.
>
> The perfect example of American tenacity and ferocity may well be our very own Private Henry Alston, who, going on patrol into no-man's-land more than a week before the armistice, disappeared. In anticipation of a

continuation of an attack, his squad had been ordered to scout a way through a heavy concentration of machine-gun nests deployed against their front.

Under cover of night, on November 1, Private Alston slipped out of the trenches through a sap and, with the other men alongside, slithered into the desolation that was no-man's-land. In short order, a Very light shot up from the Huns' trenches, exploding into a brilliant white light; a fierce barrage of German artillery shells soon rained down, followed by the deep-throated *rat-a-tat-tat* of heavy machine guns. American artillery and machine guns opened up in response, answering blow for blow. The firing continued on and off for about fifteen minutes. Periodically, for the next hour or so, American soldiers in the trenches reported occasional solitary answering shots out in no-man's-land. The soldiers in the front line recognized these as American by their sound, something frontline soldiers became adept at.

When Private Alston's patrol failed to return and no sign of them could be spotted hunkered down in no-man's-land the following dawn, the American command could only assume the squad had been captured, wounded, or killed. That suspicion was confirmed when another patrol returned later that week, having identified most of the squad, though unable to find Private Alston due to enemy sniping that sent them back to the safety of the trenches. At that news, our doughboys, having already lost many of their friends to the war, bowed their heads, whispered a prayer for the deliverance of their souls, and continued to stand watch.

The reader can then only imagine the surprise on the faces of Private Alston's trench mates when he found his way

> back to the American lines on the morning of November 11, moments before the armistice went into effect, with twenty German soldiers in tow. The Americans' joy was somewhat tempered by Private Alston's confirmation that the other members of his squad had been killed in action against the enemy.
>
> At the appointed hour, the armistice went into effect. We trust the Germans have learned a much-needed lesson and will never consider starting another war.

John refolded the article, placed it back in its protective baggie, pressed the air out, and resealed the bag. From the box, he pulled out the three other plastic baggies, each containing a follow-up and a more detailed installment of the Great Henry Alston story—a story that, through the haze of time, had grown with each telling and each passing year until crossing into the land of lore. Regarding the plastic baggies, he considered momentarily whether to read the next installment. In the end, he opted not to, knowing the story by heart, having heard it over and over since he was young.

By simply recalling the story, epic images of his grandfather as a young, valiant soldier flooded his mind. He could easily picture him standing atop the trench, astride sandbags, wearing that cocksure smile of his—the same one featured in the portrait—as he peered down at his fellow soldiers. In a German *feldgrau* uniform, surrounded by twenty captured Germans he had brought across no-man's-land, he could tell from the Americans' expressions that they were not sure it was him. Maybe they were simply stupefied by his sudden and unexpected resurrection.

"Did you think I was dead?" he reportedly asked. "Why? Because the others didn't make it? You should've known I'd survive; I've told you all along I'm bulletproof."

"Sergeant!" a soldier yelled out. "You won't believe who's come back to life."

At that instant, a short fusillade of machine-gun fire from across no-man's-land, kicking up mud and thudding into some nearby sandbags, sent Henry scurrying into the trench. By the time he and the other Americans came up to check on his prisoners, they could see only the Germans' backsides as they quick-timed it back to the German lines.

"Shit! There goes my medals!" he exclaimed, shaking a fist in the air. "You have to vouch I brought in those Boches. You had a chance to count them, right? There were twenty."

A few nearby soldiers nodded assuredly.

A smile returned to his face. "I'm going to be the best kind of war hero—a live one!" Henry said.

"Didn't I tell you? The war's all but over!" the sergeant screamed at the top of his lungs. "Who is shooting? And why? What do you want—the Huns to shoot back?"

The sergeant stopped in his tracks, seeing in front of him Private Alston in the flesh. "Alston, is that you? How in the hell did you get here, and what the hell are you doing in that uniform? You're lucky the war's over for all practical purposes and I ordered no one to shoot at anyone unless attacked. You could've been the last casualty of this godforsaken war."

"It's me, sir—really," Henry replied. Looking at his uniform, he added, "I've been hiding out in barns and any other places until a couple days ago. That's when I started to make my way back. To move around, I put on this German uniform; I was afraid the whole time I'd get caught and shot as a spy. I started capturing the Germans just in case."

The sergeant looked up and down the trench in search of the Germans. "What Germans?" he asked.

A soldier piped up, holding up his right hand. "Sarge, I swear he brought in a bunch. They weren't much to look at. They looked hungry and tired. Some of them couldn't have been more than boys. They were right there in front of us when the shooting started.

Henry, along with the rest of us, dove for cover; that must've been when the Huns ran like jackrabbits back across no-man's-land."

The sergeant grabbed his trench periscope and scanned no-man's-land. Seeing nothing and no one, he turned toward his wayward soldier and, after regarding him for a moment, added, "Well done, Private. I'll need to hear your story to determine if any commendations are in order."

"I'm just happy to be alive, sir. There's no need for that, sir. But if you feel you must ..." Henry replied, snapping a crisp, jaunty salute to his sergeant.

JULY 24

Three

"Who knows any German?" Monique, the youngest of the four, asked. She looked first to John, the oldest, who didn't respond, and then to Steven, just older than her, who didn't seem to be paying attention. "I know I don't." Finally, she turned to her sister, Donna, who was sitting on her left, and asked, "Do you?"

Donna stared absentmindedly at the store-bought cookies and brownies in the middle of her kitchen table, thinking of having one. The treats, still in their plastic containers, were within easy reach of all and untouched. Coffee or milk, also untouched so far, sat in front of each of the four siblings.

Had a stranger walked in and looked at them, that person would easily have pointed to Donna, Steven, and Monique, who were all sitting on the same side of the table, and said with confidence that they were related, maybe even siblings. All three took after Grandma Jeanne—they were short and stocky; they had deeply recessed eyes, dark coloration, and brown eyes; their natural hair color was brown tending toward black; and their facial structures were similar. The stranger would probably have seen John as a spouse or maybe a neighbor or acquaintance. The inside joke was that John not only didn't resemble his siblings, mother, or father but also didn't resemble the family's milkman or mailman of the time.

John had been uncomfortably aware of this dissimilarity from an early age and felt that his parents treated him differently because of it. As a kid, he had tried to tell himself that he looked different because he was the oldest. By the time all four were in school, he still felt slighted by his parents. When he would say something about his appearance, they would quickly dismiss his concerns, but not before a quick, light hug from his mom and maybe even a peck on the top of his crew-cut hair from her. In reply, she would say, "You know your dad and I love you just as much as the other three. It's just that they're younger and need more attention. Plus, you're a super easy kid. We don't have to worry about you." She would then push him along and turn her attention back to the others.

Of his siblings, whom he saw only on rare occasions, John got along with Donna better than he did with the others, though their relationship was tepid at best. She at least understood that life was about responsibility and duty. As for Steven, the third child, well, he was unique in many ways, mostly irresponsible and immature ways. *Responsibility* and *duty* were words Steven rarely used and things he often abused. Finally, there was Monique. As the youngest, she'd had it easy, and she continued to. Their parents had regularly reminded the others, "What do you expect? She's the baby." She knew the words *responsibility* and *duty* but also knew they didn't apply to her.

Monique nudged her sister.

"I don't," Donna said, shaking her head.

Monique looked in the opposite direction and asked Steven, "How about you? You were in Germany when you were in the service."

"Yeah, that's right. I'd forgotten all about that," Donna added, and she slid the letter in Steven's direction. "Maybe you can read it."

Without bothering to look at it, Steven answered, pushing the letter back at his sister. "I never learned to read the language. I understand some and learned only enough to get certain things," Steven responded with a wry, remembering-something-fondly smile. "The question shouldn't be if we know anyone, but does Dad? And how? He's the one who got the letter. He was in Europe during the war, right, John? You're the family historian."

"That's a stretch to say I'm the family historian," John replied.

"No, it's not; you're the oldest and have been around the longest," Steven remarked, circling his right hand round and round as if he were twirling a rope. "Plus, you knew all the grandparents."

"First of all, I never really knew Mom's parents; they died before I was old enough to form memories. And I have only a kid's memories of Pappi Henry. Grandma Jeanne was the one I knew the best," John explained.

"She only ever really liked you, none of the rest of us," Steven remarked. "I always assumed that while you two were cozied up together, she was letting you in on all the family secrets."

"Second, I know no family secrets and would be shocked if there were any," John replied. "Grandma Jeanne would occasionally tell me about growing up on her family's farm in France, nothing more."

Steven shook his head at his brother. "Every family has secrets. Maybe she swore you to secrecy so we'd never find out, and over the years, you've repressed them. Who knows? Maybe something will jog your memory and make you spill your guts."

"I hate to disappoint, but I'm afraid you're going to be disappointed greatly on that front."

"Makes no difference; I still assume you know more than we do! That makes you the family historian," Steven added.

"That's your basis for making me the family historian?" John asked. "You could be just as easily if you wanted."

Steven quickly answered, "Ah, there's the hitch; I don't want to be. I have absolutely no interest in being the repository of family history. All I want are answers when I've got questions."

Steven's attitude hardly surprised John, and it was not because Steven was not intelligent; he was. He also loved history. John was not surprised because Steven hated responsibility and was lazy. He was the one in the family who had almost always found a way to skate by and still come out on the right side. Yet despite being intelligent, he had almost failed to make it through high school on schedule, but he had somehow in the end. The most likely explanation was that the teachers and school administrators had recoiled in anticipation of having to deal with him for another year. That revelation had undoubtedly caused them to reevaluate the situation and conclude he had done enough to pass. And pass him they did—off to the armed forces. That particular institution had not been Steven's first, second, or third post-high-school choice; it had worked out to be his only. Once in the service, he had managed to serve his country without too much trouble finding him, and while at it, he had seen parts of Europe and Asia. His last CO had recommended he re-up; Steven had left the minute his discharge came through. Back in civilian life, he'd worked in restaurant management for a while. When that had not panned out, he had tried his hand at sales: life insurance, furniture, copiers, newspaper ads, office supplies, and two or three others. None of those had worked out either. He claimed they frustrated his flexibility and cramped his creativity. He had pondered going back into the service and making a career of the military but decided against it after three minutes of profound reflection. His current position, Steven claimed, let him make the most of his natural talents.

John remembered having to ask, since Steven had crowed about his new job, "What is it? Sounds like a dream job."

Confidently, Steven had said, "Sales—that's what I'm really good at. I'm on the streets all day, dealing with people; no boss is looking over my shoulder."

"Sounds too good to be true. What kind of sales? You've already done about every kind," John had commented.

"I'm back in the food business but on the catering side. I like the business and the people. Plus, on the catering side, we deal with better people. We pride ourselves on great customer service. By saving our customers so much time and trouble, they're willing to pay a premium. You might even say I'm in high-end sales."

"So you've found your place! What's the name of the company?"

"Wheel Come to You."

"Don't think I've heard of that one," John had said. "W-e-apostrophe-l-l Come to You?"

"No. It's a play on word sounds. It's W-h-e-e-l Come to You," Steven had responded, his confidence sounding a bit contrived.

John had scrutinized his brother over the top of his glasses. "I'm not judging, but isn't that the company with the fleet of beat-up old hot-food canteen trucks you see at construction sites, warehouses, and factories—selling pizza by the slice, tamales, and such?"

"And your point is?" Steven had asked, stamping paid to the conversation.

John studied his brother across the table and sitting on Monique's right. "Okay, Steven, I'll play along. What would you like to know about Dad's war experience?"

Steven ran a finger around the rim of his glass of milk. "Whatever you can tell me. All I know is Dad never talked about it in front of me." Then, after a short silence, he added, glancing around, "Maybe while he was over there, you know, he hooked up with someone."

Quickly, John interjected, "I can assure you Dad never talked to me about that type of war experience."

"Wait a second, Steven. Are you suggesting," Donna asked, holding the letter up and shaking it, "this might be from a love child he fathered? Hand it to you, Steven, to come at it from that angle."

"And why not? Dad would've been, what, midtwenties? He'd have been a long way from home, and death was staring him in the face practically every day. Plus, he wasn't married. Maybe it's as simple as he was alone and lonesome and was looking for some comfort, no different than you and me. Donna, what were you thinking about at that age?"

"Love, marriage, and happiness," Donna answered too quickly.

Laughing, Steven exclaimed, "I'm calling bullshit on that! Who are you fooling? Remember Jerry Craig? Remember what you did for the first time with him when you were only sixteen? I can jog your memory if you want, since I used to sneak into your bedroom and read your diary. As I recall, all you wanted to do after that was more of the same."

Donna, opening the container with the brownies and picking one up, blushed.

"And you're trying to say that out of the house for the first time—no parents, no curfew, no rules—you were thinking of love, marriage, and happiness? Bullshit, I say. You were thinking of the same thing all of us were thinking about. Period. Tell me—why is it people want to think their parents better, purer, or wiser than themselves? Why don't we give them the freedom to have been as big of screwups as ourselves?"

"If he were lonely, weren't there places for him to go?" Monique asked. "He could've gone there for company, right?"

"That's right; he could've," Steven said. "But that's not the type of company I'm suggesting. Let's not lose sight of the situation over there; shortages were widespread, as were sufferings and hardships, all caused by the war. It had to have been particularly difficult for girls and women."

"What are you insinuating by that?" Donna asked, irritated with the direction Steven had taken the conversation.

Opening the cookies and grabbing one, Steven answered, "I'm not insinuating anything. What I'm saying is Germany had lost the war and was being occupied; death and destruction were everywhere. No part of Germany was immune. Almost every family lost someone. The only men around were, well, either too old to help or physically unable. And in all cases, there was competition. Food was in short supply, as was fuel, medicine, and clothing, not to mention housing from the bombings and the Allied occupation. There were only a few ways to get what you needed. One was to buy it, but since unemployment was sky high, not many people had money. The other was to barter what you had to someone who wanted it. In practice, it just might've been the perfect economic laboratory: two people, each having something the other desired, willing to ..." He dunked the cookie in his milk and then took a bite.

"Stop! Don't say another word," Donna screeched at her younger brother, and then she reached around her sister and rapped him lightly upside the head.

Steven held up his free hand to ward off another attack. "Okay. I was just explaining," he mumbled.

"You're suggesting that Dad could've offered things he had or could get in exchange for ..." Monique started and then decided not to finish.

Steven leaned away from his older sister before answering his younger one. "*Comfort* is the word I'm using; I'll not say more." Steven shrugged while breaking off a small piece of a cookie, dunking it into his glass, and then popping it into his mouth. He then pushed the crumbs around the table.

"Try not to make a bigger mess than you've already made," Donna, shaking her head, said to her brother. "And you're suggesting our dad could've taken advantage of some innocent young woman under those circumstances for ...?" She would not let herself complete the thought.

Screened by Monique, Steven swept the crumbs into his lap. "She may have been young and innocent but more likely was probably cold, starving, and maybe even sick. She might've even had children who were also hungry, cold, and sick. Or a parent she was responsible for—someone unable to fend for him- or herself. It could be a whole lot worse, you know."

"How?" Donna snapped. She picked up her brownie and acted as if she might chuck it at Steven.

"Seeing how squeamish you've been so far," Steven began, looking Donna squarely in the eye, "you sure you want me to answer?"

"Yeah, I'm sure. I want to hear how you think it could've been worse," she replied, setting down the brownie.

"Here's how: maybe Dad forced himself on some woman. Maybe this letter is from that child who claims to be our older brother or sister. Rape was rampant and went virtually unpunished."

The group fell still.

"I read somewhere," Steven continued, "an estimated million German women committed suicide between the final days of the war and the end of the occupation, mainly due to the fear of being raped or the shame of having been. And God knows how many children were born in the mid to late 1940s in Germany as a result. I'm not saying definitively that's the case here. All I'm saying is we need to be ready just in case."

"That's disgusting! I can't believe you're even thinking that, let alone saying it out loud," Donna replied. "Dad's an ordinary guy."

Steven cleared his throat. "Donna, so was that old guy from Ohio in his late eighties. The German government claimed he was a SS guard at an extermination camp in Poland and played a role in the gassings. Despite his age, he was extradited, prosecuted, convicted, and then sentenced. He was an ordinary guy by all accounts, except for that deep, dark secret. I'll bet anything no one in his family knew that secret, and yet—"

"Why would they go after that old man?" Monique asked. "What had happened was so long ago. What about his family?"

"Germany needed to prove justice would be served no matter how long it took or who was affected. You know, in our case, with advancements in DNA testing, it'll be easy to prove or disprove paternity," Steven added.

"Stop! Stop it right now!" shouted Donna. "I've heard enough and have had enough."

"I only mention that in case," Steven added after a moment. "You know, in the final analysis, it may make no difference what you want to hear or believe."

"I know, but I still don't want to hear any more for now." Donna studied her younger brother for a long second and finally added, "I have to admit you're right; that'd be worse."

Suddenly, a shiver ran through Donna. She then added, "I'd hate to think what I'd do if I was in that situation. I wonder if ... you know." A moment later, Donna asked. "John, what *do* you know about Dad's service in Europe?"

"He was in France right after D-day. Since he spoke fluent French, he was attached to a unit following frontline troops into liberated areas. He interrogated locals to gather intelligence on enemy units, their strength, and movements. He ended up in Germany as a liaison and was stationed there as part of the occupation forces. It was at that time he was shot by the Nazi sympathizer."

"Dad was shot? I don't remember that," Monique commented.

John added, "He took two bullets—one in the shoulder and the other in the leg, just below the hip. He almost bled to death. He was in a convalescent hospital for months."

"Enough; we've gotten sidetracked!" Donna shook the pages of the letter. "We need to get back to this. Let's go over what we know. The letter's in German. I can't make out the signature. It was postmarked from Mannheim."

"Where was Dad stationed in Germany, John?" Monique asked. "Was it near Mannheim?"

"Heidelberg, I think. My German geography isn't very good, so I'm not sure whether it's anywhere close to Mannheim," John responded.

Looking at Steven, John asked, "Where's Heidelberg in relation to Mannheim?"

"I've got no clue," Steven quickly replied, shrugging. "Don't think I ever went to either town while I was there."

Shaking his head in disgust, John added, "Don't make it easy on us." Looking at Donna, he asked, "Do you have an atlas?"

"Here, I'll make it easy. I've got my phone with me," Steven remarked, pulling it from his pocket.

"Put that away. The screen's too small to do any good. I can't read it, even with glasses." John turned to Donna. "If you've got an atlas."

Donna got up and disappeared around a corner. From the kitchen, the three could hear the concussive banging of a succession of cabinet doors. Reappearing minutes later, she had a large world atlas in her hands. The right-hand side of the front cover was missing, and the spine had been repaired with duct tape that had at one time been a shiny silver but was now a dull gray. The tape on both ends was frayed.

Standing at the table's edge, she opened it and leafed intently through. She moved her lips as if talking to herself and occasionally shot disparaging glances at her younger brother. Stopping, she placed the open atlas on the table. Her three siblings stood up, almost in unison, and as if in a church service, they leaned reverently over the open book, their fingers devoutly steepled and their eyes downcast.

Sinuously, Donna's right pointer finger moved around the map of West Germany, as if on a Ouija wand. As it meandered its way across the page, she leaned in closer and closer, inch by inch, squinting harder and harder at the pages.

Like a lightning strike, her finger stabbed a place on the map. She declared, “There’s Mannheim.”

Replacing her right finger with her left, the right one took off again on its crusade. Starting in the south at the Austrian border, her finger swept methodically back and forth, migrating north. Within moments, her finger had again come to a stop.

The three sets of eyes escorting Donna’s finger also stopped. If the narrow gap between her two fingers was any gauge, Heidelberg was not far from Mannheim.

Donna raised her eyes and looked from one sibling to the next. “No more than thirty or forty miles apart tops, I’d say. Maybe not even that.”

She again cast her eyes down onto the map. “Before we jump to any more far-fetched conclusions,” Donna said, the disgust in her voice palpable, “maybe we shouldn’t lose sight of other possibilities. We need to keep what we know in front of us.”

“What do we know?” Monique inquired, her voice having a beseeching quality.

“That Dad is a good and decent man—a man devoted to his family. And that all this crap Steven has brought up is just that—crap!” Donna enumerated.

“I like that,” Monique remarked in support. “What should we do next?”

“John, why don’t you go talk to Dad?”

“Why me, Donna? So you won’t have to? And what’d you like me to talk about? Why he and I don’t get along?”

Donna replied, “You need to find out if there’s even the remotest chance he, you know, might’ve done … You know what I’m getting at. It’s precisely because you don’t get along that you could have this conversation. None of us could.”

"Or do you mean *should*?" John asked cynically. "I can see it now. I walk in and say, 'Hey, Dad. Your kids got together to talk about that letter you got. Though we have no idea what it's about, some think it may be from a bastard child you fathered, consensually or not, while you were in Germany. Now that we're on to you, care to come clean?'"

Monique interjected. "You may not want to use that word to describe the child. You know Dad doesn't like profanity."

"Hey, Mon," Steven said, "the word *bastard* isn't actually a profane word."

"I don't care; I don't like that word," she said, rebuking him. "And I don't like you calling me by that name."

Steven had an annoying habit of reducing names to a single syllable. In some cases, it was okay; in others, not so much. If someone was fortunate enough to have a single-syllable name already, Steven would find another way to modify it, usually equally irritatingly so.

Steven glanced at his watch. "Hey, it's almost nine thirty. I've got to go—need to get to bed. I got to be at work at five. Good luck, John Boy. Talk to you later, Don and Mon."

With Steven's departure, Monique took hers. John made no move to leave.

"Something on your mind, John?"

"Yeah, I didn't want to say anything in front of those two, but something happened yesterday at the museum."

"Care to share?"

John remained quiet for a moment and then said, "I don't think the letter is from anyone Dad knows. I think it's from someone he's never met."

Donna arched her eyebrows, a look of puzzlement on her face. "Oh yeah? Does this have anything to do with you picking up the photo albums and Grandma Jeanne's journals?"

John pushed his coffee cup to his left. "It does; hear me out. There were three Germans in the museum yesterday—two brothers and a sister. I met them."

"Germans, you say? And you met them? All of them?"

"Yes, all of them. Actually, a better way to describe it would be that they met me."

"And?"

John pulled his coffee cup back in front of himself. "And it seemed they were on a quest."

"A quest? What kind of quest?"

"Don't know, but it was like they were staking out something, someplace, or someone."

"Describe them to me."

"They were older than me—the youngest probably by about ten or so years and the oldest by fifteen or more."

"Anything else?"

John pushed his cup to one side. "I'll get to that."

"Do you think it was a coincidence?" Donna said. "You know—their appearance and the letter's, one right after the other?"

"No, I don't." He pulled his cup back in front of him.

"Tell me why."

"There was just something about them for it to have been a coincidence. Call me crazy, but like I said, I have a hunch they came searching. I doubt Mapleton Valley, even with its world-class museum, would attract three older German tourists." John pulled his coffee to him and wrapped both hands around it.

"That *does* sound crazy, John. If I didn't know better, I'd say you were off your rocker."

"I wouldn't blame you; I was thinking that last night."

"Okay."

"There's more. I've told you before that I've been mistaken for other people. It happened again yesterday, right before I ran into the Germans. I told the guy not to feel bad, that I had a story he wouldn't believe."

Donna rolled her eyes in mock disbelief. "Let me guess; you told the one about the lady who thought you were her son."

"Yeah. I'd literally just finished, when I was mistaken again—this time by one of the German brothers. No more than three or four minutes passed before I was again mistaken, this time by the sister. I'd guess I'm mistaken at least once a year—on rare occasions, twice. Never three times in a year, let alone in a single day. Then, to top it off, there was a fourth. It's always been somebody else who's mistaken me for somebody they knew. It's never been me making the mistake."

"*You* mistook someone, not the other way around? And you're saying that would be a first?"

"I did, and it was." He pushed his cup away.

"Who did you think the person was?"

John swallowed hard, looked down at the table, and muttered, "Me."

"You?" Donna asked, half choking on her own question. "Did I hear right? You mistook someone for you?"

"Yeah, I did." John looked up at his sister. "But an older version—what I'd look like fifteen years from now."

"Let me guess; it was the third German, jah?"

"That's not funny, Sis, even by your warped sense of humor. But how did you know?"

"You'd mentioned they're brothers and sister, and the other two had already mistaken you. Obviously, the other two thought you were their brother; since you weren't, it could only be the third German."

"That's right."

"And because of that encounter, you wanted the photo albums to see if you could find any resemblance?"

"That's right."

"Even though you know there's not a soul in the family photo albums that looks like you?"

"That's right, but I can hope, can't I? Anyway, it'd been decades since I'd looked through them. Who knows what I might've—"

Donna squinted at her brother. "Tell me, John, now that a full day has passed. If you ran into this person tomorrow, would you still think this person looked like you?"

"What are you suggesting, Sis?"

"Only that with the earlier encounter, your frame of mind was such you were predisposed to look for resemblances. That's all."

"I didn't mention, did I, that at the end of the day, a security guard mentioned to me he saw someone in the museum who looked a lot like me? Though, thinking about what you've just said, I'd like to think you're right—that my mind was preprogrammed to see similarities. But there was another volunteer who saw a strong resemblance with the German."

"What was his name?"

"Ed."

"Ed? That's a weird name for a German," Donna remarked.

"No, that's the volunteer's name. The German's name is Johann."

"Johann? Spelled J-o-h-a-n-n? Isn't that John in German?"

"I'd guess so. I didn't ask him how to spell it. Neuberger is his last name."

Donna reached for the letter and pulled it to herself. She flipped to the last page. Slowly turning it around toward her brother, she asked, her finger planted above the signature, "Could that be Johann Neuberger?"

With an exaggerated motion, John reached up, deliberately removed his glasses, and placed them alongside the letter. He leaned his head back, looking down his nose, and considered the signature. A moment later, he picked up his glasses and, moving them up and down as if they were a magnifying glass, carefully studied it. Straightening up, he put his glasses back in place, regarded his sister, and exhaled. "It's hard to be certain because of the flourishes, but it sure looks like it could be. Seeing this and running into the Germans at the museum, I'm starting to wonder if perhaps this family does have some secrets."

Donna wrapped her arms around herself, her hands rapidly rubbing her upper arms. "I'm with you. What could this be about?"

John picked up the letter in front of him, lined up the sheets, and tamped the bottom on the tabletop and then one side. He folded it into thirds and slipped it into the pocket of his sports coat. Regarding his sister, he answered, "I don't know, but I have a sneaking suspicion we're about to find out."

Four

Magdalena, Wilhelm, and Johann walked into the dimly lit hotel lounge just off the lobby, stopped, and glanced around. As only a few tables were occupied at this hour, they would again have their choice, just as they had the previous two nights. On a small stage immediately to their left, the same tuxedo-clad man with slicked-back raven-black hair was crooning tunes popular several generations before. Accompanying him was the same piano player, also in a tuxedo, but one less ostentatious than the singer's.

As the song came to its end, the singer glanced around at the smattering of applause and, recognizing the three Germans, nodded, a genuine smile breaking out on his face. Magdalena flashed a hasty smile back and then motioned with her head for her brothers to follow her.

They sat at a small cocktail table in the back reaches of the lounge, about as far away as possible from the stage. A cocktail waitress materialized from somewhere behind them, a haggard and forced smile on her face.

"Good evening. My name is Gita," she said flatly.

"Good evening, Gita. Is your name short for Brigitte?" Magdalena responded, emphasizing the German pronunciation of the name.

"Yes, it is. Not many people guess correctly." Gita's face lit up, and she asked a bit more brightly, "Can I bring you something to drink?"

Magdalena remarked, motioning with her hands, "Please bring me a glass of Chablis and scotch, neat, for these two."

In silence, they waited for their drinks, listening intently either to the music or their own thoughts. After being served, each took a tentative sip and then another.

In a whisper, Johann asked, "Do you think the man and the woman who left the house before John are related?"

"Do you mean are they brother and sister?" Magdalena asked. "Or are they married?"

"Brother and sister," Johann responded.

"I'd think so. They left in separate vehicles," Wilhelm replied. "I'm more interested in knowing what took so long for John to leave. It must've been another half hour or more after those two." He reached for some pretzels in a small bowl at the center of the table.

"Almost forty minutes," Magdalena answered. "It's possible he told them about us."

"That's what worries me," Wilhelm explained, covering his mouth to keep any crumbs from flying out. "If he did, that might scare them off, making it more difficult."

Magdalena shrugged. "That's always been possible. But let's assume the two who left early are sister and brother, and the woman who met them at the door when they arrived is also a sister—that'd mean there are at least those four, plus spouses and children. Some of their children may even have children of their own."

"This is becoming even more complicated. Back home, it seemed so simple; we'd find out if there was a relation and, if so, exchange what we know for what they know—maybe even exchange addresses—and then go home. We'd have found out what we'd come for. Now it doesn't seem so simple or so sure. I'm wondering if it's still worth it," Johann commented.

"How can you question this? First, the resemblance between John and you," Wilhelm said, motioning toward his brother, "is striking. Can there be any doubt of a blood relationship?"

Johann swirled his scotch glass around several times. "Sure, there can be doubts," he finally responded unconvincingly.

"Be serious." Wilhelm repeated the question, tapping his glass on the table at each word. "Can there really be any doubts?"

Johann took a sip. "No, I don't think so," he answered, shaking his head. Then he added, "But ..." He left his statement unfinished.

"But what?" Wilhelm asked.

"It just seems so irrevocable," Johann responded.

"What seems so irrevocable?" his sister asked.

"What we're about to do," Johann responded. "This is something *we* want. Who knows if they have any interest or even any inkling? We've only thought of ourselves and have given no thought to anybody who finds themselves on the other side."

Magdalena nodded, adding, "That's true, but as we discussed amongst ourselves before leaving home, there are holes in the family history we're entitled to try to find out. We're as much innocent victims of circumstances as anybody else. Our only way is to pursue this as far as we can, or as far as someone lets us. If we're turned back, then we'll need to respect that, but we are going to try."

"I agree we are as innocent as anyone else, but the difference is we at least know. Where does that leave them?" Johann asked. "They might be completely ignorant."

"I've got to believe they, whoever that turns out to be, would want to know," Magdalena interjected. "I know I would."

"I'm not so sure you can say that with any certainty. How long did we take before really starting to put together our plan? Months? Years? Don't forget how difficult our discovery was for us. It's only because we've had time ..." Johann let his comment hang in the air.

Wilhelm grabbed some pretzels. "Come on, Johann. It's probably true we know more, but we hardly know anything. I've got to believe John and his siblings have to know something—if not them, then their father." The pretzels disappeared into his mouth.

"I'd say we probably know more, but I don't agree they know something. As far as I could tell, John knows nothing," Johann answered.

"How can you say that?" Wilhelm retorted after swallowing the pretzels and taking a sip of his drink.

Johann stared at his brother. "You didn't see the look on his face when he turned and saw me for the first time, did you?"

"Of course not; I was facing you. So what?" Wilhelm asked.

"So what? You'd be crazy to say that if you'd seen what I saw on his face. I've never seen a look like that before—ever." Johann fell silent. "John caught his breath, and his eyes went wide; there was a look of fear in them. It might be better described as terror. His jaw dropped, and then he quickly tensed, as if to brace himself. I'm telling you—John knew his world, as he knew it, had changed irreversibly at that moment. He just doesn't know how much or why. Having seen what I saw, I'm not as comfortable with our plans as before."

"Are you suggesting we give up and go home without even trying to get what we came for?" Magdalena asked.

Wilhelm interrupted before Johann could answer. "I don't care if you are; I'm here, and I'm going to find out as much as I can."

Wilhelm had been the one who was at first the least interested in the undertaking. Magdalena and Johann had had to work on him for months before he came around. But once he had, he, like most converts, had committed himself fully and completely; he was now the most gung-ho. He had tracked down the Alstons in Mapleton Valley and had made travel arrangements. It was Wilhelm who was intent on finding out the full story, including the how and why behind their never-seen grandfather's death. To Johann, it seemed Wilhelm cared little about who found themselves in his path.

"As I said, the situation is getting more complicated, and potentially more people could be involved," Johann pointed out.

"That's unfortunate but not of our doing. Let me be clear; I'm not interested in abandoning the plans. This may be our one and only chance," Wilhelm responded in a challenging tone of voice.

Johann mulled over his brother's comment. "You may be right, but I've been thinking."

"Thinking of what, Johann?" his sister asked in a kind tone.

"That since we've made preliminary contact, we'd return home and write another letter, giving more details of what we know—but this time, to John," Johann explained. "The initial shock would've worn off by the time he got it, and I imagine he'd have had ample time to think things over. We could then make mutually agreeable arrangements to return. That was what I was thinking."

"Bad plan, Johann. John may not read the letter. In fact, we don't know if the first letter has been read," Wilhelm interjected. "Furthermore, John's father may already be too old or too ill. Or one of us, in the interim, could become incapacitated. No, I can't and won't get behind your plan. I say we stick with what we agreed upon; if we're going to do this, we do this now. There may not be a later."

Magdalena reached out an arm and gently patted Wilhelm's arm. "We're just having a conversation. It's important we listen to one another. We did that for you when this saga started. The least you could do is the same. There's no need to draw lines in the sand yet."

She turned to Johann. "I hear what you're saying and even share some of what you're feeling. That being said, I'm with Wilhelm; if we're going to do this, we need to do this now. There may not be another chance, and we're so close. Declining health and advancing age are reasons enough to not put this off. Plus, I really think we owe it to the family."

"Which?" Johann inquired acidly.

Magdalena eyed her brother and then responded matter-of-factly, "The family, whoever that is, wherever they are, and however they're related."

Wilhelm signaled to the cocktail waitress, making a circling motion in the air, asking for another round. The three sat in silence until the drinks arrived.

Johann asked, "What's our next step? We know where John lives and, presumably, a sister. We don't know where the other two live. How about John's father? Since we have his address, are we still planning on stopping by?"

"I'm in favor of going there as soon as we can," Wilhelm commented. "We might as well see if there's a conversation to be had."

"Not so fast," Magdalena replied. "It'd be imprudent to go barging in. Who knows what John may have already told him? He may not answer. Also, in line with what Johann has pointed out, he could be in ill health. The shock might be too much for him if we show up unexpectedly."

"And he may not be in ill health, and he may very well be expecting us," Wilhelm replied.

"Bruder, we'll get one chance. We need to give ourselves the best chance of success. Let's figure out where and when John works; we follow him for a day or two to get a sense of his schedule. Maybe he'll stop by his dad's. Since John knows who we are, we can knock on the door once he's inside. His presence should allay any shock caused by our sudden appearance. How does that sound, Johann?"

"I've already been outvoted, so I don't think you really care what I think. But in case you do, I'm okay with that plan. We have to agree to react appropriately once we're inside."

"What does that mean?" Wilhelm interrupted. "We can't go searching through his house for stuff or interrogate him under bright lights?"

"If you'd let me finish, you wouldn't have had to ask," Johann said. "I meant that if John's dad shows signs of stress or starts to push back, we have to back off. Agreed?"

Almost instantaneously, Magdalena nodded her agreement and then asked her other brother, "Wilhelm, what do you say?"

Wilhelm studied his two siblings before replying pointedly, "I'll agree, albeit reluctantly. But I want you to know I don't like it."

Five

At home, John went straight to his bedroom closet and pulled the shoe box down from the top shelf. He carried it into the kitchen and set it on the table. Purposefully, he walked to the cabinet where he kept both his bottle of scotch and favorite scotch-drinking glass. He poured two fingers and walked to the freezer; he added two ice cubes. His rule of thumb was one ice cube for each finger of liquor; adding more diluted the magic of the distiller's potion.

He set the glass down on the kitchen table and then sat down, allowing the ice a moment to do its job. Lifting the glass, he swirled the elixir slowly around. He loved the soft, tinkling sound of ice against the glass, like a crystal wind chime in a slight breeze. He brought the glass to his nose and inhaled deeply, loving its enthralling and intoxicating bouquet. His habit, savoring a sniff before the first sip, heightened the anticipation of the explosion of complex, oaky tastes of this twelve-year-old single malt.

He took a sip. Swishing it gently around his mouth, he savored the exquisitely subtle flavors slowly revealing themselves.

He set the glass down and lifted the box lid. From inside, he pulled the three plastic baggies holding the longer newspaper installments of Private Henry Alston's exploits behind German lines that had gone unopened the night before. Identifying the first installment, he removed the neatly folded article from the baggie, carefully unfolded it on the tabletop, and pressed it flat with his palms.

He looked into the distance and then again lifted the glass to the light. He admired the honey-ocher color, seeing in the liquid swirly lines as the ice melted. Bringing the glass to his nose, he again sniffed deeply, the liquor's vapors slightly burning his nostrils. He took another sip and hoped it would help steel his resolve to read, word for word, the first installment.

As he was no longer a child with a child's understanding of the world or the words, a more careful reading, he hoped, would provide insights into a troubling sense of something that had roiled around in his mind since he'd first run into Johann and his siblings. He had hoped this evening's conversation with his siblings would clear his head, but it had not. The truth was that it had failed to assuage anything, only heightening his growing disquiet.

He took another sip and set the glass down on top of the empty plastic baggie. He removed his glasses from his shirt pocket, held them up to the light, and, seeing how dirty they were, cleaned them on his shirttail. Putting them on, he leaned over the article.

> Paris, November 21, 1918—Now almost a full two weeks after the armistice, the victors are making their way to their duty stations along the Rhine River, following the German army as it trudges its way home. Under normal circumstances, Private Henry Alston would be among those soldiers slogging along, burdened with supplies and equipment. But for Private Alston, nothing is normal. He has been too busy being recognized for his exploits behind German lines.
>
> Here is Private Henry Alston's story, in his own words:

It was pitch-black that night when the squad slipped into no-man's-land and moved forward, hunched over. We'd been out there ten or twelve minutes, when a Very light shot up from the German lines and exploded in a burst of bright light, making it look like midday. Unfortunately, our squad had three soldiers new to trenches. While the rest dove for cover at the first hiss of the flare, those three stood watching it soar upward, frozen in place, and remained immobile as if hypnotized as it slowly wobbled downward, swinging side to side and creating strange shadows. Within seconds, they were cut down. Machine guns on all sides then opened up, strafing the ground around us. Three more were killed, and another, Private Corley, was badly shot up.

Private Clifford and I were pinned down in a shell crater about ten or twelve yards from Corley. I yelled to him to quit making so much noise, that if he didn't stop pleading for someone to come and get him, it'd be the machine guns that would. But he wouldn't stop, and each time he called out, the machine-gun volleys got closer.

"Shut up; I'll come get you," I finally told him. Turning to Clifford, I said, "Do something as a diversion." I assumed he agreed, even though he hadn't responded.

I made my way to Corley, whispering the whole time for him to keep his mouth shut. Reaching him, I placed my hand over his mouth. "I'm going to pull you by the collar. Don't make a sound—got that?" He grunted.

"Clifford, I'm ready. Do something," I called out at half volume.

Nothing happened. I again called out, louder, and waited. I could hear a whimper and a low moaning coming from the crater.

"For God's sake, Clifford. Corley and I need you to do something. Now!"

Again, nothing happened. I said to Corley, "Oh hell, here goes. We'll go slowly."

I gently pulled until I could feel his uniform hitch up under his arms. Corley let out a scream. I hit the ground. The machine guns opened up, spraying their deadly contents around us. We lay still, neither moving nor making a sound. I half thought about trying to knock Corley out to make it easier to get him to the shell hole.

A moment later, I again pulled. Corley shrieked. The machine guns again went at us. I grabbed a nearby carcass—no way to tell anymore if it were German, French, English, or one of ours. I yanked it in front of Corley as a shield. Just as I finished, the machine guns swept us. I can still hear the dull, sickening thud of the bullets. I'll never forget the lurching of the lifeless corpse as they struck home.

"Corley, you still with me?" I called out. No answer came. I reached a hand out and placed it on his face. It was wet and sticky. Drawing my hand back, I knew it was blood—his. He was gone. There was nothing more I could do, so I left him.

I scrambled back to the shell crater. Clifford had fallen apart; he was crying and mumbling, "I'm going to die, and I'm too young to die. I don't want to die. Not yet. Not here."

I tried to quiet him down, telling him we'd be okay as long as we kept our heads about us, kept our mouths shut, and stayed put.

"I don't want to die," he wailed.

"If you listen to me and stay with me, you won't," I reassured him tersely.

That calmed him momentarily. We must've stayed there for another six or seven minutes before Clifford yelled, "I can't take it any longer!" He made a run for it, yelling, "If I'm going to die, make it quick!"

"You can't make it!" I yelled at him, grabbing him and pulling him down. "The Huns know where we are."

As a reminder of our predicament, a machine-gun burst sprayed the top of the crater, spewing rocks, mud, and fragments of what had once been soldiers all over us.

My efforts went for nothing; Clifford jumped up again. I lurched for his ankles before the bullets could do their job, but his shoes and puttees were slick from the mud. He slipped from my grasp. He had taken no more than four or five steps, when the machine guns let loose. He didn't stand a chance. I heard the same sickening thud as the bullets hit him. Violently, his body twitched as the bullets struck full force. He was dead before hitting the ground.

I lay for a long time there, foundering deeper into the muck. Clifford lay sprawled nearby. I could hear the scurrying of rats as they found him. Every once in a while, a machine gun would rake the lip of the crater, or a bomb would explode nearby, dissuading me from fleeing. In early November, in the Argonne area of France, sunrise happens late. I had several hours before I could even get a visual of where I was.

As the minutes crept by, I became more and more certain I'd die there, shot up so badly no one would be able to recognize me—if anyone ever recovered my body. So many of the dead had disappeared, blown to bits, rotted away in no-man's-land, or shredded on the barbed wire. I was sure I'd lie there, dead and exposed. Within hours, the rats would pluck out my eyes and devour them; within days, they would've stripped my flesh from my bones, and within weeks, my uniform would've started to disintegrate.

I did the only thing I could think to do in that place and in those circumstances; being Catholic, I made the sign of the cross. I clutched my hands tightly together and prayed for my deliverance or, if not deliverance, salvation and forgiveness when I would face God in judgment.

He refolded the article, put it back in the baggie, and placed the baggie back in the box. John pushed the box to the table's edge and sat back. Lifting the glass to his lips, John gazed into the amber liquid and then downed the last of it in a single gulp.

He got up from the table and ambled off to bed, leaving an empty glass behind and a whole series of questions ahead.

JULY 25

Six

Arriving home ninety minutes later than usual, John rushed inside and headed straight to his bedroom. After changing into shorts and a T-shirt, John grabbed sandals from the closet and made a beeline to the kitchen. At the table, without caring where it landed, he flipped the lid off the box with the back of his hand and reached in for the plastic baggies. With a flick, he dispensed with the first two and opened the second installment. Laying it on the tabletop, he studied it carefully. In the past, he had only ever scanned the articles, without paying much attention to the byline, date, or, to tell the truth, content.

Standing over the article made the incident, as recounted through the years, come back to life. His grandfather had gone on patrol; found himself stranded and alone in no-man's-land after a brief but intense gun battle; been captured by the Germans; escaped almost immediately; found refuge in a small farm owned by a French woman; saved her from a German deserter intent on further conquest before the war ended; left the farm immediately for fear of being hunted down; wandered about in an attempt to get back to the American lines, capturing twenty Germans en route; and somehow found his way back without so much a scratch, just as the fighting was to end. He could remember no more details, nor could he have recalled, prior to just a few days before, exactly how many days had passed between the start of his grandfather's patrol and his reappearance.

He slipped on his glasses, and the date of the article was the first thing he noted. It was almost three weeks later than the first detailed installment. That was news to him. He wondered why there was a gap.

From the table, John snatched last night's scotch glass, carried it to the sink, rinsed it out, and placed it in the bottom of the sink, on top of other dishes. Turning to his right, he opened the refrigerator to see what his dinner choices were. He had leftover spaghetti from three nights before and an unopened bag of salad turning a brownish-rust color. He pulled the salad out, pulled open the bag, and took a whiff. Spaghetti was for dinner, he decided, as he dumped the salad down the disposal.

While he warmed the spaghetti, his thoughts went back to the gap between the first and second installments. To help lubricate his thinking, he poured a generous glass of a cheap cabernet sauvignon from a five-liter cardboard box with a plastic spigot; he thought more clearly with a glass in hand. He took a sip; walked back to the table, curious about something; and pulled the final installment from its baggie.

Only three days separated the final installment from the second.

He took another sip, returning to the stove. He either had been unaware of or had long ago forgotten about that gap. Either way, it had not colored the way he had viewed his grandfather. But now it did.

It was, John thought, unlikely that the famous war hero would have been sent on occupation duty along the Rhine. He could have been busy making the rounds of the other victorious armies, gathering up his cache of medals. His absence as a result of that particular tour of duty would easily have accounted for the gap.

After another sip of wine, another possibility came to mind: the flu.

He remembered reading something somewhere about it and how deadly it had been. Maybe either the reporter—the same person had written all four pieces—or his grandfather had been laid low by it. That was possible, maybe even probable, since during this time, the Spanish flu's scourge was at its height. Thousands of daily new cases were being reported. If flu was the reason, then whichever one had had it could have counted himself among the fortunate for having survived, considering the millions who did not.

He found it sad and ironic that soldiers could have survived the war and all the dangers that went hand in hand with trench warfare, including getting shot at by a rarely visible foe, only to die from an invisible one. But if one of them had been hit by the flu, three weeks was not too long a period to recuperate. Even then, depending on the illness's severity, the stricken one may still have been very weak and fatigued.

He took another sip of wine, contemplating other possibilities. He wanted to believe one or the other had gotten sick; that was logical and easily corresponded with what had been happening at the time. He had, however, an uneasy feeling that the flu had nothing to do with it. Another sip failed to elicit further insights.

He stuck his finger into the spaghetti and realized it was ready. After lifting the pan from the burner, he spooned its contents onto his plate. With glass in hand, he carried his feast to the table. He moved the article up and away from his plate, hoping to keep sauce from splattering on it.

Out of habit, John pushed his glasses farther up on his nose.

> Paris, December 10, 1918—The reader will remember that we left Private Henry Alston in the bottom of a crater somewhere in no-man's-land. The men who had gone on patrol with him had been killed. German machine guns

swept the area from time to time. Private Alston was sure he would never get out alive and so was busy praying.

> I must've fallen asleep. I dreamed about hearing an English voice calling out to me, as if to guide me to safety. When I came to, it was still dark, and it was quiet. I could hear English being spoken. That was a sign, as far as I was concerned. I figured that if I could hear them, they ought to be able to hear me, unless the wind worked against me. "Psssst," I called out. After a moment, I heard an answering "psssst." Again, I called out. Once more, there was an answer. The third time I called out, I paid closer attention to the direction of the response. I realized it wasn't very far away.
>
> I called out in a hoarse whisper, "I'm going to try to make my way to you."
>
> A response came: "Take your time. We'll cover you."
>
> Believing my chances were better trying to get to safety than waiting to be rescued, and better still under the cover of darkness, I slinked over the lip of the crater and worked my way slowly toward where I'd heard the voice. I whispered, "It's me—Henry. Am I going the right way?"
>
> It took a while, but finally, I got an answer, also in a whisper: "Keep coming, Henry. You're almost there." I didn't recognize the voice but thought nothing of it since whispered voices often sound different.
>
> I finally came across a thick field of barbed wire. That made me feel I was home safe. I slipped

through, crawled over the sandbags, and then fell into the safety of the trench.

Looking at my watch, I saw that it was almost five o'clock in the morning; I'd been out there over seven hours. Standing up, a smile on my face, I saw unfamiliar faces, as well as rifles pointed at me. My smile faded. One soldier stepped forward, disarmed me, and said in English, "The good news is the war is over for you. *Willkommen, Kamerad.*"

Later, I was taken to the rear, guarded by the English-speaking soldier. My hands were bound behind by back, and my ankles were loosely shackled with a rope. As we trudged along, I kept working on the ropes around my wrists, hoping to loosen them. At the first stop, they had become loose enough for me to get my hands free. The German was watching.

"Where did you learn to speak English?" I asked, hoping to get him to drop his guard.

His mother was an American who'd had grandparents living in Germany. She had visited every summer. During a visit, she'd met his father; they'd fallen in love and later gotten married. She had spoken English in the home, wanting her children to be able to speak both languages fluently. She'd had three sons; the one guarding me was the youngest and the sole survivor. The other two had already been killed in the war.

He spoke as though she were no longer around, so I asked him.

"She died of consumption several years ago."

"How old are you?" I asked, because he looked to be in his early fifties. He was thin as a reed, and his face was gaunt and gray. He had dark circles under his eyes.

"Almost eighteen," he replied. "This war has been very hard on all Germans, not just the soldiers."

With a motion of his head, he indicated it was time to move on.

As I started to get up, I tripped and fell down. "Ouch," I screamed. Kicking furiously, I added, "Got caught up in these ropes around my ankles. Can't you untie them?"

He shook his head but said, "I'll help you up." He came over and reached down with his left hand. Grasping my arm, he pulled, trying to help me up. At that moment, I sprang up, both hands free, and knocked him to the ground. I was on top of him in no time. I strangled him. His eyes bugged out, his face turned bright crimson, and then the eyes went lifeless, though they were still staring at me.

I dragged his body into some bushes and stripped off his uniform, replacing mine with his. I hid in that area until night fell and then went looking for a place to hide until I could figure out how to get back to the American lines.

I found what was left of a grange. I tunneled into the debris and waited. Lucky for me, there weren't many rats, but I did crush one with a rock and then gutted it, peeled off some of the meat, and ate it raw.

By the next night, I'd figured out, by the artillery flashes, which way I had to go. I slipped away and looped around to the north and west, figuring if the Americans continued to advance, I'd run into them. I happened across a couple of small farms; most buildings had been damaged but not enough to be useless.

As the Americans had advanced in late September and early October, pushing the Germans back almost fifteen miles, I'd seen what total destruction looked like from over four years of fighting. I've heard the word *desolation* used to describe the front; I thought it was worse than that. To me, desolation was empty and lifeless, but these areas were filled with carcasses, shattered buildings, and splintered trees. Where I found myself behind the lines had hardly suffered in comparison.

The third night, I found another grange. It was on the edge of a village. Scattered nearby were several dozen houses, an open market and bakery, and, of course, a Catholic church in the village center, with the cemetery on its far side. A plaque on the church listed the villagers who'd died in 1870 during the last war with the Germans, though they were called Prussians then. The buildings' stone had turned gray and green over the years. The name of the village was Beaulieu-en-prés. I'm told it means "beautiful place in the meadow."

The grange was in pretty good shape. The doors were on and still closed, and the roof was mostly intact. I climbed up into the loft, burrowed into the hay, and listened as a steady drizzle came down. The next thing I knew, the sun was up, and I was staring at a pitchfork's pointed end. A young mademoiselle held it, prodding my chest and saying something I couldn't understand.

Figuring I was still in France, in my best French, I said, "I don't *par-lay fran-say.*"

"*Deutsch*?" she asked.

I answered, reverting to English, having used two of my three French words, "No, my name isn't Dutch; it's Henry."

She laughed before asking, "*Anglais*?"

I realized then that she hadn't been asking my name but was asking me if I was German. My uniform must've made her think that.

I shook my head and used my last French word: "*A-mer-i-cane.*"

She jabbered about who knows what. I didn't recognize but a few words. Finally, frustrated, she motioned for me to follow. She climbed down.

Half expecting to be shot as a spy because of the uniform, I decided to strip to my skivvies. Maybe she had seen me come in the night before and had alerted somebody. I scooted to the edge of the hayloft and peered over, not knowing what to expect. She stood at the base of the ladder, pitchfork on the ground next to her; she was holding both sides of the ladder and motioning for me to climb down. No one else was around.

I did as asked, and we went into her house. She had a young son. He might've been three or four. The place was bare except for a few essentials, including two beds, a chest, a table with two chairs, a few pots and pans, and a handful of kitchen utensils.

She pulled some men's clothing and a beret from the chest and handed them to me. I changed behind a blanket hung between the two beds. The pants were about three inches too short and three inches too big around the waist. The shirt wasn't much better. The boots she gave me were the only thing that fit.

It was only then that I had a chance to look her over. I would've guessed her to be in her midtwenties. Her complexion was sallow. She was very thin. Her son, who kept an eye on me the whole time, looked like her.

Each day, I hid in the grange; she must've been afraid I'd be found. I don't know what the consequences would've been for harboring an enemy soldier, but with what she was risking for my sake, I wasn't about to do anything to find out.

At night, she let me in the house, but only after her son had gone to sleep. I had to be quiet and not wake him.

For the next five days and nights, she shared everything.

John got up and refilled his wine glass. Leaning with his back against the countertop, John alternately sipped the wine and savored what he had just read. Biting his lower lip, John focused his thoughts on that last phrase. Reading between the lines, it seemed as if Henry were boasting or confessing, the latter being nothing more for John than a private form of the former.

In his mind, there was never a question what exactly she had shared; his father's existence—and, by extension, his own—was proof enough she'd shared more than just the basics. This young mademoiselle, really a *madame veuve* at the time, was his paternal grandmother by virtue of having given birth to his dad about nine months following Henry Alston's exploits.

He laughed to himself at his use of two words: *virtue* and *exploits*. At first blush, the word *virtue* sounded out of place, all things considered. As for the word *exploits*, it was the perfect word to retrospectively describe Henry's actions and the results. If Henry's exploits were as John now imagined, was it possible virtue was involved?

His first thought was *Certainly not. But why not?* was his next. Perhaps the virtue she had shared was of another kind than *her* virtue. Perhaps in the chaos of the final days of fighting, it remained unclear whether she would live to see the end. This young madame, whose husband's name, he would later learn, had already been added to the lengthy casualty list, had been alone and lonely for so long that she wanted only to feel connected and intimate again. Perhaps all she wanted was to one last time express love as she knew how to express it. Perhaps she was so fed up with the privations of the war that she would not deprive aid and comfort to this fugitive soldier.

There was that word *comfort* again. At Donna's the other night, Steven had used it. In this context, it carried the same connotation as Steven's.

He thought, *I'm in no position to know her predicament or her motives, and I refuse to judge her or her actions. She could've been feeling love. Maybe not the storybook type, but love, albeit fleeting, in the moment.*

John took a sip of wine and muttered to himself, "To have willingly put herself into that position had to have involved risks for her and her son—risks different than those she had dealt with during the occupation. She must've sensed the war drawing to an end and her liberation at hand. The Vandals would be driven out, and she could put her life back together—what was left of it. She simply had to stay out of the way. Yet she hadn't. Why? I'll probably never know, but she had to have had a reason."

Another thought popped into mind: *Maybe she felt she had no choice.*

John emptied his glass. He knew the reason for the gap between the first and second installments. It had nothing to do with the flu, though nausea was a shared complaint. He knew, instinctively, Grandma Jeanne must have gotten word to Henry that she was with child. At the news, Henry had to have returned to make her understand he wanted to make her his intended.

John glanced at the wine box, thinking about another glass, when another epiphany burst upon him—one he had not previously considered and one that demanded serious consideration. If what he now thought had occurred had occurred, and for the reasons that had come to mind, by taking Henry in, she, not his grandfather, would have been the real hero.

A slow smile formed on his face. She could have lain low and waited out the war. In the end, though, she had decided against it, opting for the daring. With little regard for her own regard, she had taken Henry Alston in and provided sanctuary, sheltering him from a potentially tragic denouement to his wartime drama.

His smile transformed itself into a beaming, comprehending one. Setting the glass down on the countertop, he pushed himself off and steadied himself against the edge for a split second. His head was spinning.

John knew what she had had to share—something much larger and much greater than herself, something irreplaceable and invaluable. She must have decided to no longer be part of the death and destruction surrounding her. She must have decided she would take no more; she would give. And what she gave was life.

JULY 26

Seven

In the intimacy of his den, ensconced in the cozy, creaking rocking chair Grandma Jeanne had left him, the one in which they had spent many hours together, John gazed down at an old, leather-bound photo album resting in his lap—one of the five he had retrieved from Donna. A lone floor lamp standing guard behind cast its tight, bright circle of light upon and about him. Beyond the liberties of the light, in the blackness of the house, the chimes of his grandfather clock sounded. He lifted his head, listening attentively to the last stroke of 10:00 p.m. resonating through the solitude.

On the floor to his right, within arm's reach, sat a not-so-tidy pile of the other albums; some were leather bound, and others were covered in fabric. All were awaiting their turn, though John was unsure if he would get to them this night.

On the floor to John's left, a handheld mirror sat facedown. Moments before, John had spent several minutes in self-examination, concentrating first on his eyes and then on his forehead, followed by the size and shape of his nose, the structure of his cheekbones, and, finally, his chin. He had established this mental checklist and order to make the most of the little time he had allotted to leafing through his family's photographic history.

Rubbing his hand over the front cover, he noted the discolored and deep creases in the joint between the cover and the spine. When he opened the album, the oldest of the five, the heady smell of timeworn, well-traveled leather, dried glue, and musty cotton-bond paper wrapped itself around him. The pages, rough to his touch and the color of cold café au lait, felt thick yet brittle. Small black arrowhead-shaped holders secured some photos; others sat at jaunty angles, their holders gone, liberated from their years of captivity.

Over the years, many of the ragged-edged, sepia-toned photos had faded, making it hard to distinguish features. Others were already nothing more than ethereal shapes, causing him to push his glasses onto his forehead, lift the album closer to his face, shift it around to catch the best light, and strain his eyes.

From one page, he pulled out a photo to examine later, in better light and a better frame of mind. On its bottom border, someone had scrawled something, though the words were practically indecipherable. He flipped it over to see if he could find any other markings. Finding none, he placed it on the floor to his left, starting a pile in anticipation of adding others from his forensic examination.

As the grandfather clock sounded 10:30 p.m., he put the first album on top of the mirror and then reached for the next. This album contained black-and-white photos, and as in the first, the people in it sat rigid and unsmiling. Their clothing, hats, and hairstyles bespoke another time, a different era. As in the first, the people in this one, no matter how young at the sitting, all looked old. He pulled no photos from this one.

John was well into the third album when 11:00 p.m. tolled. For the first time during this exercise, John recognized people he had known: Grandma Jeanne and Pappi Henry, as he was known, on his dad's side of the family. Also, photos of his dad's only sister, Mary, who had died suddenly and unexpectedly shortly after Grandma Jeanne passed, appeared for the first time. He closed this album, again feeling the sting of looking like no one in the photos.

By 11:30 p.m., John had made his way through the remaining two albums, the photos in these more recent than the first three and populated with people—grandparents, grandaunts and granduncles, parents, aunts, uncles, siblings, nieces, nephews, and cousins—whom he had known for the better part of his life.

Closing the last album, he looked down to his right at the journals and decided as he yawned, stretched, and rubbed his eyes that he had gotten through what he could. The journals would have to wait.

He cast a glance down at the pile of photos that he had deemed worthy of closer scrutiny. There was but the one photo. Picking it up, he considered it, shifting it slightly right and left and tilting it front and back. He could not remember what about it had made him pull it out and set it aside in the first place, there being no obvious resemblance whatsoever to the person in the photo.

"I'll put it back before I forget where it goes and then go to bed," he murmured.

He thrust his hand into the pile of albums, felt for the bottom one, grabbed it by its spine, and gave a forceful yank. A muffled sound of leather ripping greeted him. He exclaimed, "Shit!"

Holding up the spine, which had several pages still attached, he helplessly watched as a dusting of leather and paper motes settled onto his lap. Muttering, he said, "Goddamn it. Donna will make me find some book repair place. Probably cost me a fortune. Goddamn you, Johann. It's your fault!"

He set the album on his knees and, reaching up with both hands, massaged his temples, the hint of a building headache just behind his eyes.

John let his chin slump to his chest and closed his eyes; he realized he was dead tired, having gotten only about three hours of sleep the night before—and a troubled three at that. No matter how hard he had tried to relax and drift off to sleep, he could not banish the thought that something unsettling and upsetting was looming. Worse, he was convinced that whatever it was was tied to the Germans. By two in the morning, just as he felt himself nodding off, Johann's face popped into his mind. He found himself once again staring at his own image.

I need to get some sleep, he thought to himself, rocking rhythmically back and forth.

He reached for the severed album covers and wayward pages. Gingerly, he took hold, wriggled them free, and lifted them onto his lap. He set the tail of the book against his stomach and flipped open the front cover, swinging it to his left and letting it come to rest against the left arm of the chair. Leafing through, he found the place where the still-attached pages belonged. He reinserted them and flipped through the remaining pages.

Confident the photo album was back in its proper order—as best as he could remember—he grabbed the rear cover to close it. He noticed, for the first time, a slit running along its backing. This slit ran true and neat, as if made with a sharp blade and on purpose. Remnants of brownish, flaking tape no longer serving a purpose were visible in the bright light.

Running his hand over the backing to smooth it down, he suddenly stopped. He had felt something. Lightly, he again ran his hand, in an ever-widening motion, over that area. Again, at the same spot, his hand came to a stop.

Certain something was there, he cautiously lifted the top edge of the slit. Peering inside, he could just make out what looked to be an edge of something. Careful not to rip the paper, he gingerly inserted the pudgy fingertip of his pinkie in an effort to free what he saw. After several clumsy failures, he glanced about for something to use.

On his desk, to his left, a glint of light reflecting off his stamp-collection tweezers caught his eye. Grunting from aching knees and a balky lower back, he lifted himself out of the chair with his left hand, the photo album clutched tightly in his right. He stood momentarily still, arched his back slightly backward in relief, and then shuffled over to his desk. He grabbed the tweezers and, as a second thought, a small clear-plastic tape dispenser.

He returned to the rocking chair. Wriggling up and down and back and forth, he got comfortable, making sure the best light fell onto his lap. John slipped the tip of his left pinkie into the cut and wedged it slowly and slightly deeper. He took up the tweezers and slid the elongated, rounded prongs into the cut. Then, with the patience and deft touch of a kid playing the board game Operation, he inched the tweezers in.

Several cautious attempts later, he felt the tweezers grasp the object. Lightly wiggling it back and forth, he loosened whatever it was. Once he had liberated it from its long imprisonment, he instantly recognized the back of an old photo.

He inserted the tweezers between his lips and let them dangle like a cigarette. A slight cramping of his right hand caused him to flex it several times and then massage it to restore circulation.

He set the back cover back down and nonchalantly pushed the photo to one side. John tore off a small piece of tape, pressed it in place, and then repeated the process twice. He then vigorously rubbed the tape to make it turn invisible.

The grandfather clock struck midnight. "I've got to get some sleep," he said aloud, and then he sighed.

He picked up the emancipated photo. As he was about to drop it on the floor next to the photo albums, he stopped. "I might as well take a peek."

He flipped it face up; staring back at him was a face. It was of a young man in an army uniform.

The soldier had to be German, since he was wearing a pickelhaube, one of those funny-looking helmets with a spike on the top. Along the photo's bottom edge, in a distinct hand he recognized as his grandmother's, the word *Franzis* was written.

Bringing it close, he studied the face and eyes carefully. What John saw caused him to gasp, just as he had the other day in the museum. Reaching up with his left hand, he removed his glasses and brought the photo closer, almost to his nose. He exhaled loudly through clenched teeth, making a whistling sound. Holding the photo in his right hand, he snapped it a couple of times with his left middle finger and then slipped it into his shirt pocket.

He knew sleep would again prove elusive.

JULY 27

Eight

"How many more days are we going to do this?" Wilhelm remarked from the backseat. "I told you that when he pulled out of the parking lot he was going to go straight home. He goes the same way every time."

Magdalena glanced into the rearview mirror. She kept quiet.

Johann, sitting alongside her, replied, "What's the problem?"

"The least he could do is to take a different route. I couldn't do it; I'd go crazy after only a few days. I vote we rethink our plan. Following him mornings and nights and going to museums in between is not what we came to do."

"You went to the hotel pool today, so it's not just museums," Johann said.

"I didn't come here to do that either; I came to learn about what happened to our grandfather," Wilhelm replied. "Pay attention, Magdalena. He's going to turn left at the next street."

"You think you're the only one who knows?" Magdalena commented, glancing in the rearview mirror. She gave him a sarcastic smile.

Magdalena was following at a safe distance as John's car turned first onto Redwood Drive and then onto Baobab Drive, followed by a left onto Cypress.

"I vote we go straight to Herr Alston's house," Wilhelm threw out.

Magdalena replied, "This is what we agreed to do, remember?"

"I remember," Wilhelm replied sarcastically. "You remember I only reluctantly agreed?"

Johann turned around. "How could we not? You constantly remind us."

The three fell silent as John's car turned onto Poplar Street, John's street. John's house was the fifth one on the right—a large, attractive two-story white house with a three-car garage. Magdalena stopped in the middle of the intersection as his car pulled into the garage.

"Shall we vote on my suggestion?" Wilhelm asked as Magdalena drove off.

Johann replied, "Yes. To prove how fair we are, we should vote. I vote no."

"Me too," Magdalena added. "You lose. Anything else you want to put to a vote?"

Wilhelm sat back in his seat and returned his gaze to the outside. "It's not fair. How long are we going to continue to do this? It's futile from my perspective."

Johann craned his head to his left and, eyeing his brother, replied, "Not too much longer. Earlier today, Magdalena and I talked about needing to do something different."

"You did?" Wilhelm asked hopefully. "Where was I?"

"At the pool, sunning. While I'm on that subject, I don't think it's proper for a man your age to wear such a tiny swim suit," Magdalena replied, catching her brother's eye in the mirror.

"I have faith women find it attractive," Wilhelm responded.

"Need I point out that faith is rarely grounded in fact?" she replied.

Wilhelm exhaled. "Let's get back to the matter at hand. What did you discuss during my absence?"

"Are you really interested or just acting like it?" his brother asked.

"I want to hear it," Wilhelm answered sincerely. "Any plan has got to be better than the current one."

"Are you finished? If so, we'll share our thoughts on what's next," Magdalena remarked, pulling onto Broadway Boulevard to go back to the hotel.

"Yeah, I'm finished. Tell me—what are we going to do differently?" Wilhelm responded.

Johann nodded at Magdalena. She nodded back to him.

Taking the lead, Johann started. "We've decided we're not going to the hotel lounge tonight. We know all the songs by heart."

Interrupting, Wilhelm remarked heatedly, "This is what you discussed while I was at the pool?"

"Of course not." Magdalena laughed. "We thought it'd be funny to see if you were paying attention."

"I can hardly control myself," Wilhelm added.

Johann finished, "We're going to follow John home from work one more day. If tomorrow he goes straight home and not to his father's, we'll go knock on Herr Alston's door. It's time to move this along. How does that sound?"

"Gut!" Wilhelm exclaimed. "Now that that's settled, what are we going to do for dinner? Anyone want barbecue again? I'm told LaPorte's is good. We haven't tried that one."

Nine

A ringing phone greeted John as he came in from the garage. In the background, he could hear the whirring of the garage door closing. Glancing at the stove clock, he realized he had been stuck in that late-afternoon meeting an hour longer than he'd originally thought. Had he listened to the radio on the way home, as was normal, he would have already figured this out. Instead, the radio had remained off; he had been preoccupied with the photo he had found the night before and the last newspaper installment.

Striding across the kitchen, he reached for the wall-mounted phone. Lifting the handset, he could hear only a dial tone.

"Good! I didn't want to talk to whoever it was anyway," he muttered. "In fact, I don't feel like talking to anyone tonight."

He laid the handset on the counter and then set his briefcase on the floor. Reaching down, he pulled off his high-gloss black tasseled loafers. The big toe of his right foot stuck through a hole in his sock. Grinning, he remembered he had to go shopping for badly needed socks and underwear. He yanked off both socks and then tossed them into the trash.

He went to the cabinet where he kept his scotch, and he pulled the bottle out. He retrieved last night's glass from the kitchen sink, rinsed it out, and, leaving the other dishes untouched, dried it on a crumpled towel.

He held it up to the evening light streaming in through the window over the sink and saw in the slanting rays that he had done a good enough job. Whatever the hot water hadn't taken care of, the alcohol would. He was about to pour two fingers.

Across the way, the phone started making the obnoxious noise it made when left off the hook too long. He set the bottle down, shuffled across the kitchen, grabbed the handset, and stuffed it into a drawer filled with dish towels.

"That'll take care of that," he said softly to no one, and then he added, "I've got to get out of these clothes before I do anything else."

In his bedroom, he changed into his favorite shorts and T-shirt, the same ones he had worn the last three nights. Sitting on the edge of his bed, he slipped his sandals on and then glanced at the photo of the German soldier on the nightstand. He picked it up, regarded it for a minute, and then, with it in hand, returned to the kitchen.

He set the photo on the table and went to the pantry, looking for something to eat. His choices were limited; John decided to fix a peanut butter and jelly sandwich.

"I should probably have milk with dinner. I doubt scotch and peanut butter mix well," he said aloud to himself.

With dinner on his plate, he sat down at the table. The shoe box was to his right, where he had left it. He lifted the lid, reached in, and pulled out the last installment. He gently removed it from its baggie and, going through a similar routine as he had with the first two, unfolded it, straightened out the creases, and put his glasses on.

He took a long pull of milk.

> Paris, December 13, 1918—Our very own Private Henry Alston had now been gone for more than a week, still

unaccounted for and believed dead. His sergeant had listed him as missing but conceded he had likely been killed in action, simply up and disappearing like so many before, not leaving a trace. Since going out on patrol, Private Alston had been lured to the German trenches, captured, escaped, and been on the lam, trying to make his way back to the American lines. For days, he had found refuge on a small farm with a French woman and her young son.

Private Alston continues his story.

> The last day there, I was in the hayloft, watching through the slits as the Frenchwoman scrubbed the few clothes she and her son owned and then hung them to dry in a chill north wind.
>
> Almost every day, she had been visited by the village priest; this day was no different. He'd stay fifteen or so minutes each time. After he left, she always seemed upset, but after this visit, she seemed more so. I tried to ask what he'd wanted and why she was so upset, but I'm not sure I made myself clear. She muttered something, no doubt trying to explain, but like her, I didn't understand. Finally, she pointed at me, acting as though she were shouldering a rifle, and then raised her arms.
>
> My first thought was she wanted me to surrender, but I finally came to understand she meant the Germans, after she made a gesture on her head to indicate a pickelhaube. That meant the killing was almost over.
>
> If true, I needed to make my way back to the American lines, not wanting to explain how I'd

ended up behind enemy lines and out of uniform. I decided to sneak off under cover of darkness that night. Grateful for all she had done for me, I was of the mind it'd be best if she didn't know; I'd just slip away.

Late that afternoon, she brought me some dark country bread, a few slices of cheese, and a bit of wine. I made a gesture to ask where her son was. She gestured back by pointing at the house and then tilting her head to one side, placing it on her hands, and closing her eyes. I think she suspected something, because the helping was larger than usual, and she stayed longer than usual. Finally, she climbed down and went back inside. Afterward, I lay down, hoping to rest.

I was awakened by loud voices coming from the house. I scurried around the hayloft, peeking through various openings and slats. I didn't see anything. I climbed down and moved to a corner of the house. I peeked in. A German soldier was inside, his back to the window; he was shouting and gesturing. I moved to the other side of the window. From there, I could see her son; he was peering around a blanket, fear on his face.

As the soldier started to take off his uniform, the Frenchwoman motioned to her son to get behind the blanket and close his eyes.

The previous several days, German soldiers had straggled through, looking for something to eat or drink but not causing any trouble. I had kept a watchful eye just in case they'd something else in mind. This one obviously was after something else.

She and I made eye contact; her eyes then darted to the table. A long knife was in clear view but out of her reach. I nodded and then, pointing to myself, gestured with a finger across my throat. She nodded and turned away. By now, the soldier was ready.

I slipped around the corner of the house and slowly pushed open the door. The boy was lying on his stomach, his forehead resting on his crossed arms. Lifting his head, he looked directly at me. I put a finger to my lips, gesturing to stay quiet. He buried his face in his arms.

I could hear the German speaking between grunts. I could understand what he was saying; he was speaking the King's English. He was saying, really more taunting, that he wasn't going back to Germany without one final violation of France.

I laid my hand on the knife and carefully slid it to the table's edge. Holding it firmly in my right hand, I tiptoed to the edge of the blanket and peered around. Her eyes were shut, and the soldier was too busy to be aware of my presence.

I lunged, yelling, "Take this!" I'm sure he was shocked, if he'd time to notice, to hear another voice speaking English. The knife went in. His head came up, and a scream escaped from his mouth. I yanked the knife out and then grabbed his hair and jerked his head farther back, exposing his throat. The knife found its way across his neck.

With a heave, the French woman pushed him off. He fell to the floor with a dull thud, his head lolling off to one side.

She pulled the blanket down and wrapped herself up. Taking her son up in her arms, she cradled him, cooing to him.

A split second later, she motioned for me to get the body out of the house.

I dragged the German out of the house and into the grange. I went back to the house and gathered his belongings, leaving his rifle just in case. I dug a hole and put his things in. When finished burying his belongings, I arranged some things over the hole to cover it up.

I didn't think it wise to leave her and her son alone, but I knew I had to get out of there. I was afraid German patrols might be about, rounding up stragglers and deserters. A patrol may have tracked this soldier here. If so, it wouldn't take long to find me, no matter where I hid.

I went back in; she'd cleaned herself up and was busy scrubbing the floor. The little boy sat at the table, not moving, as if in shock. As I washed, she kept muttering, *"Merci, merci."*

I explained with gestures that I'd be leaving. She nodded and then gathered a small parcel of food for me.

I put back on the German uniform I'd been wearing when I'd first shown up, and I slipped off without saying good-bye, taking only the rifle and the food. I stumbled around for most of the night before I found another place.

My last day, as I made my way closer to the front, I disarmed and captured the German soldiers I'd bring over. Most I surprised as they rested or retreated. None gave a sign of wanting to be a hero. They happily threw their weapons down and their arms up and said, smiling, "*Kamerad.*"

We kept on the move. By late morning, I was less than a half mile from the front. Everything on the German side was chaos. In some places, red flags were flying. We came across one group who busied themselves with former officers. I kept a suspicious eye on them as we skirted around, hoping no one would try to stop us. They let us pass without as much as a word or gesture.

Forming the group up in front of me, we trudged across no-man's-land. I was surprised by the eerie near silence; in the distance, I still heard sporadic shelling and firing. But for the first time in I don't know how long, there was little of the shrill whining of overhead shells or the deep-throated rattle of machine guns. More than anything else, I remember the disquieting quiet. The world as we had come to know it was about to change again.

The rest of the story you know.

Thus ends the behind-the-enemy-lines exploits of our war hero, Private Henry Alston. Even in the last days of the war, caught behind enemy lines, he did what he had to do

> to protect innocent victims from German brutality and kept his head about him, capturing twenty enemy soldiers. He has received several commendations thus far and likely will receive many more for his valor.
>
> The future is a murky thing, but this reporter predicts the country will celebrate Private Henry Alston's heroism for years to come.

John removed his glasses and rubbed the bridge of his nose. He refolded the article, put it away, and closed the box. He got up, stretched his arms upward, and arched his back, stiff from having sat too long. Deciding to get some sleep, he grabbed the box and tucked it under an arm. He carried his dishes to the sink and set them in the bottom, on top of the others. Before quitting the kitchen, he opened the drawer, freeing the phone from captivity. It was still making that obnoxious noise. He put it back on the hook. Almost immediately, the phone rang.

He picked it up. "Hello?"

"Where in the hell have you been, and where's my letter?" a strident voice on the other end asked.

"Hi, Dad. How are you? It's good to hear your voice after so long. I'm fine; thanks for asking," John replied.

"Knock it off. I've been calling since about five thirty. It's now almost nine. Have you been avoiding my calls?"

"That's not possible. I don't have caller ID, so I have no idea who's on the phone when it rings. If I did, I might've not picked up."

"I would've called all night long if I had to," his dad retorted.

"No need; I picked up. If you must know, I didn't get home from work until seven thirty, and when I came home, I took the phone off the hook, wanting some peace and quiet."

"Good God, do you always work so late? And to think, I couldn't imagine you working as hard as your brother."

"Not usually, but something big came up at work. I've had to put in some longer hours and sit through a couple meetings. Thanks for comparing me with Steven. That's a real compliment. It was intended as a compliment, right?" John delivered the last two lines in a sarcastic tone of voice.

"If you want to take it that way, there's nothing stopping you."

"We'll leave it at that."

"I only asked where you were because, like I said, I've been calling most of the night. I want my letter back. I even thought about calling you at work," his dad commented.

"Thanks for not calling work. I wouldn't have been able to pick up there either, and I'd prefer you not jam up my voice mail."

John had standing orders with his assistant that if his father called, she was to tell him that John was unavailable and would call back. Not once had his assistant had to deliver that message.

"Hell, the only thing stopping me was I don't know your work number; in fact, I have no idea where you work these days. Are you still hanging out with those parasites in the real-estate business?" Francis asked.

"Still in real estate, but I've latched on with different parasites," John replied, wanting to not delve too deeply into the subject with his father.

"That's your business, not mine; just don't call me if you find yourself in trouble. I won't help. I've repeatedly told you to get out of that business and into something honest."

"Don't worry about it; I won't. Anything else?"

"Yes! Do you have it?" Francis inquired, a hint of worry in his voice. "You haven't sent it off somewhere to be translated, have you?"

"We must be back to the letter."

"Good God! Of course we're back to the letter. What else would we have to talk about?"

"Since we've already talked about my work, you could ask about my kids," John commented dryly.

"I doubt you know any more about them, their whereabouts, or what they're doing than I do. Am I right?" Francis asked, and then he added, his volume rising, "Can't we just keep the conversation on point? I want to know where my letter is."

"Okay, okay, okay. I've got it, and no, I haven't done anything with it yet. I've been too busy to pay much attention to it. I'll find someone tomorrow. I promise."

"Don't bother. I want it back. Why don't you drive it over tonight? I can't chance anyone reading it, and I won't sleep until it is back in my possession. You never know who you can trust."

"Listen, I'm tired. I'm not bringing you the letter tonight. I can bring it with me the next time I stop by."

"I'll likely be dead at that rate."

"Okay. What if I drop it off tomorrow after work? That'd be somewhat on my way. Don't you want to know what's in it?" John asked.

"I'll figure that out myself. I want the letter back. I told Donna, when she took it from me, you wouldn't do anything with it. Turned out I was right," his dad shot back.

"Whatever you say, Dad. I've offered to swing it by tomorrow. Will that work? And will you be home?"

"Where else would I be? Since my car's been taken away, I'm stuck with no other means to get out, except for my kids, when they care to come by, you not being one, and the white van that swings by once a week filled with old people. That thing smells inside, and the people inside smell. So to answer your asinine question, of course I'll be home, and I guess that'll have to work. Don't forget it."

The line went dead.

John held the phone in his outstretched arm, his jaw clenched, staring at it. Deciding one call was enough and wanting not to chance another, he set the handset on the counter, where it would stay for the night.

He gathered up the box and photo and resolutely strode to the other side of the kitchen. He put the box down and laid the photo on top. He reached for the scotch bottle and his glass and poured a finger of ambrosia. Not bothering with ice, its bouquet, or its color, he downed the drink in one swig.

"Ah, just what the doctor ordered," he said softly, thinking about what he had read and how it fit with all that had recently occurred. Having reread the newspaper articles, having met Johann and his siblings, and having found the photo hidden away in the backing of the photo album, a clearer picture was forming.

After the armistice, Henry had learned that Jeanne was pregnant. He went back to Beaulieu-en-prés, which would account for the time gap in the articles. He had explained that he'd return to take her and their child back home with him; granted, it wouldn't be until 1921. Her son, Alain, stayed behind with his dad's family. Grandma Jeanne returned every other year, always alone, to visit. She saw her older son for the last time in 1938, when Europe was again in a headlong rush toward war. Alain died in May 1940, defending his country from the latest generation of German invaders. She didn't get to his grave until 1948. After that, she never went back and never mentioned his name.

Henry also did the right thing after the war, just as he had during. How difficult it must've been for him to bring home a foreign bride who didn't speak the language at first and then spoke with a noticeable accent the rest of her life—a woman who'd been married before and widowed early, with a child who'd died in childbirth and a living one from her first marriage who had stayed behind. Yet Henry remained true to her and his mission. They had a daughter in 1922 and stayed married until Henry's death. Francis adapted quickly and well to his new circumstances, only returning to France during World War II as an American soldier. Shortly after his return, he met the woman he'd marry. They had four children in short order and stayed together until her death.

John shot a glance at the photo and then aimlessly glanced about, focusing on nothing in particular. Thoughts surged through his brain. Again, he thought about how he was not like his grandfather; that saddened him. Yet he was not like his father; that didn't sadden him. Though they hadn't gotten along for a long time, he couldn't remember their relationship being as strained as that night's phone conversation had suggested.

Not like my grandfather and not like my father. He returned his gaze to the photo, tapping it several times with a finger, and then cocked his head to one side. *I wonder.*

MAPLETON VALLEY

FORTY YEARS EARLIER

Ten

Standing silently outside the door to his grandmother's small bedroom, his back against the wall, John spied in through a six-inch wide crack. Despite the murky light from the gathering dusk and the nearly drawn curtains, he could see her clearly lying on her bed, a thin ray of light from the overhead hallway light spilling in and washing over her face and body. She had kicked off the covers. She was practically naked, a threadbare night shift hanging loosely off a shoulder and hiked halfway up her thighs. Peering in, he watched as her head thrashed rhythmically on her pillow. Her eyes were shut, the muscles of her face taut. Suddenly, her hips bucked upward, arching higher and higher. She threw her head back as another spasm coursed through her body. He could hear her panting. Though only twelve, John knew enough about life to understand what he was witnessing.

Engrossed, he dared not move but cast an embarrassed and guilty look in the opposite direction, one filled with hope of not being found out. Turning back toward her, he noticed her body had just as suddenly relaxed, going practically limp. He heard a soft, wistful moan escape from her slightly moving lips. Her tongue flicked out and sensuously circled her lips. The cadence of her breathing had slowed. Then began her muttering; words, really more like pleas, escaped in a low whine, rose into the room, and were then completely swallowed in the midst between them.

He slid sideways toward the door, nudged it open with his left shoulder, crossing his fingers that a squeaky hinge would not give him up, and stole into her room. As he inched closer on tiptoes, her words became clearer to him. He knelt next to the bed and gently reached for her hand.

Her eyes opened with a jolt and stared hypnotically at the ceiling. Feebly struggling to free her hand, she whimpered, "*Non, non. S'il vous plait. Je ne peux pas. S'il vous plait, je ne peux pas.*" On the cusp of weeping, she repeated, "*Arrêtez, s'il vous plait. Non. S'il vous plait, arrêtez. S'il vous plait, ne me commandiez pas ça.*"

To John, what she was muttering was clear. He had grown up speaking French with her; he was the only grandkid Grandma Jeanne had taught. When she wanted to make sure his siblings had no clue what they were talking about, she and he spoke in her mother tongue.

His grandma's eyes closed again, and her head rolled gently away from him. Her breathing settled into a shallow and rapid pant. The raspy rale in her throat, which he had heard for the first time just days before, had grown more noticeable. Hers had the same distinctive timbre John had heard when his Pappi Henry had lain dying. He had died in this room just over two years before.

John shivered at that remembrance—not only because he had been particularly close to Pappi Henry but also because Pappi

Henry had died within days of developing his rale. Plus, John recognized the overpowering reek that had crept into her room in the past day—the same one that had been present when his grandfather had died. And as it had during that time, it was stealing into a place where it was hardly or heartily welcomed. He remembered the harsh truth he had learned back then—death never came to call; it came to cull. John knew it would not be much longer before she too departed. He swallowed hard, fighting back tears, breathing slowly and deeply through his nose.

John glanced around the bedroom from his knees, seeing that not much had changed in the interim. Cataloging it for his own sake, he noted the outdated, brownish wallpaper with thick, sinuous vines and large, randomly blooming, formerly red but now faded to puce flowers clawing their way toward the ceiling; the jaundice-colored lace curtains that at one time had been bright white; and the old-fashioned matching rock maple dresser, armoire, nightstands, head- and footboards, and rocking chair, this last piece sitting in front of the window. The dresser and nightstands each had a squat table lamp; each lamp had a shade the same shade as the curtains. Also yellowed from age, tattered lace doilies sat under the lamps on the nightstands, protecting the beautiful dark-grained wood.

He pressed his hands against the side rail, pushed himself up, and walked to the rocking chair. He pulled the chair to the bed and sat down. The chair creaked, bringing a smile to his face. It had creaked every time he and Grandma Jeanne had rocked together. She had held him in an all-encompassing embrace; he'd felt safe and secure in her lap, one of the few places he'd had a sense of belonging. Leisurely rocking, she'd told him stories of her youth on the family farm in northeastern France. Getting drowsy, he would bury his face into her meager bosom and breathe deeply, certain what he smelled was goodness.

Stroking his hair as they rocked, she'd repeatedly murmur, "*Tu te ressembles fortement a ton grand-père, Jean. Qu'il était beau et fort. Que je l'aimais; plus que je croyais possible.*"

"Why do you say that Grandma—that I look like Grandpa?" he would ask. "I don't think I look like anyone in the family. And I'm not handsome or strong like you say I am. And, Grandma, how is it possible to love someone more than you thought possible?"

She would hold him tighter and whisper, "*O mon petit,* you do look just like your grandfather."

John had been almost ten years old when Pappi had passed away. The year prior to his passing, Pappi had been mostly bedridden, weakened by the cancer that consumed him. John's best-surviving memories of his grandfather, the ones he kept alive in his memory, were of his grandfather as a short and stocky man with white hair, a wrinkly face, and soft, translucent-looking skin—skin with a pale bluish shade on his hands from the underlying veins being too close to the surface. Pappi had worn rimless glasses with funny-looking wraparound earpieces. John used to think Pappi had worn those to keep his glasses from falling off when he fell asleep, his chin dropping by degrees to his chest, while reading. When his grandfather had removed them with that unhurried motion of his to clean them with the hankie he had always kept in the back right pocket of his pants, the deep red indentations on each side of his grandfather's nose had stood out. Course, wiry stray hairs had bristled from his ears and eyebrows. He'd had a strong, almost overpowering odor; John had thought it might be from being old, though it might have been from Pappi's shaving cream or aftershave. Also, John remembered that Pappi Henry had groaned practically every time he had stood up. Once on his feet, he'd had to momentarily stand in place, a hand resting on any nearby piece of furniture or person, before he would shuffle off slowly and stiffly to wherever he was headed, which many times turned out to be nowhere in particular and his next resting spot.

With his grandfather's passing, John had looked at photos of him as a younger, healthier, and happier man. There was no likeness.

As John had snuggled in his grandmother's lap, he'd thought about what his grandmother had said. He'd figured it was probably one of those things he would understand when he got older, whenever that was.

"Grandma, do you think someday I will love someone as much as you loved my grandfather?" he had asked frequently.

She would always answer him the same way: *"Tu pose trop de questions, mon petit, mais j'espère que oui,"* and she would then muss his hair, pulling him even closer.

"I hope so too. I'm sorry I ask too many questions. But, Grandma, if you'd answer, I wouldn't have to ask," he'd replied breathlessly.

"Which don't I answer?" she had asked.

"Only one, Grandma, and always the same one. How is it possible to love someone more than you thought possible? I don't understand."

She would smile knowingly and kiss the top of his head, wrap her right arm caressingly around his shoulders, and hug him still tighter. She would say, her voice almost as caressing as her embrace, "You'll understand when you're older."

In those moments, he'd thought his grandmother was the saddest person he knew.

John had become convinced of that when, at Pappi's funeral, he had learned his Grandma Jeanne had been married once before and had had other sons. She had never told him about them; in fact, she had never even spoken of them.

The priest, standing at the pulpit, had carefully put his reading glasses on and then glanced out at the congregation. His gaze had locked onto Grandma Jeanne.

Reaching into a recess in the pulpit, he'd pulled from it a sheet of paper folded lengthwise in half. Clearing his throat, he'd straightened it out and then begun. "For everything there is a season, a time for every activity under heaven, a time to be born and a time to die."

He'd paused for effect.

"This is a time of celebration, for through death, Henry has been born again into the presence of the Lord."

The priest had cleared his throat again, covering his mouth with his clenched right hand.

"Jeanne, death is no stranger to you. In fact, it has visited you many times—first, when your first child was stillborn in 1913; then when your first husband, Jean-Pierre DuFour, became a casualty of the First World War; and, thirdly, when your second son, Alain DuFour, became one of the Second," the priest continued, pronouncing the last name as *due four.*

A commotion had rippled through the congregation. Obviously, others in attendance had also been caught unawares. John remembered glancing about, seeing eyes shooting looks at one another and then, as inconspicuously as possible, heads tilting toward neighboring ones and lips moving at the speed of buzz saws. He had been able to hear the high-pitched whirring of whispers all the way in the front pew, where he'd sat next to her. Turning his head slightly, John had looked up to his grandma, sitting on his left, surprise etched into his features.

Stoically, she had sat, staring straight ahead.

He'd grabbed her right sleeve and given a gentle tug, his eyes still glued on her face. "Is it true?" he'd whispered skeptically.

"Pay no attention. It is nothing. Besides, it does not concern them," she had whispered sternly out of the corner of her mouth to him, her eyes staring straight ahead.

Then, turning her head slightly toward him, she had momentarily shifted her gaze in his direction, half smiling at him. With that, John had understood he was to ask no further questions about this.

Eleven

His head on the bed and her hand in his, John dozed.

Idealized landscapes of a small farmstead filled his dreams. A man and a young woman were in front of the farmhouse. They were speaking. The voice of the young woman was his grandmother's—not her voice as a young woman but the one he had known his entire life, raspy and breathy. The man's was unfamiliar but filled with presence and commanding respect.

They were arguing in French—no, not arguing. The man was ordering her to do something. She, in turn, was imploring him not to make her, the strain in her voice distinctive. John could feel her anguish. The man's voice came from someone dressed in black whose face was untouched by worry or the sun and whose practiced hands were soft and smooth. Menacingly, he stood over her, staring at her. On her knees and leaning back on her heels, the young woman had to crane her neck back severely to look into his face. Tears flowed from her eyes.

The man, pointing a long, bony finger in her face, glared contemptuously at her. He said, "If you don't do what I say, it'll be very bad for you once the fighting is over. You have until tomorrow."

The woman replied, "Please give me more time. I need more time; I can't decide by tomorrow. It's too soon, too soon."

"Tomorrow or else," the voice responded.

John woke with a start as he felt her hand slip from his. His grandmother balled up her hands as if in prayer and began to sob. She clutched her hands together on her chest, just as she had in the dream; tears were coursing down her cheeks, just as they had in the dream. From her mouth came the voice he had so clearly heard in his sleep. *"S'il vous plait, je ne peux pas. C'est impossible que je fasse ce que vous me demandiez. Je ne veux pas le faire. C'est impossible. Je l'aime."*

"It's okay, Grandma; you don't have to," John reassured her.

Her eyes opened slowly and guardedly shifted about. She turned her head toward him, surprised to find John next to her.

"Il veut que je," she whispered.

"Who's he? Who are you talking to?" John asked.

When she failed to answer, he continued, his voice soothing, "There's no one here but me, Grandma. You're in your house. You're safe. I'm here with you."

Lovingly, she smiled at him, her lips badly chapped and barely parted. Beads of sweat had formed on her face and neck. A small pool had gathered in the indentation at the base of her throat.

"J'ai soif, mon petit," she murmured.

"I'll get you something to drink, Grandma." He lifted himself up.

He returned with a cool, wet washcloth and dabbed her forehead. She sighed. Stroking her face with the back of his hand, he could feel the searing and feverous heat decimating her body. As the washcloth came near her mouth, she would involuntarily turn toward it and make a sucking sound, her lips moving like a fish's.

John gently brought an ice cube to her mouth and then rubbed her lips with it. Instinctively, her tongue flicked out, lapping at the moisture. Bringing a glass to her lips, he guided the straw for her and then watched powerlessly as she struggled to drink through it. He tossed the straw to the floor, raised her head up, and brought the lip of the glass to hers, slightly tilting it so that she could more easily drink. She took several sips; relief washed over her face.

"Merci, mon petit. Tu étais à jamais mon favoris," she whispered conspiratorially to him.

"Don't say I'm your favorite, Grandma; it makes me feel bad," he replied. "The others love you just as much."

"C'est vrai que ton frère et tes sœurs m'aiment autant que toi, mais, je ne les aime pas autant," she replied haughtily, a slightly wicked grin breaking across her flushed face.

"Don't say you don't love them as much!" he scolded, conflicted about how to feel about her statement.

Motioning with her head for him to come closer, she whispered, *"Ecoute, mon petit; il faut que je te parle."*

"What is it, Grandma? What do you have to tell me?" he asked timorously, again dabbing her face with the washcloth.

"You remember the priest at Pappi's funeral? And what he said?" she asked.

Cautiously, he nodded. "I remember him, Grandma, and what he said. I didn't think you wanted to talk about it."

"I must before I go," she replied in a low and scratchy voice.

"Are you sure?"

She nodded.

"Okay, Grandma. What is it?"

Her voice hoarse, she started. "I was seventeen when I married in 1912. Jean-Pierre was like most men of that time: brutish, harsh, unloving, and unforgiving. He treated his pigs better than me. And he drank. But I was no longer a burden to my family; I had learned to hardly expect better. Soon enough, I was with child."

She caught her breath.

John raised the water glass to her lips, giving her a sip. He gently laid her head back on the pillow and rubbed an ice cube around her lips.

"My first son, Jean-Baptiste, died at birth. I was very sad. Then my son Alain was born in 1914. I fell in love with him at first sight. With him to care for and distract me from my sadness and marriage, I thought life would be okay. Then the war came. I was not sorry when Jean-Pierre had to go off, even if I had to run the farm. I thought the fighting would last but a short time. Just as the Germans marched in, Alain got very sick. That kept us from fleeing."

She stopped to catch her breath, which was becoming shallow and irregular. She coughed hard, and her face turned crimson from the strain; veins on both sides of her neck popped out, and froth formed at the corners of her mouth. With the cloth, he dabbed her face.

Grandma Jeanne rolled onto her right side, her feverous eyes staring directly into those of her favorite grandson. Her breathing had become more rapid, and her skin had taken on a chalky pallor.

"I only saw Jean-Pierre alive one more time. He died in 1917, near the village. He had deserted that spring and tried to return. I am so ashamed."

John ran the washcloth over his grandma's face as she rested. "Why are you ashamed, Grandma? He was trying to get to you."

Opening her eyes again, she continued. "I was ashamed because I had never wanted to see him again; I did not love him and never had. But mostly, I was ashamed because after he was dead, I was glad."

Not knowing what to say, John sat self-consciously while she dozed off. Minutes later, she stirred. Looking at her grandson, she said, "What I have to tell you is this: I killed your grandfather."

Startled, he replied, "No, you didn't, Grandma; he died of cancer. He died right here in this room."

"Non, mon petit. You do not understand; I killed him. I did not want to, but I had to. You must know I was forced to—or else."

"Or else what, Grandma?" he asked, unsure what to make of this revelation.

"Or my baby would have been taken away," she stammered.

John answered quickly, "Who, Grandma? Who would've done that?"

"Père," she replied in a halting voice.

"Your father?" he asked, surprised.

She took a breath as if to answer, but rather, her eyes widened, and an expression of joy spread across her face. In a low, soft, caressing voice, she whispered, *"François, je t'aime. Attends-moi. J'arrive!"*

"Francis? Do you want me to get my dad?"

"No; it would do no good, child. He is angry at me; he is ashamed of how he came into the world. He wants nothing more to do with me. But he will understand later," she replied.

John, a confused look on his face, answered in a whisper, "Okay, Grandma, but why are you asking Francis to wait for you then?"

"Ne t'inquiète plus mon petit. François est là, devant moi. Il m'attend. Je vais lui rejoindre," she said. Lifting her right arm, her fingers outstretched as if trying to grab on to something, she added, *"J'arrive."*

"Grandma, who are you talking to? I'm the only one here; there's no one else," he answered.

Her eyes closed. She drifted off.

Remaining next to her, John waited for her to wake; he had questions. It was only later, as her hand turned cold in his, that he realized his questions would go unanswered.

JULY 28

Twelve

Sitting in his car along the curb, John stared up at his dad's front door. He had come straight from work, leaving a little earlier than normal. He felt guilty sitting there—not because he had left early, having put in his time that week, but because he had forgotten the letter. He had almost arrived at work, when it had dawned on him; he had left it on his chest of drawers, under his watch, thinking there was no possible way to forget it. "Oh well," he had said softly aloud. "I'll still swing by and explain. Plus, I'd like to discuss Alain with him."

John always pronounced his never-before-seen and only marginally more mentioned dad's half brother's name in an exaggerated French accent.

Having sat for more than twenty minutes, he knew he should get out and go up to the house, even if unsure how to broach what was on his mind. John's father would probably view his appearance without the letter as an unwanted and unwelcome intrusion. No matter—John knew he should go knock, particularly since, for the second time in less than five minutes, he had seen his father's face peering out the window in the front door. His dad would be wondering who was parked out front. John knew that at any moment, his dad could pick up the phone and call across the street to the Fredericks, if he had not already.

John stared at the Fredericks' house. They had lived in theirs for almost as long as his dad had in his, now going on fifty-two years. They would get the first call, having the best view of the car and being block captains for the watch group. The problem with calling the Fredericks was their eyesight—bad to begin with, it had gotten worse with age. Mrs. Fredericks had had cataracts removed from both eyes within the past decade. That surgery had been deemed a success, improving her vision from blurry and filmy to just blurry. Plus, in her mental condition, she would scurry around looking for her glasses, having a hard time remembering where she had last set them. As for Mr. Fredericks, he had worn an eye patch for as long as John could recall. He was the only person John had ever known who used a monocle.

If John waited much longer, his father would place the call, setting in motion a series of predictably erratic events. Upon fielding the call, whoever answered would call out to the other, and together they would wander over to their front window, the telephone in hand and its long extension cord strained to its limits, and peer out, their faces conspicuously plastered against the glass, adding to the already numerous oily smudges. Failing to recognize the car, they would then tell his dad they would have to call him right back. They would then place a call to the Bournes, neighbors whose house was catty-corner from theirs and just north of his dad's. The Bournes were, of the three, the newest kids on the block, having been in their house a mere twenty-three years. Those two worked, and at this hour of the weekday, they would be at their jobs.

The Fredericks, whose collective mental acuity was no sharper than their collective vision, would not remember; they would get worried when their call went unanswered. To the Fredericks, an unanswered call could signal but one thing: the car parked down the street from the Bournes' was somehow involved. That would be proof enough for the Fredericks to make the next call—not back to his dad but to the police, requesting immediate assistance. Then, for good measure, they might lob a call into the fire department just to make sure someone of authority responded. Mrs. Fredericks had done that in the past.

Staring at the Fredericks' house, John discerned no outward sign of neighborly collaboration yet. Wanting to avoid explaining himself if an emergency vehicle pulled up, John opened his car door and stepped out. Leisurely, he yawned, stretched his arms to their full extent, and slowly turned so that anyone who could see that far could see who he was.

Three-quarters of the way around, John stopped. Another car was parked against the curb, down the street from his, facing in the same direction. It was a newer vehicle, plain like a rental. Squinting and moving his head slightly from side to side, John thought he could make out silhouettes of heads inside, but he was not sure because of the sun's near-blinding reflection off the windshield.

Probably just the headrests, he reasoned.

Still peering at the other car down the street, he could just make out, in the distance, a faint wail of emergency vehicles. Fearful he had waited too long and the Fredericks had placed the phone call, he glanced again in the direction of the Fredericks' house. Still, he saw no outward sign of life.

He listened again. The sirens were moving away. He let out a low whistle of relief and then strode up the steps of the front porch and rapped on his dad's front door.

The inside door immediately opened. His dad, whose left hand was on the doorknob, stared at him through the rickety, weathered screen door, surprised it was him. After a passing standoff, Francis remarked, with a glance at his wristwatch, "You're not who I was expecting—at least not yet. Did you get a new car? I didn't recognize it."

John shot a look over a shoulder and nodded. "Might be new to you. I got it about three years ago. Has it been that long? Did you call the Fredericks? They might've called the police and the fire department."

"I better call off the dogs," Francis responded. "The last time she also called for an ambulance." Pushing the screen door open, he added, "I suppose you want to come in."

"If I could." John reached for the screen door.

"If you must," his dad replied, and then he took three steps back.

"What made Old Lady Frederick call all three?"

"On Halloween, some delinquent egged her house. I guess he didn't like those damned popcorn balls Myrtle hands out."

"She's still handing those out? She was handing them out when I was trick-or-treating."

"Could be the same ones, as far as I know; she told me once they keep. She just doesn't get that today's parents aren't about to let their kids eat anything not hermetically sealed. Anyway, when the ambulance arrived, the paramedics quickly determined there was no medical emergency. When asked why she'd called, she told them it was a precaution just in case her husband had a coronary when he saw what had happened."

"Did he?"

"No, he wasn't even home. He was over at one of the grandkids' houses, helping hand out candy—stuff kids would actually eat," his dad answered. "I better call them back."

His dad walked down the hall and disappeared into the kitchen. Then, peeking around the doorway, he motioned for John to follow.

"That's taken care of. Mrs. Fredericks told me to say hello. Sit down. Do you want coffee?"

Taking a seat at the old dinette table where they had eaten meals as kids, John responded, "Don't go to any trouble. If you've got some brewed, I'd love a cup. Otherwise—"

"I brewed some this morning; I keep it on the warmer all day. I'll pour you a cup."

"Dad, you know you shouldn't—" John was looking at his dad; he had seen that look of annoyance all too often.

"Don't start! Your mom's daughter Donna is always after me for that. I'm old enough to know what I should and shouldn't do. Besides, I survived a war and that crazy Kraut. I can take care of myself," he replied tersely. "Anyway, it's my house, and I'll do what I want, how I want, and when I want. Any questions?"

"Nope. Got it," John answered without conviction. "Why do you say my mom's daughter when she's your daughter also?"

"I'd never try to tell someone how to live their life, so she can't be mine. Your mom would and did, so she has to be hers."

John opted not to remind him of their phone conversation of the night before.

Francis handed him a cup, its acrid aroma reaching him well before. His dad's had a strong, burned smell, whether freshly brewed or not. Glancing into his cup, John noted the usual qualities: viscous as sludge, black as newly laid asphalt, and tacky like roofing tar. Bringing the cup to his lips, he faked a slurp. "That's good, Dad. Thanks."

Holding his hand out, Francis said, "Give me the letter. You brought the letter with you, right?"

John cleared his throat. "I forgot it. Last night, right after our phone call, I put it under my watch on the dresser, thinking I couldn't possibly forget it. I did. I left the house and got to work before realizing it. Sorry."

"I told you last night not to forget, and yet—"

"I know; you don't need to remind me. I feel bad already, okay?" John explained.

"Since you don't have it, why did you come by, John? You could've just called, you know?"

"Alain DuFour," John replied, using an exaggerated French accent.

"You, of all people, shouldn't be butchering the pronunciation of his name, having learned French from your grandmother."

"Sorry again; it's been a long time since I've used it. Can we discuss Alain?"

"Certainly; that subject won't take long. But before we do, when will you bring it to me?"

"How about if I bring it with me the next time I drop by?"

"At that rate, I'll be dead."

"You've already used that line. You can stop with it now." Pausing, John eyed his father, hoping to see the slightest hint of jest on his face. Seeing none, he continued. "Certainly don't want to deprive you; I'll bring it tomorrow. I'll make a special trip."

"It's only special because you forgot it this trip."

"Okay, you've made your point. I said I'm sorry; no need to drive it home any further. But if you ask me, it's a shame you want it, since I still don't know what it's about."

"I'm not asking you, and I know."

"You know I don't know yet, or ...?" John asked in a trailing voice.

"Or what?"

"Or you know what the letter's about?"

"Knew the minute I looked at the return address," Francis replied. "It could only have come from one family and mean only one thing."

John studied his dad's facial expression, trying to read whether his dad really knew. If so, it was possible what Steven had insinuated the other night could have some truth to it. Yet if his dad was about to be found out, he seemed no more worked up than he normally was when his older son was around. Had his dad reconciled himself to the fact that whatever it was was about to get out and that it was too late to do anything about it? Or because of his age, did he no longer care?

"If you know, why did you let Donna take it?" John asked incredulously. "Care to share?"

"In due time, in due time," his dad replied. "Let's get to why you're really here."

"I had a weird dream the other night. Your half brother, Alain, was in it."

"I don't know why you insist on calling him my half brother; I barely lived with him in France when I was a baby, and he never lived with us here in the States. I have no memories of him," Francis said, cupping his hands around his coffee cup.

"That may be, Dad, but it doesn't change the fact. Since you were both born of the same mother, you are, by definition, half brothers."

"I'll concede that. You didn't come here to clarify that. Why are you really here?"

"I'd like to know what you can tell me about him. That's all," John responded matter-of-factly.

"What piqued your interest in Alain, dead now going on seventy years?"

John raised the coffee cup to his lips and took a sip. Its bitterness made his mouth pucker up. "It wasn't a dream; something happened at the museum the other day. It made me pull out the old family photos and Grandma's journals."

"Still looking for the missing link? You think it might be Alain?" his father replied.

John shook his head. "No, not really. In two of the older albums are a few photos of him. There's no resemblance; he must've taken after his father. I know so little about him; I thought I should know the basics since he's family. That's all."

"Family in name only. Here goes. He was born in 1914, survived the First World War, stayed in France with his dad's family when *our* mom moved over here, and died sometime in May 1940, fighting the Nazis. There, you now know what I know," Francis recited perfunctorily. "Do you want to stay for dinner?"

John stretched out his legs to one side of the table. "Sure, if I'm invited. I was hoping for a bit more flesh on the bones, if you know what I mean. Like why didn't he come over to America?" John pushed his coffee cup away.

"I'd guess he didn't want to."

Exasperated by the offhand comment, John said, "That's ridiculous, Dad. Alain wouldn't have been more than seven or so when she came over. He wouldn't have been old enough to make that decision."

"He would've been seven. Maybe his dad's family didn't want him to go. Since his father was killed during the war, Alain would've been all that remained of him. Is that a less ridiculous explanation?"

"It's at least more plausible. Was there bad blood between Grandma and her first husband's family?"

"Where are you hoping to go with that question?" Francis asked. "Do you know something?"

John straightened up in his chair and shook his head. "Know something? I don't know anything. How could I?"

"You're the one looking through old photo albums and reading the journals. That's how."

"I've only had time to look through the albums—haven't had time to get to the journals. Rest assured; I don't know anything. That's why I'm asking questions." John added caustically, "Do you?"

"And if I did?" his dad answered.

John caught his breath.

Something about the way his father was acting made John uneasy. Sliding his left hand into his outside suit coat pocket, John fingered the edge of the photo of the German soldier, the one whose name was the same as his father's but spelled with a *z*. John wondered about his options, considering if this was the moment to pull out the photo. Sensing not, he continued. "Do you know anything about how Alain's dad was killed? I ask because Grandma Jeanne told me he died near her village. He'd deserted around the time of the Chemin des Dames debacle. Does any of this sound right?"

"Right? What's right when it comes to anything your grandmother ever said to you? I'm not sure that word should ever be considered in your situation."

"What does that mean?" John asked, surprised by the response and tone.

"It means she was really good at rearranging and reordering facts, particularly if the real facts reflected poorly on her or didn't support the way she wanted you to see her."

"Should I assume the truth may have been somewhat different than what she told me?" John asked skeptically.

"No, you should not assume the truth may have been somewhat different," Francis replied flatly.

Whistling lightly through his teeth, John made an exaggerated motion of wiping his brow with the back of his right hand and feigning relief. "That's good. I was starting to think I couldn't believe anything I'd heard from her."

Francis regarded his son. "You probably should and shouldn't."

"What does that mean—should and shouldn't?" John asked. "I shouldn't believe what she said was true, but I should believe what she said might be?"

"You probably shouldn't believe how, but you should probably believe what."

"That's blurry; I'm not sure I get what you mean. Can you give me more?" John scratched his scalp.

"Here's more. The seed of what was said is probably, in the end, true, but the real story behind it is almost certainly different than told."

"Almost certainly different? I'm not sure I understand that, but ..." After a moment, John countered, "If that's true, then how should I react to what she told me on her deathbed? I was there when she died. I was only twelve."

"I remember."

"Well?" John asked.

"Well what?" his father replied.

"Well, how should I react to what she told me on her deathbed?"

"What did she tell you?"

"She killed my grandfather; those were her exact words. I'll never forget them. She said she was forced to or her baby would've been taken away. What doesn't make any sense is that she had to be talking about Alain, right, since she didn't have any others? Pappi Henry had nothing to do with Alain. That puzzled me."

"Did she say who was going to take the baby away?"

Lifting his eyes skyward, John tried to recall the long-ago conversation. "I think she said ... She said her father."

"How was that possible? Her father had been killed by the Germans within months of the start of the war," Francis offered.

"I'm positive she said—" John hesitated for a second. "Though it's been a long time. No, I'm sure she said *father.* Doesn't matter—it's probably not important."

"No, it probably is." Francis stared straight into his older son's eyes.

John returned the stare before continuing. "Anyway, I told her she couldn't have killed my grandfather, since he had died just two years before; I reminded her Pappi Henry died of cancer, in the house. Since she was old and dying at the time, I figured she must've gotten confused. So I assume I *shouldn't* believe that, right?"

"No, you *should*."

"What? I should? But ..." John fell quiet, pursing his lips and arching an eyebrow.

"But what?" Francis asked after a moment.

"But you just told me I should assume the truth is somewhat completely different. Remember that?"

"Actually, what I said was you shouldn't believe how it was told; the story's not to be questioned."

"What does that leave?"

"The truth."

"What is the truth?"

"That's up to you to find out."

"Where? In what Grandma Jeanne told me?"

"Partially."

"In what she really meant?"

"Partially."

John thought for a moment. "If the truth may partially be in what she said and partially in what she meant, could it also partially be found in what is not known?"

"That's possible, though a better way to say it may be 'in what has yet to be told.'"

"In what has yet to be told? That'd mean there might be others who might know a piece of the truth?"

"Yes."

"I might have to look beyond what I know, or think I know, or who I know, or who I think I know? Will I have to go outside of what is at hand?"

"Might, but probably not. The truth is usually invisible to us, though it's staring us square in the face. It's only necessary for us to unlearn what we've been taught and to adopt a different perspective."

"Do you know the truth?"

"I know more than you. I don't know it all, not yet. That part is headed this way; I'm convinced of that now."

They fell silent, as if to catch their breath.

Francis broke the hush. "What happened at the museum?"

Instinctively, John was afraid of saying too much, but in the end, after considering what and what not to reveal, he told about meeting the Germans and how uneasy he had felt at the end.

"What exactly made you uneasy?"

"It was the third German who made me uneasy. When I turned to meet him, I was essentially looking at myself."

"What does that mean?" Francis asked.

"I was looking at a man who looked just like me—a spitting image, Dad. His name is Johann."

"Johann, not John?"

"Yes. Johann, not John."

Francis sat back in his chair, letting out a low whistle. "And they're Germans? Did they say anything about who they were or why they were there?"

Ding-dong, ding-dong. The front doorbell chimed as Francis finished.

"Saved by the bell," John joked. "You going to get it, or do you want me to?"

Francis sat immobile, showing no sign of getting up to answer the door. He was mumbling over and over, "German."

"Dad, are you going to get the door?"

He regarded his son before commenting enigmatically, "German—you're positive?"

"Yes, I'm positive. Is something wrong?"

"As I said earlier, the part I don't know is headed this way."

"No need to get melodramatic; it's probably just the Fredericks checking on you, or the police. Are you going to answer?"

"I've been getting myself ready for this for forty years. Now I'm not sure I'm ready."

"What the hell are you talking about?" John asked. "Ready for what, Dad?"

Ding-dong, ding-dong. Again, the doorbell chimed. Again, his father made no move to get up.

John stated, "Someone's got to get the door. What if it's the police? The Fredericks could've already called, you know, and I don't believe the police can choose not respond to a 911 call. It'd be smart to go see, don't you think? You don't want anyone forcing your door, do you?"

Still, his dad gave no indication of getting up.

Ding-dong, ding-dong. Ding-dong, ding-dong.

"I'll go," John added. "I'm afraid of what might happen if it's the police and no one answers."

As he walked from the kitchen, John heard the scrape of chair legs on the worn, gray-streaked pale green linoleum floor. Glancing over his shoulder, he saw that his dad had pushed back from the table and was now in his lee. As they approached the front door through the murky hallway, John could see a silhouetted figure through the sheers covering the window. John reached for the doorknob, turned it counterclockwise, and slowly pulled open the door.

"*Guten Tag*, John," Magdalena offered. Pointing at his car, she added, "We recognized your vehicle."

Her brothers were standing off to her side. Leaning to her left to glance around John, Magdalena smiled at his father, saying, "*Guten Tag*, Herr Alston. My name is Magdalena. These are my brothers, Wilhelm und Johann. Did you receive our letter?"

"Your letter?" John asked, shocked by the question.

"The one that we sent to your father," Magdalena responded

"I got your letter," Francis replied, giving his son a perturbed look, "though I don't have it."

Magdalena translated. Expectant and beaming smiles lit up her brothers' faces.

Placing a hand on John's shoulder, his dad gently moved him aside. He reached for the screen door and pushed it open. Motioning for them to enter, Francis commented, "*Willkommen; Ich habe Sie erwartet.*"

The Germans looked from one to the other, relief breaking upon their faces.

Turning to his son, Francis said, "That's the only German phrase I know. I learned it long ago just for this moment."

"What are you talking about?" John asked, perplexed. "And what did you say?"

"You'll find out soon enough." Turning his head toward the Germans and smiling, Francis answered his son's last question. "I told them I've been expecting them."

"What do you mean you've been expecting them?" John inquired, shocked by his father's statement.

"Just that, John," Francis responded matter-of-factly. "I've been expecting them. That's not so difficult to understand, is it?"

"Yes and no. No, because I understand the words; yes, because I don't understand their meaning."

"Why didn't you say that? I'd have answered. Remember what I've been telling you since you were young?" his dad asked.

The Germans stood silently to one side, embarrassed bystanders to the conversation.

Having stolen a glance at them, John turned and studied his dad, waiting for him to once again remind him of what he needed no reminder of. John turned slightly to the Germans. "My father"—John motioned with his right thumb as if hitchhiking—"used to lecture me on being very precise about what I said." He knit his brow and dropped his chin an inch or two. In a deep and gruff voice, he mimicked what his dad would say and how he would say it. "John, if you are not precise about what you say"—he stopped for effect and waggled his right pointer finger in Magdalena's face before finishing—"what you get is exactly what the other person wants you to hear based on that person's interpretation." Turning to his father, John asked, "What did you mean by what you said?"

"Just that—that I've been expecting them."

"Them specifically?" John pointed at Magdalena and her brothers before motioning into the ether with his eyes screwed up to the heavens. "Or them conceptually?"

"Them conceptually, of course," his dad replied. "I had no idea who might show or how many. I've just been expecting someone to show."

"Now we're getting somewhere. How long have you been expecting someone, Dad?"

"About forty years, since right before your grandmother died. I'd almost given up, resigned to the fact I might never know."

John held up a hand. "Whoa, stop right there. Know? Know what?" Stunned again by what his dad had said, John covered his mouth loosely. He shot a glance from his dad to the visitors and then back.

Flipping the hall light on, Francis took a good look at the three visitors. "John, these must be the people from the museum. I see how much you and Johann look alike. Eerie, isn't it?"

John swallowed hard and motioned toward Johann. "Like I told you, we're practically mirror images."

"I didn't believe it until now. But she"—Francis pointed at Magdalena—"said hello when you answered the door. So obviously, what you told me really happened."

"Thanks for having so much faith, Dad."

Johann said something to Magdalena. Shaking her head, she refused to translate for Francis and John. Johann repeated his comment, and again, his sister shook her head.

Their turn to watch an uncomfortable family squabble unfold, Francis and John watched. It was obvious that whatever Johann had said was causing her difficulties. Johann and Magdalena stared at one another, neither showing any sign of backing down.

Wilhelm, in his halting and broken English, commented, "My bruder tells my sister that she should tell you who we are."

Magdalena nudged Wilhelm with her shoulder while saying something in a cross tone of voice.

Wilhelm continued. "Magdalena says that I am not expressing myself properly. She says that I am like John." He pointed at John, pronouncing his name as "Yon." "That I am not saying exactly what I should be saying." He nudged her with his shoulder.

"Wilhelm does not mean to say that we should introduce ourselves. What he means is that we should make clear who we are und why we have come."

"I'm anxious to hear," Francis commented. Turning and making his way down the hallway, he added over his shoulder,

"Let's go back to the kitchen; we can sit down. Would you like coffee? I have some on."

Intensely, John shook his head. Magdalena translated Francis's question for her brothers. They chuckled at John's reaction.

"Please sit down; make yourselves at home." Francis motioned to the table. "Anyone want coffee? John, want a warm-up?"

There were no takers.

"Okay," Francis said. "So tell me who you are and why you're here."

"It is not so easy to begin, because it started long ago," Magdalena started.

"When did it begin?" John asked curtly.

"My guess is 1917," his dad interjected.

"My dad's full of surprises today," John murmured. "He obviously knows more than he's letting on."

Magdalena regarded Francis. "It actually started in 1914, when my grandfather went off to war. He left behind his wife, our grandmother Hilda, und two young sons: Herman, who was born in 1911, und Alois, who was born in late 1913. At the start of the war, our grandfather could have stayed out because he was a teacher; he instead chose to go with his unit."

"Which was your father?" John asked.

"Neither. My father, Konrad, would not be born until 1918—nine months after our grandfather's last home leave. That would be the last time that my grandmother would see him. After the war, she went to where he had been buried. It was in a small French village by the name of Beaulieu-en-prés."

John straightened up and quickly looked around the table.

"His last known whereabouts," she continued, "placed him in that village the last morning of the war. He must have died there or close by. His body would never be found, but ultimately, a gravestone in a nearby German cemetery would bear his name.

How und why he died, we do not know. That is what we have come to learn, if it is to be learned."

"Continue," Francis commented.

"Though they were separated, they shared their separate lives through letters. He wrote every day that he could. Toward the end, the letters became fewer und fewer."

"He probably had a hard time finding time," John commented dryly. "The Allies were advancing, pressuring the German armies and pushing them back toward their borders."

"That is true. It was what we believed. But we," Magdalena added, pointing to her brothers, "came to suspect, like our grandmother, that there might have been another reason; the other reason involved another woman."

"This is all very interesting, but what's it got to do with us here in Mapleton Valley?" John inquired hesitantly.

"He is the reason." Magdalena pointed directly at John's father, who was wearing a slight smile.

"What?" John replied incredulously. "Him?"

Magdalena answered, "Please allow me to explain."

Wilhelm leaned in, whispering something to his sister. She leaned back in his direction, saying something in return and causing Wilhelm to glare at his sister.

"He wants me to get to the point," she commented, eyeing her brother severely. "But I am telling the story. It is a story that I have thought about for many years now. I have practiced it in my mind so that I could tell it properly when the time came. Now it is time; I will tell it my way und at my own pace," she said, her eyes on Wilhelm.

With a deep breath, she continued. "It was while we were cleaning out our father's things after his death that we learned of the other reason."

"What did you find?" John asked suspiciously.

"Boxes filled with letters und photos. My grandmother wrote letters to her sons und gave them photos of their father. She did this so that they could know him, particularly my father. My father, Konrad, obviously never knew his father, since he had never seen him. By knowing his story, at least as much as she knew, she could make sure that her sons would understand what happened."

"Your grandmother never remarried?" John asked.

"No, she never married again. The only father that my father would know would be the one his mother, Hilda, told him about; he only ever saw his father through his mother's stories und photos."

"It's interesting you've mentioned everyone's name except your grandfather's. There's your grandmother, Hilda; your uncles, Herman and Alois; and your father, Konrad. What was your grandfather's name?" John asked.

"You do not know?" Wilhelm asked, surprised by the question.

John responded, his tone clipped, "How could I?"

Francis cleared his throat. All eyes turned to him.

"Do you know?" John asked.

Francis nodded. "His name was the same as mine, except it was spelled with a *z* instead of a *c*. That's how the name is spelled in German."

"That is correct," Magdalena answered. "His name was Franzis with a *z*."

"I should've known since you'd already said you came because of him," John answered, pointing at his father. "That and the fact the letter you claim to have sent was addressed to Franzis with a *z*. That makes sense. But what does having the same name have to do with anything? There are thousands of men with the name of Francis in the world."

"It is not simply sharing a name. Your father, Franzis, was named for his father," Magdalena explained.

John laughed nervously. "His father was Henry Alston. We called him Pappi Henry. You might've even seen his portrait in the museum, the war hero. Unless Pappi Henry changed it at some point, I'm not aware his name ever contained a Francis, no matter how you spell it."

"You are mistaken," Magdalena replied, even voiced, "but without realizing it. We have a story that you should know. Ours is a story yet to be told."

"Did you say a story yet to be told?" John asked, his eyes shooting in his father's direction.

"I did say a story yet to be told. We know only the beginning; we do not know the end. What we hope is that you have the ending. We hope"—Magdalena pointed first at one brother and then the other—"that you can tell to us the rest. That is why we have come to your city und to this house." Magdalena reached into her purse and pulled from it a small piece of paper with ragged edges. She placed it face down on the table and then covered it with her right hand. "Und this," she added, casting a glance downward, "is the beginning of the story."

Eyeing Francis, Magdalena patted the piece of paper. "I am going to let you see this." She pushed it to Francis. "If you turn it over, you will see someone you have never seen before."

Apprehensively, Francis reached out with his left hand, which shook slightly. "Is it who I think it is?"

"It is who you think," Magdalena answered.

"Is it him?" Francis asked.

John interjected before Magdalena could respond. "Is it who?"

Without hesitation, Francis answered, "My father."

"How could it be your father? How could they"—John pointed reproachfully at the guests—"have a photo of Henry Alston?"

Francis replied softly, "It's not Henry Alston."

"I'm completely lost!" John exclaimed, pushing back from the table.

Taking hold of the paper, Francis asked, "May I?"

"*Bitte*," she replied, lifting her hand from the paper.

Francis placed his left hand on the paper's edge and flicked it a couple of times with his thumb. He lifted a corner. It was a photo. Lifting his eyes to his guests' faces, Francis noted cautious smiles.

He flipped it over and began to say something but then stopped. He placed the photo facedown and slid it back to Magdalena.

Moving her eyes to John, Magdalena pointed at the paper. "You are going to have a chance to see this, und when you see who is on the other side, as Germans say, *Blinde werden sehen*."

"What does that mean?" John asked hesitantly.

"The blind will see."

John's right hand fingered the paper. It looked like the paper in his jacket pocket. He felt an edge, deciding it was the same thickness as his. The edges were irregular and wavy, just like his.

On the back, written in neat, square letters, was the word *Franzis*. With the exception of the different handwriting, the photo was just like the one in his pocket.

Inconspicuously, he dropped his left hand into his lap and then moved it to his jacket pocket. He withdrew his photo and set it faceup on his lap. He glanced down. A German soldier at parade rest looked back at him. He wore a pickelhaube. The soldier's glare was resolute, his chin firm. John looked just like him. He slipped the photo back from where it had come.

Grimacing, John worked his way through what, if Magdalena's photo was of the same person, it had to mean. John gazed down the length of the table; his father's face had a serene look on it, as though some great and mysterious truth had been laid bare and a great weight lifted. Bringing his left hand back onto the tabletop, John planted both hands, palms down, on either side of

Magdalena's paper. He slid the photo along the edge of the table and then lifted the top half. He saw a faded and grainy photo of a young soldier at parade rest. He wore a pickelhaube. The soldier's glare was resolute, his chin firm. John's mouth suddenly went dry, and his mind was blank.

An insidious and deafening stillness stole through the house. John heard barely a sound, the exceptions being the coffeemaker, which had the temerity of making a metallic, clicking sound from time to time, and, in the hallway, the grandfather clock ticktocking away.

"That is our grandfather Franzis." Magdalena pointed.

Francis added, "And yours."

John said, "How could this be my grandfather? The name written on the back is *not* Henry. You did notice that, right?"

"Yeah, the name Francis was written on the back. Francis with a *z*," Francis replied.

"Pappi Henry was my grandfather on your side of the family. Mom's dad's name was Charles. Unless—"

"Unless what?" Francis inquired.

"Unless one of my grandmothers was married before to a man named Francis with a *z*," John replied.

"I can assure you neither grandmother was ever married to anyone named Francis, with either a *c* or a *z*," Francis remarked.

"You're sure?"

"Absolutely. One hundred percent."

"I'm confused then," John commented.

"How's that possible? The truth is looking you square in the face."

John caught his breath. His dad had, minutes before, brought up this notion. Looking up, he saw that Johann was looking squarely into his eyes. "Okay. Maybe I'm not confused. Maybe I'm troubled," John replied.

"That's probably true," Francis said. "About what?"

"About how the guy in this photo"—John waved the photo in the air—"could be my grandfather, when all my life, Pappi Henry was. For that to be the case, that'd mean Grandma Jeanne would've ..."

John stopped and glanced around. "That'd mean my grandmother would've had to have ... You know what I'm getting at."

"Why is it people want to think of their ancestors as better, purer, or wiser?" Francis commented pensively.

"Wait a second," John interjected. "Steven, not too long ago, said something along those lines."

"There must be some truth to it then; Steven's pretty intuitive. Remember, I told you tonight the truth is usually staring you square in the face."

"Okay, I know Grandma Jeanne was married twice—first to Jean-Pierre and then to Pappi Henry. Mom's mom was only ever married to Grandpa Charles. I'm not aware of any other grandfathers, but you tell me the man in the photo is mine." Holding the photo, John acted as if he were studying it; all the while thoughts whirled about in his mind, such as *If what they're saying is true, that'd mean this man would be my father's ...*

John eyed his father, studying his physical features, though the examination was a complete waste; his father looked like his mother, not Pappi Henry, and nothing like the man in the photo. But John did. He was a spitting image of the man in the photo and of Johann, sitting across the way. That could only mean ...

The ticktock of the grandfather clock rolled through the house like a time bomb, and with each tick, John shifted his gaze from his father to Johann and then back. John took a deep breath and licked his lips. "That'd mean this man, Francis with a *z*, is your ..." John could not force himself to utter the last word. Massaging the back of his neck with his left hand, John snuck a peek at Magdalena, who, sitting there calm and composed, leaned slightly forward in her chair with her hands folded serenely on the table. He cast a lightning-quick glimpse at the other players in this drama. Wilhelm sat motionless in his chair, his posture rigid, his chin set, and his eyes glued on Francis, as if sensing that Francis had known what was coming. Johann focused his attention on John.

John pushed the photo toward Magdalena and looked across the table at Johann, studying his features. Now he knew why he looked like no one else in his family; he had been looking in the wrong family. Johann's features were his: the brow and receding hairline, the jowls, and the eyes, particularly the eyes. They had the same shape and color.

He pondered what their thunderbolt—his father was a half something to Johann, Wilhelm, and Magdalena—meant and would mean to him and to his sisters and brother. What were these three to them—also half somethings? Was there such a thing? If so, was it possible to be a half anything in a whole way?

At no time had the Germans mentioned family—wife, husband, or children. But then again, why should they? They had been the only ones who'd suspected or known of a family connection; there was no purpose in mentioning it. All three wore rings that looked like wedding bands. At their ages, they likely had grandchildren and maybe even a great-grandchild or two.

Francis did. John had two sons whom he hadn't spoken to since his nasty and divisive divorce. Sean, the older one, supposedly lived not far away. That one, he'd heard, had married several years back. Donna had mentioned at some point that Sean and his wife had had a child. Did that make John a grandfather? He guessed so, but only in the strictest sense. In practice, he was anything but. As for Brian, the younger one, John had no idea where he was or what he did.

Donna had been widowed almost ten years. Her husband, George, had fought long and hard before succumbing to cancer. They had two daughters. The older was getting a master's in social work at a university on the West Coast. The other was a junior at the state university about two hours east. Steven had never married but had a son from a relationship of convenience—his, not hers. Steven rarely saw the boy and even more rarely brought him to family get-togethers. Monique was too narcissistic, immature, and insecure to be in a lasting and meaningful relationship. She floated from one to another, proclaiming the latest would be the last, which, technically, it was until the next.

How would they react to the new family dynamic? Would this revelation end up being anything other than an interesting footnote in the family annals? Would his siblings see Magdalena, Wilhelm, and Johann as real family? Would the German side of the now much-expanded family consider them blood relations? And if they had family, would he and his siblings accept them—and be accepted, in turn, by them? His head hurt, and the whole situation was becoming fuzzier by the moment.

John realized that what they were claiming was true. There could be no other explanation for the physical resemblance. However, they had not made clear the circumstances by which Jeanne DuFour had had a child by Franzis Neuberger. But John knew the circumstances. The *Mapleton Valley World Journal* had reported the circumstances. Franzis must have been the one who had forced himself on her. There could be no other explanation. In the article, Pappi Henry had witnessed it.

With a vengeance, ugly images—clear, crisp, and horrific—of that scene sprang to mind. Could this be why Grandma Jeanne had chosen not to speak of this period of her life? Or had she chosen to act as if it had never occurred? In the situation she had found herself—hungry, cold, sick, fearful for her life and her son's, and under the thumb of an occupying force—she had probably been powerless to do anything but submit.

Fury and hatred surged through him, causing his temples to throb. Across the table sat three smiling people, clueless to the underlying reality. They were not just smiling people but family whose grandfather had fathered a child with a woman, his grandmother, in an occupied zone of a war-torn country. Was it not bad enough the woman had lost four years of her life? Was it not bad enough she had lost her husband to the war? Had it also been necessary she lose herself as well?

These people had some nerve to show up unannounced, naively expecting to be welcomed as long-lost family members. These things were supposed to happen only in books and movies, not in real life.

John got up from the table. "I need a drink. Dad, you have any booze in the house?"

Francis nodded in the direction of the cabinet above the stove.

John opened the cupboard and pulled out two bottles. Turning to the table and holding them aloft, he asked, "Anyone game?"

Magdalena asked, "What does that mean?"

"Do you want a drink? There's scotch or bourbon." John matter-of-factly motioned first with one bottle and then the other.

Francis lifted a finger and pointed in the direction of the bourbon. "Straight up. One finger for me."

Magdalena translated for her brothers. John understood without translation that all three wanted scotch. He poured four scotches over ice and one straight-up bourbon, carried the glasses to the table, and passed them around.

His dad raised his glass in salute and toasted, "Prost!" He took a sip.

Wilhelm raised his glass. "To family."

All but John responded in kind.

"John, that's rude not to toast!" Francis exclaimed.

"Sorry if you think I'm being rude, but I'm not sure I like the idea we're family. It's not that I no longer disbelieve we're family, though the evidence up to now is all hearsay and circumstantial," John said. "Yes, there's too strong of a physical resemblance"—he motioned toward Johann—"but in and of itself, that's not enough. It's just that ..."

The Germans waited for John to finish.

Shifting his gaze to Magdalena, John commented, "When I answered the door, you said you thought that was my car. You even motioned toward it. How did you know?"

"That is a strange thing to ask," Francis commented.

"It could be, but I'd still like to know."

Magdalena cleared her throat. "The other day, at the museum, we stayed until you went home. We watched you get in your car und drive away."

"Is that all?" John asked.

Magdalena furrowed her brow.

"I asked is that all?"

Magdalena cast her eyes to the table. "We followed you home. The next day, we followed you to work, und that afternoon, we again followed you home. We have done that each day, hoping that you would eventually come here." She tapped the table for emphasis.

"What else?" John asked, tapping his glass on the table.

"The night after the museum, we followed you over to the other house. Does that belong to a family member?"

"Yes. The house belongs to Donna. She's the older of my two sisters and just younger than me. How long did you wait outside?"

Looking from one brother to the other, Magdalena hesitated to answer.

"Well? Were you outside still when Steven, my brother, left?"

She lifted the glass to her lips and then, before taking a sip, set it back down. "Yes. We waited until you left. We talked about knocking on the door und introducing ourselves. We could not agree on what to do."

John continued his interrogation. "So then you saw my younger brother, Steven, leave. Monique, my younger sister, would've left right behind him."

Magdalena translated. The two brothers nodded as she finished.

"Okay, so you know where I live, you know where Donna lives, and you know where my father lives. Are you planning on visiting the other two?"

"We would like to meet all of your family."

John downed his scotch in one gulp. "Why?" John asked. "Haven't you accomplished what you set out to do? To make clear who you are?"

"That is not the only reason we have come. We also came because we know some of our grandfather's story, but there are things that we do not know. We want to share with you what we know; we want you to tell us what you know."

Francis asked, "How long do you plan on staying?"

"We will stay as long as we must. Our families understand und support us, though they are also nervous und angry like John," Magdalena commented.

Francis turned to his son. "John, you're suddenly quiet. What do you think?"

John bit his lower lip. "What do I think? I'm not sure I'm all that interested in knowing more than I do. What's the old saying—'Ignorance is bliss'? More than anything, I think it's extremely rude for them to show up," he remarked, again pointing an accusatory finger in their direction, "and expect to be accepted as family.

As far as I know, their grandfather forced himself on Grandma Jeanne. Now they want to make nice."

Magdalena interjected. "I am not sure I understood precisely everything you said, but I understood the tone. What I can tell you is that my grandmother's letters make it clear that my grandfather would never have done what I think you are suggesting. Grandmother Hilda's letters say that Franz was a gentle und good man."

John snapped back, "Letters from someone who had something or someone to protect shouldn't be relied upon. She probably wrote that to make herself and you feel better. Anyway, I don't put much faith in what you say. For me, the only one whose opinion matters is my dad's."

All eyes turned on Francis, who, for the longest time, twirled his drink glass around and around. Finally, taking a deep breath, he remarked, "There are things I know, things my mother only told me about right before she died—things about the man who I never knew was my real father until that time. Yet there are many things about this man you call my biological father I don't know and would never be able to learn without you having come."

Francis fell quiet, rubbing his chin in thought.

"I'm old and have wondered for forty years if what my mother told me could be true. She had a way of stretching and twisting the truth. Looking at the resemblance between these two"—Francis pointed to son John and then to Johann—"I now know that at least a portion of what I heard was true. What scares me more than anything is what if the rest of what she said is true?"

He dropped his eyes to the tabletop.

"Dad, are you okay?" John asked.

Francis nodded. "I'm willing to tell you what I know as long as you tell us what you know—quid pro quo."

Magdalena translated.

"I suggest we meet here starting two nights from now," Francis commented. "I'll invite my other children, at least for the first session. I'm thinking it'll take more than one night. It'll be up to them if they want to stay around after that. John, what do you think about them staying at your place? You've got a couple of extra bedrooms. That would save them some money, and you'd get a chance to know them."

"Are you crazy?" John replied. "How can you even suggest that? Invite these people to stay when I have no idea what the circumstances were surrounding how you were conceived?"

"Let's suppose what you say is right. Why should I hold it against them? They had nothing to do with it. Their father never even knew his father—never even saw him, except for photos. If what they say is correct, then my father is their grandfather. You want to hold them responsible for what he may or may not have done? I don't know about you, but I wonder if we"—Francis pointed first at the three Germans and then at himself—"shouldn't view ourselves as late casualties of the war."

"I don't see it that way, but it's obvious you want bygones to be bygones. Why? I don't get it. How can you be willing to live and let live under unknown circumstances?" John lived in a world of absolutes. There were two ways of doing something: his way and the wrong way. People were of two kinds: his kind and *them*. He was right, and everyone who disagreed was wrong.

"Do you want to know how I can be willing to live and let live?" Francis asked.

"Yeah, I want to know."

"Here's how. I've experienced war and seen death and destruction. I know there are other casualties besides the soldiers, flyboys, and sailors. I've seen how everyone—societies, neighbors, and particularly families—suffer, especially the innocents. War only ends for those who have been killed in or by it. I sometimes think it would be best if all warriors perished on the battlefield. That way, they couldn't take their pride, hatred, anger, and vengeance back to infect the next generation. But that would presuppose conflict is not a genetic trait."

Magdalena translated.

"That's crazy talk, Dad."

"How would you know? You've never experienced war," Francis snapped in response. "I have, and I've seen what hatred and rage and anger and jealousy and desire to revenge wrongs—and isn't every act a wrong to someone?—do to people. These cause wars and keep them going. They're the reasons fueling the next, not-too-distant future one." Francis swallowed hard. "I had a buddy, Jimmy Conray, who was sitting right next to me"—Francis pointed at an imaginary spot to his left—"get vaporized in a spray of blood and flesh by an artillery shell. Nothing happened to me, except a ringing in my ears for weeks. One moment, I was talking to him, and the next, he was gone. Not enough of anything left to bury. Even now, I wake up almost every night in a sweat, thinking it could've been me. It's been how long—sixty years—since the official end of the war? Mine's never ended. I'm tired of the fighting, killing, hatred, vengeance, and injured national pride. The only difference today is that our current enemy has a different name. Their people"—Francis pointed at the three guests—"were our enemies for almost four years. We killed millions of them, and they killed hundreds of thousands of us. Then, practically overnight, they became our ally when the Soviet Union turned away from us. Instead of Hitler killing millions, it was our former ally Papa Joe."

"Everyone knows it was an alliance of convenience," John remarked smugly. "Its only purpose was to rid the world of Hitler and the Nazis. You, of all people, should recognize that!"

"And what a price to pay; we're still paying today!" Francis exclaimed. "What makes you say I, of all people, should recognize that?"

"Because of that Nazi—the one who tried to kill you."

In a hushed whisper, Magdalena translated.

"What about him?" Francis asked tersely.

"He was a German!" John exclaimed, pointing at the three guests. "Just like them."

"So are you, if what they say is true." Shaking his head, Francis said, "Why have you not included yourself? From what I've heard, if not for a German, you wouldn't be here."

His father's riposte stunned him.

"Listen, Son, I've read the same articles you have. But I know things you don't. I can appreciate why you might feel the way you do, but—and this will come as no surprise—I don't share your viewpoint. The story has yet to be completely told, and that is the reason I am willing to live and let live. I'm going to say something; it'll seem beyond comprehension. Are you ready?"

"Yeah," John responded casually. "Say whatever it is you have to say."

"The truth—remember that?—will come out of the story. You have to hear the whole thing. I have some of it, but part of it has to come from them." Francis gestured with his eyes toward Magdalena, Wilhelm, and Johann. "If you listen and keep your heart open, you will understand eventually. When you understand, you'll find compassion. When you find compassion, you'll be able to accept them."

"Got it, Dad," John responded, becoming reflective.

"We'll reconvene in two nights," Francis continued, tapping the table. "Let's say seven p.m. The story will have to be told in parts. We'll take as long as it takes." Francis asked Magdalena, "Does that work?"

She conferred with her brothers. All three nodded.

"Yes. We would not want to impose on your son," Magdalena replied, nodding in John's direction. "We will stay at our hotel. That way, we will have a place for ourselves, if necessary. We appreciate the thought."

"Suit yourselves." Turning to his son, Francis added, "I'm willing to spend whatever time is needed. Are you?"

"I guess so, as long as we get together in the evenings; I won't be able to take any time off work. In the end, though, when the story is out in the open, I suspect, having just recently reread the articles, they will owe us an apology."

His voice soft and subdued, Francis replied, "Son, I don't think that's the frame of mind you want going into this. If you're going to be closed minded, then ..." Francis collected his thoughts. "The truth is, when all is said and done, I fear it will be them who will be owed the apology."

JULY 29

Thirteen

Sitting in his cubicle in the late afternoon, John looked again out a nearby window. He was having a hard time turning his attention back to work. It seemed nice outdoors—sunny and bright, with a slight north wind, if the rippling leaves were an indication. This usually meant low humidity and comfortable temperatures, a nice break from the usual humidity and heat for Mapleton Valley. It would have been an ideal day to call in sick.

He had slept well for the first time in weeks. That morning, lying in bed longer than normal, even with the maddening *nyaaaaaaaaaaaaaaah* of his purposely out-of-arm's-reach alarm going off, he had contemplated the pros and cons of not going in.

The pros had consisted first of not having to show up. Being self-employed as a commercial real-estate agent, he, technically speaking, did not have to show up ever. But since he would make no money if he failed to, his self-employment status was just that—a technicality. The other would have been the chance to more leisurely leaf through his grandmother's journals, reading entries that caught his eye, versus the hurried and superficial way he would have to skim them in the evenings. During his frenetic after-work searches, he would need to keep one eye on the clock so as not to lose track of time and stay up too late while the other searched for key phrases relating to his quest.

The list of cons had consisted of one item: he would have been unable to chase the rabbit.

"Chase the rabbit" was his latest term for how he made a living; a truer description would have been how he lived his professional and personal lives. Prior to adopting this phrase, he would have described his life, had he given it much thought, as living the dream.

Ambition, single-mindedness, drive, and doggedness were all qualities of living the dream. These would lead to wealth, power, influence, and position—qualities everybody could embrace. Well, almost everybody—his ex-wife and his two worthless sons did not. John blamed his sons' outlier viewpoints on jealousy or laziness—in the case of the younger one, both.

Living the dream had embodied the essence of what was important to him: financial success, social status, and, lastly and above all, recognition as a role model for those aspiring below. Living the dream was a noble and laudable pursuit. But living the dream no longer held sway over him. Chasing the rabbit had replaced it.

Living the dream had been rudely and ruinously crushed one night in a blur of fur at a dog track. In hindsight, John had reconciled himself to what had happened and where, understanding that others' dreams had also been crushed there.

During the first races, he had been too busy getting drinks and identifying lonely looking, mildly inebriated socialites to cozy up to to watch. After three quick highballs followed by three equally quick strikes, he'd turned his attention to the track. Having never been and having no clue what to expect or how it worked, he'd sat alone and watched.

At the bell, dogs had bolted from the gate and, almost instantaneously hitting top speed, chased after the mechanical rabbit as it made its way around the oval. Mesmerized by what he was seeing as the dogs made their way down the back straightaway, he'd inched forward on his hard plastic seat and straightaway understood that no matter how fast the dogs; no matter how many the dogs; no matter the track conditions; no matter the wind; no matter the dogs' color, size, breeding, or sex; and no matter how big or little the crowd or how noisy it was—in fact, no matter anything—the prize was to be forever beyond reach.

The dogs, being dogs, had seemed oblivious that the gig was rigged and that they had no chance and never would. So at each succeeding race, when the bell had sounded, the gates had sprung open, and the dogs had burst forth, their heads down, running at top speed, keeping their eyes on the elusive quarry, looking neither left nor right, and pushing and jostling any others that got in their way—all to chase after something that could never be.

Sitting in the grandstands after the races, most of the grandstanding crowd he had come with having dashed off, his head had spun. He was waiting for it to clear before he too raced away.

Brattick Terrier, a young up-and-comer at a different commercial real-estate company, had called out, "Yo, dog, you okay?"

His head still down but his ears perking up at Brattick's questions, John had barked back, "Doing fine—just a little too much tonight."

Brattick's salutation, in the split second delivered, had crystalized for John his true situation. The unexpected and profound parallels between the dogs' existence and his had stunned him. In that instant, the sickening recognition of his true place had come, impelling him to his new term.

Arriving home, he'd vowed to make changes to his life, starting the next morning. True to his word, change had occurred. The next morning, instead of bolting out of bed at 6:00 a.m., his normal wake-up time, he'd bolted out at 5:30 a.m. and hit top speed within seconds. He was ready to push and jostle any who got in his way if it would let him nose ahead. He reasoned that since living the dream was not a dream but a delusion, he meant to chase after something that could be his: money. Every morning since, whether on a weekday or weekend, his alarm clock had sounded at the new time, and his feet had immediately hit the ground.

This particular morning had been atypical. Lazing away twenty-nine minutes in his contemplations, he had ultimately decided, at 5:59 a.m., to hit the ground and go to work, the bone being the burgeoning piles of deals he had to deal with. If he stayed behind, he would find himself left behind. As surely as the sun would rise the morrow in the east, new deals would brighten his life next week. As it was, he was barely able to keep up. If he did not go to work, how would he find time for this week's next?

Pulling into his driveway after work, the little hand approaching the six on his watch face, he again glanced over his right shoulder to see if the car the Germans were driving was following. He had not noticed it that morning on the way in to work—not that that was conclusive. They could simply have been staying farther back or blending in better with traffic. Or they could have turned their car in and picked up a different one. But if they were following, their reasons, after yesterday, were unclear.

He pulled into the garage, gathered his things, and went inside.

"I'm not drinking tonight; I don't care what," he mumbled without much conviction. "And if the phone rings, I'm not answering."

In his bedroom, he set his briefcase down next to his dresser, removed his watch, set it again on the letter his dad had received, and laid his gadgetry next to it. Quickly changing out of his weekday uniform, he donned his formal summer evening attire—shorts and a T-shirt—forgoing his sandals, opting instead to go barefoot.

"It might help to go out on the deck with a beer and relax for a minute. That should get me in the right frame of mind to tackle the journals. Oh, can't do that; told myself I wouldn't drink tonight." He paused for a second. "I meant real drinking, not beer drinking," he muttered. He walked to the refrigerator, grabbed a bottle, opened it, and tossed the cap onto the counter. He took a long pull. "Ahhh, that tastes great."

He drew the cold, sweating bottle across his forehead and then took another pull. Two more emptied it. He set the empty on the counter, opened the fridge again, reached in, and grabbed his second. "Three will be my limit tonight no matter what." He chuckled. "Too bad I didn't buy quarts."

He strolled out onto the porch and glanced up and around at the sky, enjoying the brisk air. "Might need a sweatshirt before too long," he muttered. "Maybe I'll even fire up the chiminea."

He set his unopened beer on the railing and leaned forward, flattening his palms on the rail. He shut his eyes, let his head roll forward, and then slowly rolled his head clockwise. Stopping after several rotations, he reversed direction.

Finished, he glanced to his right, at his neighbor's fence line. Magdalena, Wilhelm, and Johann were standing there, watching him.

He exhaled. "Can't you leave it alone for just one night? Good God, when's enough enough?" he called out.

Speaking for the group, Magdalena answered, "We are sorry for disturbing you. We have one question."

"I doubt you have only *one* question. I'm not in the mood tonight anyway. Go away, and show up tomorrow, as agreed."

Magdalena continued, "We are sorry for disturbing you, but our one question is very important."

John glared at them before answering. "I'm sorry; I'm not in the mood. Like I said, go away. I'll see you tomorrow at my father's house."

The three did not budge. Magdalena again opened her mouth to say something.

John held up his hands. "Don't say you're sorry again. I don't think you are, and even if you were, I don't care. And I know—you have one question." John opened his beer and downed about a third.

The three Germans watched in silence.

"You're trespassing, you know. Do you understand what that means?" John called out.

"I understand what that means, but I am pleased to inform you that we are not," Magdalena replied.

"What do you mean you're not?" John inquired, confused and startled by the response.

"We asked permission of your neighbor."

"You what?" Shaking his head, John regarded them. "You asked my neighbor?" John downed another third.

Magdalena nodded. "If you feel that you must, you should question him yourself. He is fascinated by how much Johann"—she motioned toward her brother—"looks like you. He saw it immediately when he opened the door."

"Whoa there, little cowgirl," John interrupted. "You're telling me you talked to my neighbor?"

"He is a nice man." Magdalena added, "I told him that you would probably tell him the story."

"I doubt he'd be interested no matter how it turns out. But why in the hell did you do that?" John asked peevishly.

"We figured that you would not answer your door if we rang your doorbell. We thought if we waited in your neighbor's backyard, you would have to speak to us if you came outside," Magdalena explained.

"I'm not so sure you're right about me having to talk to you out here." After a momentary silence, John added in an irritated tone, "Okay. I give up. What's your one question?"

"Last night, you were paying very little attention to what I was saying until ..." She let her thought hang.

"Until what?" John asked, drawn in.

The three talked among themselves for several seconds. Magdalena turned to John. "You were paying very little attention until I mentioned the name of the French village," Magdalena said. "Johann thinks that you know something. Do you?"

John swallowed hard. When she had mentioned Beaulieu-en-prés, he had reacted; he knew that. Immediately after, he had glanced around, convinced he had been able to mask his reaction. Now he was shocked to learn someone had seen it.

"Do you?" Johann asked in passable English.

This startled John; he had thought Johann neither spoke nor understood English. Pondering how to extract himself, John brought the bottle to his lips and tilted it upward, finishing it.

"Do you?" Johann again asked, more tersely.

"I suggest you go," John remarked. "If you don't, I may not show up tomorrow, and you may never find out the whole story."

"We will leave, as you suggest, but we will find out," Magdalena remarked.

JULY 30

Fourteen

John rested his brow in the crook of his right hand, his thumb massaging his right temple, and the ring finger and middle finger massaging the left.

His third and final beer, the cap still in place, sat on the kitchen table to his left. A small ring of water, condensation from when the beer had still been cold, had formed around its base, encircling the bottle protectively like a moat. John's left hand was wrapped around its neck, his knuckles white as if in a death grip. The left thumb tapped out the same constant, rhythmic beat as his grandfather clock, which had, moments before, gonged once.

John glanced at his watch, thinking it couldn't possibly be 1:00 a.m. Had he not just sat down with the five journals and the cold beer shortly after the Germans had left? His watch read 1:02. He shook his head and took another look. It now read 1:03.

He slipped his glasses on and then pulled the open journal back toward himself. The last entry was dated May 28, 1917. All subsequent pages had been removed—and purposely so, if the clean, neat edges were an indication. It looked as though someone had taken scissors or a straight edge to them.

The missing pages from the 1917 journal were only one of two mysteries concerning the journals. Each of the other thick journals had been for a specific year. The one for 1914 commenced with a January 2 entry and ended with a December 30 one. The unused, excess pages—and there were many—remained in the journal. The first entry for 1915, dated January 1, was the opening item in the next journal. It too had blank pages in the back after a December 31 entry. That was also the case for 1916. Then the pattern changed. The portion after May 28, 1917, was gone. That particular year opened with an entry dated January 3 and went to this date; after that, there was nothing.

He had flipped through the portion of the journal for 1917 twice to make sure his mind was not playing tricks on him at this time of morning. Sure enough, he realized the May 28 entry was the last entry and the last page.

He closed the journal and again looked at the front and back, comparing it to the others. It was identical: same color of leather, same binding, and same faded gold lettering on the front. The only difference was that it was about half as thick as the three preceding ones and the one following. Where were the rest of the pages for 1917? Based on the evidence, he had to surmise that the pages had simply disappeared.

The other mystery was that the journal following was for 1919, not 1918, as it should have been. There was no trace and no mention of the latter, even for the portion of the year following the armistice and the liberation of the occupied territory. With the Germans marching back home, she would have theoretically been free to do as she wanted without fear of consequences or reprisals. Yet there was no journal for 1918.

Had there been one? And if so, where was it?

John half expected there would be no 1919 journal, but there in front of him was the 1919 journal, with all of its pages. He had flipped through twice to make sure.

Any number of explanations for the absence of a 1918 journal came to mind. First, perhaps Grandma Jeanne had not had a matching journal book, so she had not kept one, or second, she had kept one, but it had been lost at some point in the past.

John thought the first possibility was unlikely, almost inconceivable. He acknowledged that she might not have already had one or had not been able to find a matching journal book, yet he was confident that, having seen her dedication in keeping her journals, she would have found a way. Besides, another factor argued against that explanation: the 1919 journal itself matched the earlier ones. He conceded that she might have been able to find one after the armistice; however, that possible explanation nonetheless struck him as improbable.

As for the second possible explanation, he discounted that as well. To have kept possession of the bookending journals seemed reason enough to give this one short shrift. While either reason could have explained the absence of a 1918 journal, they offered no explanation for the missing portion of the 1917 one.

Reasons for both absent portions were the following: first, someone had found out she had been keeping journals and had either prevented her from continuing or warned her not to continue, or second, despite warnings to the contrary, she had continued. That someone had found out and then appropriated these portions. Both scenarios were perfectly believable, provided it had been a German who had protested her journaling. But what if it had not been a German?

John looked at the beer bottle and thought about opening it, and he would've, had it still been cold.

He was convinced that Grandma Jeanne would have found a way to keep journals and keep them safe, concealing them if necessary. Plus, the journals for 1914 through mid-May 1917 had not disappeared, so why just the last part of 1917 and all of 1918? And then there was the apparent care with which the pages had been removed. Someone had not hurriedly torn them out, leaving behind ragged edges and hints of words.

Intuitively, he struck the first explanation from the list. That left the second, which seemed the more credible, particularly since it had an air of mystery about it. The puzzle of the journals fit right in with what John had experienced the past few days: the appearance of the Germans, the arrival of the letter, and the realization that the German visitors were family by blood. As such, the possibility of purposely missing journals seemed plausible.

No other possibility could explain the missing portion of the 1917 journal and the absence of the 1918 one other than that she had faithfully kept them but they had been disposed of afterward.

John sighed, massaged his brow, and removed his glasses.

But why, and by whom?

Having scanned the journals, he realized that any number of people would have had reasons, including his grandmother, probably motivated by a desire to conceal what was now obvious. His grandfather would have had essentially the same motivation but from a different perspective. Maybe Pappi Henry had come to realize his son was not *his* son. Getting rid of those portions then made sense, allowing him to protect the secret and his pride.

After all, the oft-told and well-burnished story of Henry returning to France several years later to bring back Grandma Jeanne and their son, whom they had conceived in the final passion of the war, was well known in the family. The returning and retrieving part was as equally important as the war-hero part in this story.

The only hiccup in the story was his father's birth date, Bastille Day, July 14, 1919. Counting backward from that date to early November 1918, John again came up one month short of the timeline for a normal pregnancy. He knew that in and of itself was not conclusive proof of Henry not being the biological father; children were born prematurely every day and had been since time immemorial.

When Henry had returned with the two in tow, his family would have been unable to seriously question the child's lineage, as Francis took after his mother. As such, there would be no physical reason to outwardly question the story. If someone had, Grandma Jeanne would only have had to recite some made-up birth information regarding height and weight, making it hard to credibly refute the paternity. In the end, having purged the pages and disposed of the journal, Pappi Henry would have made sure whatever Jeanne wrote would not come to light.

For him to have done this was more than possible; it made the most sense—that was, unless he had never caught on. Then John's grandmother would have had the most to hide, and for her to have done it made the most sense. But what if she was not the culprit?

What if neither his grandmother nor his grandfather had done it?

John's head fell backward, and he stared blankly at the ceiling. As was now obvious, Pappi Henry was not the biological father. Could the real father have found out and taken the missing portion of the journals to protect himself and his family? If this scenario was right, then finding the missing pages was highly unlikely, and learning what was written on them was even less so.

That explanation was more than possible and probably made the most sense, unless ...

John's chin dropped to his chest. He took a deep breath and mentally rehashed what he had just worked through. His machinations had led to three scenarios that made the most sense. *The good nuns in grade school taught me that the word* most *was a superlative and that superlatives were each supposed to be one of a kind. If that's so, then how can there be three scenarios that make the* most *sense?* He laughed to himself, feeling punch-drunk from fatigue.

John put his glasses back on and reached for the 1917 journal. He pulled it close, flipped it to the last entry, and reread it. For the first time and the last, Captain Neuberger's name appeared in the journals. Other names had made a single appearance—he was confident of that. Some unique mentions had been good, and others had not. But this one was neither good nor bad; it was just a mention. Previous mentions of names had been unfamiliar to him, and this one would have been in the same camp but for what had happened in the past several days. Captain Neuberger's name had become more than familiar; it had become familial.

His head was swimming from all that he'd read so far. At the point of Captain Neuberger's appearance, John would have been hard pressed to recount who was still alive other than Alain and the priest, who was not, who had remained part of the cooperative survival effort, and who had split off, going it alone in hope of …

"In hope of" meant nothing yet might've meant everything.

After three years of war, hope was all the players in this drama had left. Each person had to keep alive hope for something. And their hope had likely been distilled to the most basic of things: hope the damn war would come to an end; hope the damn weather would hold; hope the damn harvest would be bountiful, or at least no worse than the last; hope that life would not end before its damn time; hope that if life did end before its time, the damn end would be swift; and, finally, when it came to judgment, hope one would not be damned.

If hope was the currency of life at that point, what change was made from this first, sudden, and unexpected appearance of Captain Neuberger? Was he just another in the line of Germans who had come to plunder and rape?

That word continued to surface. *Rape* was such an ugly word with uglier connotations. Had he meant to use it? Or, rather, had it inadvertently slipped out?

John knew it'd been no accident. He had read the newspaper articles. His grandfather had witnessed the act and had killed the rapist.

So the Germans had come to find out what had happened to their grandfather. If that was what they wanted—to find out—he was determined they'd get what they wanted, even if, in the end, they wouldn't.

Fifteen

"You're kidding me, right?" Steven asked. "You don't really expect me to hang around to meet these people and listen to some far-fetched story about how they're related, do you? Dad, I'm more worried than ever about your mental condition."

Francis and his children were sitting around the dinette table at his house. It had been years since all of them had gathered at this table. Francis was in his usual place at the head of the table. His daughters were sitting side by side to his right. Steven, slouched down in his chair as usual, took up the side opposite his sisters. John sat across from his father, at the other end.

"No need," Francis replied flatly. "I've still got my faculties. And because I do, I think you should at least hang around to see the resemblance between your brother and the one."

"Dad, resemblance is a poor way of determining if someone's related. Just look at your own kids," Steven commented, jabbing a finger hitchhiker-style at John. "Three of us look alike, and one doesn't. I've known families with five and six kids, and none of them look anything alike. Plus, if you half believed even half the stories John tells about the number of times he's been mistaken for someone else, he'd be related to half the people in this city and half in others."

Donna, sitting across from Steven and next to her father, threw out, "Steven, the other night after you and Monique left, John told me he'd run into these people at the museum. He was even shocked by how strong the resemblance was. You've heard the story about the photo of their grandfather. He looks just like the older German man, who, in turn, looks just like John. Don't take our word for it; stay and see for yourself."

Monique asked, "Steven, how else would you explain the Germans having a photo of a man John resembles, if they're not related? The photo's more than ninety years old."

"No clue. Haven't given it any thought," Steven remarked. "And not likely to." Still talking to Monique, he added, "Hey, Mon, you don't seem too upset or too disbelieving about what's been said. I thought for sure you would, considering how you were the other night at Donna's. What are you thinking?"

"I've told you I hate when you call me that. Can't you have the decency to call me by my given name and not the one given by you?" Glaring at her just-older brother, she added, "To your point, I don't see why it couldn't be true. If the man in that photo looks like John, then ..." She shrugged and fell quiet. "It'd explain why John never looked like anyone else in the family. I'd never understood that before, but now ... Honestly, I'd come to the conclusion he was adopted and we just hadn't been told."

"What are you talking about?" exclaimed John, stunned by her statement. "How can you even say that?"

"Well, this is better, don't you think?" Monique answered.

"I don't care if there's a resemblance," Steven commented. "And even if there is, I'm not hanging around. I don't know these people, don't care to know these people, and don't much care about them. Sorry, Dad, but that's the way I feel. It's obvious you've known something about this for a long time and never said anything. Why is that?"

Francis cleared his throat and then gingerly rubbed the back of his left hand. "If you're already worried about my mental condition, what would you've said if I had brought this up out of the blue? 'Oh, by the way, my mother told me ...' I had nothing to go on other than what your grandmother had told me, for what that's worth. I suppose it would've been easier if I hadn't taken after her, but since I did ... Anyway, truth is, I had no idea how to bring this up."

Steven regarded his father, disgust written on his face. "Let's suppose I believe that—which, by the way, I don't. Your rationale went out the window the minute the letter showed up and you didn't speak up. That presented the perfect opportunity."

"For what?" his dad asked skeptically.

"To tell us what you know."

Francis shook his head. "I don't know what I know. At this point, all I know is what your grandmother told me right before she died."

Ding-dong, ding-dong, chimed the doorbell. *Ding-dong, ding-dong.*

No one made a move to push back from the table, each looking at the others expectantly.

Steven broke the spell. "Not a chance. I'm only sorry I didn't get out of here before. Later, if you want, you can fill me in." He pushed back at the same time as John. "Sorry, Frandad, Don, and Mon, but I'm out of here. John Boy, can you get the door behind me?"

"Sure," John stated, getting up from the table.

They walked down the hallway, Steven falling in behind John. Just before reaching its end, John said over his shoulder, "It's not too late. You could stay and see how this unfolds."

"I've got no interest. Besides, you're the repository of the family history, remember? Sounds like the old family history's about to get a bit more complicated." Steven chuckled, patting his brother patronizingly on the shoulder.

John opened the door. Wilhelm, Magdalena, and Johann were patiently standing on the other side. A large canvas sack hung from Magdalena's shoulder. John swung the door open and smiled. "Welcome. This is my brother, Steven. He's leaving."

Steven stepped out into the evening's twilight and studied each face. He paused at Johann's, taking longer than he had for the first two. Turning, he said to his brother, "Uncanny, John Boy—really uncanny. If I hadn't seen it, I'd have never believed it. The resemblance really is uncanny. I've got to admit my curiosity is piqued almost enough—but not quite. Wish I could, but I can't. Got to run! Excuse me, and have fun." Steven pushed through the Germans. Then, waving absently over a shoulder as he strolled down the front walk, he called out, chuckling, "So long, farewell, *auf wiedersehen*, good night."

"That's my younger brother. He's not interested. Sorry. That's just the way he is," John said, apologizing as the four watched Steven's car drive off. "He lived in Germany for a while when he was in the air force several years back."

Magdalena kept up a running translation. Turning back to John, Magdalena commented, "We understand. There are those in our family who feel the same way."

Johann said something in a barely audible voice. Wilhelm nodded at his brother while Magdalena translated for John. "My bruder says his youngest daughter is like that."

John nodded in acknowledgment.

"Johann's daughter said that she had no interest in knowing anything about you. Johann apologizes for her attitude," Magdalena finished.

"Thank you, but there's no need." Holding open the screen door, John added, "You might as well come in. The others are anxious to meet you."

"We are excited to meet the rest of the family, but we are nervous also. We hope that this goes well."

From the kitchen, Francis called out, "John, are you coming back?"

"Just a second; we'll be right there," he yelled back. "My father is impatient," John added, motioning to them to follow him.

"Before we meet the rest of the family ..." Magdalena said.

John looked at her and then shifted his gaze to her brothers. "Yes?"

"About last night," she said, restarting, her tone apologetic. "We should not have gone to your house, und we should not have disturbed your neighbor. It seemed the right thing to do, but it was not. We understand that now."

"You're right about that," John commented, a tone of reproach in his voice.

"What I am trying to say is that I should not have said what I said," she finished.

"Again, you're right," John remarked unapologetically.

Magdalena waggled a finger at him. "Though we are sorry about last night, it does not change the purpose of our visit. You must understand that we intend to find out what we have come for."

"Your actions speak to that," John remarked, and then he added, "I'll make sure you learn what you've come for."

Magdalena translated, and when she finished, all three nodded, smiles on their faces.

"John, where are you?" Francis called out again.

"Hold your horses," John called back, and then, with a sweeping motion of his right arm, he pointed down the hall.

As they entered the kitchen, they heard the metallic screech of chair legs on the linoleum flooring. John's two siblings were standing nervously next to their respective chairs on the far side of the table. His dad stood next to his at the close end.

"*Guten Tag,*" Francis remarked. "Welcome back."

The three nodded. Magdalena added, as if scripted, "*Guten Tag.* On behalf of my brothers und myself, I assure you that we are pleased to be here—nervous, jah, but pleased."

The two sisters laughed nervously and said, almost in unison, "Us too."

Then Monique exclaimed as she studied Johann for the first time, "Oh my God, John, you do look just like him. I didn't know what to expect. Not this."

Francis remarked, "Please make yourselves comfortable. Would anyone like coffee?"

They all shook their heads, trying to keep smiles on their faces.

"Twice now, there've been no takers," Francis commented. "I won't offer in the future."

His three children clapped vigorously; the Germans blushed.

"No matter," Francis added. "Please consider this your home. You probably saw my younger son at the door. You might even have met him before he hightailed it out of here. It is unfortunate that he isn't interested. Who knows? He might still come around."

"We met him at the door. It is obvious that this is difficult for him—for everybody, jah? We understand. It is difficult for us," Magdalena explained. "But we are pleased to be here, und we are looking forward to getting to know you und hearing what you know."

"I've told my kids pretty much all that took place the other night when you first appeared. They haven't seen the photo, the one of your grandfather, and haven't had a chance to appreciate the resemblance between John and Franzis. Let's get started." Glancing at Magdalena as he sat, he added, "Please, sit down and begin."

The Germans sat on one side of the table and pulled their chairs up, Magdalena in the middle. She pulled the canvas bag off her shoulder and set it on the floor. She spoke briefly to her brothers, translating what Francis had said. When she finished, an awkward silence fell over the group.

John pulled his chair around to the other end of the table, to the left of the Germans and opposite his father.

Wilhelm leaned toward his sister, whispering. She leaned back toward him, saying loudly, *"Nein, Ich werde am Anfang anfangen."*

Turning her attention to the other side of the table, she said, "Wilhelm can be an impatient man; he does not want me to start too early. Und he is a persistent man, always wanting his way. I have told him that I am telling this story. So I will begin at the beginning. I will take you back to July 1914, to Mannheim, Baden-Württemberg. It is in this town where our grandparents lived at the start of the war."

Monique interrupted. "Why did you say Bad-and-worm-burg? I thought they were from Germany."

"Mannheim is in Baden-Württemberg," Magdalena explained. "It was a small country in the German—" She stopped and looked to her brothers, asking, "*Wie sagt man Konfederation in Englisch*?"

Her brothers shrugged.

Francis answered, "I think the word you're looking for is *confederation*."

"Danke," Magdalena responded with a slight nod of her head. "As I was saying, Germany was a confederation of many countries—some large, some small. Baden-Württemberg was a small one. But it is not very important to our story to make the distinction, so I will say that it is in Germany."

"Okay, if you say so. Thanks for the explanation," Monique responded, smiling. "You can go ahead if you want."

Magdalena described the assassination by Serbian nationalists of Archduke Ferdinand and his wife in Sarajevo toward the end of June 1914. She told of the Austrian ultimatum of late July 1914 to Serbia, which, within days, led to a break in diplomatic relations with Serbia. An Austrian declaration of war against Serbia soon followed.

At the end of Magdalena's explanation, Donna asked, "Then what?"

Magdalena took a minute to speak with her brothers. Johann nodded as she spoke; Wilhelm just glared at her. "I wanted to make sure that my bruders understood what I had been saying. I apologize. You asked me what happened next?"

"Yes. What happened next?" Donna asked.

Before she could respond, they heard the sound of a closing door and approaching footsteps. All heads turned toward the noise. The footsteps came to a stop, and Steven peeked sheepishly around the corner.

Francis asked, a twinkle in his eye, "Did you forget something?"

"Yeah, I did forget something."

Half standing and looking around, Francis asked, "What did you forget? I don't see anything that doesn't belong."

"I forgot I wanted to see that photo—the one of their grandfather."

Magdalena rummaged in her sack and extracted a small photo album. She opened it and pulled from it a photo.

Moving closer and motioning with his fingers, Steven said, "Let me see." After a glance at the photo and another at Johann and John, Steven let out a low whistle. "I'll be damned. Spitting images."

Scratching his cheek, Francis added, "Now that you've seen that, was there anything else you forget?"

"Yeah. I forgot I didn't have anything else to do. Plus, you didn't really think I'd let you do this without me, did you?" Steven asked with forced bravado.

Magdalena translated. Johann's face broke out in a smile.

"Come on in then. We were just about to start," his dad replied. "You've seen these folks on the porch. This is my younger son, Steven."

The Germans nodded in his direction and then introduced themselves.

"There's a folding chair in the hall closet. You know where it is," Francis stated. "Get yourself something to drink if you want, and sit down. Magdalena just finished setting the proverbial table."

Moments later, Steven scrunched himself between his sisters, taking the best spot, directly opposite the Germans. "Well, now that I'm settled in, what do you say we get this rodeo under way?" Steven said, a big smile on his face.

Magdalena wore a confused look on her face, failing to understand the idiom.

"He means he's ready to start," Francis explained.

With a nod, Magdalena reached for her canvas sack and dug out a folder. She set it on the table, opened it, pulled out several sheets, and spread them in front of her. She placed the bag back on the floor and glanced at her newly found American family. "I will take you back to the end of July 1914, when our story begins."

MANNHEIM, GERMANY

JULY 30, 1914

Sixteen

Hilda stood immobile in shadows in the dining room, on the far side of the doorway leading into the kitchen. The doorjamb partially obscured her face. The hazy, slanting rays of the dying day's sun poured in through the kitchen window, casting a pale light. Methodically, she took inventory, assuring herself everything was where it belonged. The well-ordered kitchen, perfectly mirroring her life and lifestyle, pleased her. She had recently laundered the curtains over the sink, air-dried them in the summer sun and breeze, and crisply ironed them. Her cast-iron kettles and pots were in their appointed places, black as the day purchased and within arm's reach of the stove. A yellow-and-white-checkered hand towel, folded into thirds, was draped over the oven handle, her married monogram clearly visible.

With confidence, she knew that if blindfolded, she could easily navigate her way around. From the sink to the stove, she needed only to take two steps to the right; from the sink to the butcher table was another six steps, also to the right; and from the sink to the icebox was only four steps to the left. If put to the test with the blindfold still in place, she would easily find the drawer in which she kept her kitchen utensils—flatware in the top drawer, knives and serving utensils in the middle one, and all others in the bottom. Barely turning her head to the left, to the area between the sink and the icebox, she gazed, a smile coming to her face, upon her favorite spot in the kitchen. There she mixed, kneaded, and rolled out her pastry dishes. She was famous for these, at least in the neighborhood. Her boys loitered nearby while she baked, hoping to snatch morsels without getting caught or to clean the mixing spoons and bowls when she was finished. Beneath this counter, concealed by a yellow-and-white-checkered table skirt matching the curtains, the mixing bowls and baking pans, the tools of her trade, were stored.

How was it possible, she wondered, that what had started out as yet another perfect summer day—just like the other ones of that summer, neither too dry nor too humid, cool in the morning, pleasantly warm in the midafternoon sun, and turning cool again in the evening—could turn so wrong so quickly? The summer had rolled by without worry or concern, and the days had clicked by as if to the well-measured pulse of a metronome. Yet by late day, gathering storm clouds were clearly visible in the distance, and she could hear the muffled rumbling of far off thunder. *Why,* she thought, *could this day not have followed course?*

She shifted her gaze to her right and looked above the butcher table at her grandmother's cuckoo clock, which was keeping perfect time. Not needing to look, she knew it was just after eight, having heard the cuckoo's call as she came down from putting her boys to bed at the prescribed bedtime.

Still standing motionlessly in the doorway, she wondered how the events of the last few days might disrupt her world.

Born in 1890, Hilda had only ever known a life filled with peace and prosperity. Certainly there had been occasional difficult economic times, but other than those rare occurrences, her world, from one day to the next, had been mostly constant and predictable. She had married right before she had turned twenty and had become a mother within a year. The second child had followed two years later. Her husband taught the King's English at an exclusive, private boys' school. He aspired to one day become headmaster, believing he would set the proper example. Though school was not to begin until after the fall harvest, which was still a month away, her husband was already planning his curriculum.

In the stillness of the moment, she realized she had everything she had hoped for out of life Her contentment welled up inside her in a wavelike rush of physical heat, starting in her toes and rapidly spreading upward to her face. She raised both hands, felt the warmth radiating from her cheeks, and then fanned herself with both hands.

Wanting her husband's attention, she took a half step forward, bringing most of her face out of the shadow; she cleared her throat. Franz, at the kitchen table with his meerschaum pipe in his mouth, a veil of tobacco smoke swirling about his head, and a dish towel draped nonchalantly over a shoulder, failed to react to the summons. Waiting for him to emerge from his thoughts, she again glanced about, noting the supper dishes sitting to the right of the sink. While she had been getting the boys settled, he must have washed and dried them, leaving them neatly stacked and ready to put away. He knew better than to do that himself. She was especially particular about how and where they belonged.

Her husband puffed away on his pipe. She imagined she could just hear the muffled crackle of the burning tobacco and envision the reddish-orange of the smoldering leaves under a thin layer of grayish ash. He looked lost in thought, deeply immersed in the mists of time and a long way away. So as not to startle him, Hilda again cleared her throat. As before, he remained unaware of her.

She cleared her throat a third time, louder this time.

Coming out of the haze, Franz looked distractedly up and around toward the sound. He saw his wife in the doorway. "Are the boys asleep?"

"Yes. Alois was asleep before I finished reading, Herman immediately after. The excitement of the day must've worn them out. It's not every day there's as much hustle and bustle in town. Herman wanted to know when the circus was coming."

"A circus? Is there a circus coming?" Franz asked.

"No."

"What made him ask?"

"Men were plastering broadsides on shop windows and on buildings and news kiosks," Hilda replied. "Last year, posters went up right before the circus came to town; I guess from the perspective of a four-year-old, posters going up could only mean a circus was coming. He was disappointed no elephants or clowns were on the posters. He asked what kind of circus had no elephants or clowns."

"What did you tell him?"

"That no circus was coming. I wasn't about to try to explain what the posters were for; he wouldn't have understood."

Franz pulled out the chair next to his and patted the seat. Hilda walked around her husband, the back of her right hand brushing against his shoulders. She sat down, scooted the chair closer, adjusted her shawl, and reached for his hand. Without a word passing between them, they held hands, looking into each other's eyes. Each could see the other's concern.

Franz asked, "Did you read one?"

"Of course, but it was difficult to get close. There was such a crowd of people. To keep the boys busy, I bought an ice cream."

"Good thinking." Franz released her hand and patted her thigh.

"What is a state of imminent danger of war?" Hilda asked. "Does this have anything to do with that assassination in Sarajevo? I can't imagine anyone being too upset anymore. That man was not well liked, except by the kaiser. It was a shame, though, his wife was killed at the same time, leaving behind those young children. What's this mean, Franz?"

"It has everything to do with the assassination," Franz replied. "Austrians—they're so inept at everything except coffee and strudel. They should've crushed Serbia when they had the chance several years back. Nobody would've lifted a finger. Had they, we'd not be in today's predicament. Plus, to think the kaiser has tied our fate to them."

"Does this mean we might go to war over something that happened in some corner of the Balkans—something not even involving us?"

"More than might. Our government has never gone this far before—not that I can remember. Not even back in 1911, when the kaiser almost single-handedly provoked a war. Luckily, cooler heads prevailed then. We can only hope the same happens this time."

"But why are the posters going up? What happened?"

"Yesterday Russia mobilized its armies as a show of support for its Slavic kinsmen in Serbia. The Russians will move against Austria-Hungary."

"Why has Russia gotten involved? Isn't this between Serbia and Austria-Hungary?" Hilda asked. "And what do we have to do with this?"

Franz explained how Austria, in 1908, had annexed an area in the Balkans that Serbia had wanted. Russia, Serbia's protector, had been unable to do anything to prevent this from happening. After Austria-Hungary had marched in, Russia had pledged that if Austria again overreached in the future, it would support Serbia militarily.

"The Russians mobilized, as promised, when Austria broke diplomatic relations. With the Russian armies threatening Austria on its eastern borders while its army is on its southern border against Serbia"—Franz stopped for a moment and took a deep breath—"our government can't stand by and allow Russia to threaten Austria-Hungary for two reasons. First, we can't allow our one true ally to be beaten, even if they're more trouble than they're worth, and two, there's no way we can be sure the Russian troops aren't on the Prussian border."

"But we're nowhere close to Prussia," Hilda said. "Isn't that Prussia's problem, not ours?"

"It is, technically. But remember, Prussia has the power to declare war and can order mobilization. That turns their problem into ours," Franz explained. "The Junkers are probably scared to death, thinking what might happen if the Russian hordes come swooping across the border."

"I understand that, but no war has broken out, has it?" she asked.

"Not much shooting has occurred, but Austria-Hungary declared war on Serbia two days ago. When that occurred, Russia prepared for war."

"What happens next?"

"The government will have to order a general mobilization, which means not only active soldiers and sailors but reserves as well. We'll need to defend against the Russian menace."

"Mobilization means certain war. Isn't there something someone can do?" Hilda asked.

Franz shook his head. "Not from a military point of view. This was preordained years back, when the kaiser scrapped the alliance with Russia, allowing the Russians to take up with the French and slip a noose around our neck."

"We never even considered going to war in 1912, when those Balkan countries fought the Turks," Hilda remarked.

"That's true, but as Europe was concerned, Christians had every right to oust the Muslims and send them back to from where they came," Franz added.

"I remember our pastor making that point during his sermons. He even led prayers to that effect. But in 1913, when the Balkan countries fought it out again, we again stayed out. If there has to be war, can't it be limited to just those directly involved, just like then?" Hilda suggested.

"It's different this time. In 1912, everybody wanted the Turks out, and they got thrown out; in 1913, none of the countries that fought were considered major powers. As long as the major powers stayed put, the balance of power in Europe remained unaltered. That's always been vital. Plus, the 1913 war lasted only about six weeks—hardly enough time for governments to work their citizens into frenzied support."

"We may not have fought in either war, but we supported our allies." Cynically, Hilda added, "If only I could be sure we wouldn't have jumped in if the outcome looked like it wasn't going to be to our liking."

"It's a certainty that we would've gone to war to influence a favorable outcome if we had to. At a minimum, we would've threatened to, hoping that'd be enough. The kaiser has done that many times. He's always prancing about in his bemedaled general's or admiral's uniforms with gold braiding and piping and those frilly, plumed caps. He loves nothing more than to rattle his saber, all the while praying it doesn't have to be unsheathed. The ink had hardly dried on the newspapers before the shooting was all over in the first war. Then Bulgaria pulled the surprise attack on its former allies in late June 1913 after Serbia refused to cede what Bulgaria had been promised as war spoils. In the end, Bulgaria only wanted what she had bargained for. Within a month, Serbia, Greece, Romania, and the Ottoman Empire had crushed Bulgaria, taking more of her land."

"Sounds like a perfect recipe for Serbia to think itself invincible; it had been on the winning side of two Balkan campaigns. Couple that with strong support from the Russians, and ..." Hilda remarked.

Franz reached for her hand and gave it a squeeze. "It might've been better if Serbia had been beaten. They would've had to have licked their wounds. Had that happened, maybe, just maybe, we wouldn't find ourselves in this mess," Franz commented. "But then again, maybe not; perhaps this has simply become inevitable."

"All this talk of war frightens me, Franz. The only good thing is if Germany goes to war, you won't have to go, since you're a teacher. Maybe it'll be a short war. Who knows? The fighting could be over before Christmas."

Franz took his wife's hands in his and gazed into her eyes. She returned his gaze, holding his as tenderly as he held hers. He remarked, "Don't bet on a short war; today's world is different than the past, and today's wars will be different. If we go to war, it could last longer than anyone thinks, depending on which countries come in and on whose side. If that happens, you can't waste anything. You might even have to consider moving in with your parents or mine or having them move in with you and the boys."

Puzzled, Hilda asked, "Why would I have to do that? You'll be here with me."

Franz lowered his eyes.

She pulled her hands free and cupped them in her lap, letting her gaze fall upon them. Franz reached for her chin, gently lifted it, and looked into her face; she forced a dry smile.

"You needn't say anything; I already know. I knew you wouldn't let your men march off without you. If you had, you'd have worried the whole time anyway, so you might as well go. Either way, I wouldn't have you, not in spirit; that's what I love most about you. You'll always do your duty for God and country—another reason I love you so much. Since you don't know when the orders will come, I'll go upstairs and start to gather your things."

She pushed her chair back from the table. With his left hand, Franz reached out for her; with the other hand, he fingered the edge of her shawl. "Put something in my valise to remind me of you."

Hilda smiled, got up, and walked to the counter. She opened the bottom drawer and pulled out a pair of scissors. Returning, she sat close to her husband and pulled the shawl across her body. With several quick snips, she cut a square.

"Will this do?" she asked, handing him the swatch.

He brought it to his face and breathed deeply. "This is perfect. Smells just like you."

"No more talk of war tonight," she ordered. "As it is, I won't get any sleep, and tomorrow the boys will know something's wrong. I won't know what to tell them. You may be ordered to report any day and—" Hilda was reasoning out loud.

Franz cleared his throat. Holding his pipe in his right hand, he squeezed hers with his left hand. "Like you said, no more talk of war tonight. I love you so much. You've given me something; I just wish there was something I could do for you so you'd know I'll always be with you."

Smiling, Hilda answered, "There is, Franz. Do that thing I like."

Franz smiled back and took several deep puffs on his pipe. In the gathering gloam of the evening, the tobacco glowed red in the bowl, casting a faint light upon his face. With his last puff, he slowly blew the smoke into his wife's face.

Closing her eyes, she breathed deeply in through her nose, letting her head fall back; a look of ecstasy swept across her face. The smoke billowed around her head and shoulders before settling onto her shawl. Bringing the edge of her shawl to her nose, she breathed in and held her breath for several heartbeats.

"I like it when you do that. I love that smell." Squeezing Franz's hands in hers, she added, "As long as I can smell your pipe smoke in my shawl, you'll be with me."

MAPLETON VALLEY

Seventeen

With a flick of her left index finger, Magdalena wiped a tear away. Awkwardly, she smiled as her glance jumped haphazardly around the table. Johann had pulled a handkerchief from a pocket and was dabbing his eyes. Wilhelm had a distant and melancholic look on his face. Monique and Donna, having moved next to one another, clasped hands and softly wept. His eyes cast down, Francis seemed far away and completely absorbed in what he had heard. Only two looked unmoved: Steven and John. Steven looked more bemused than moved. John regarded her through narrow slits of hostile eyes.

Not taking her eyes from John, she reached down and pulled her sack onto her lap. She reached in, brought out a remnant of cloth, and placed it on the table. "This is what remains of her shawl. Our grandmother kept it as a reminder—a reminder of her love and of her life before the war." She brought it to her nose. "If you hold it to your nose, you can still smell the faint hint of smoke."

Magdalena handed it to Wilhelm with a motion of her head, as if to say, *Pass it along when finished.*

Monique, the last to hold it to her nose, as John showed no inclination of taking it when offered, inhaled deeply. "You *can* still smell smoke. Dad, did you smoke a pipe?"

"Not for long. I smoked cigarettes first—started during the war. For soldiers, smoking a fag was easy compared to a pipe—easier to lug around, easier to find, and easier to smoke in the lines. I always liked the way pipe tobacco smelled. For a short time, after the war, I switched because there were, in Germany, many beautiful pipes, and like other things there, they could be bartered for for practically nothing."

The four siblings nervously eyed one another. Donna and Steven swallowed hard, no doubt their conversation of just a few nights before in mind.

Magdalena continued her story. "The following day, there were displays of patriotism. Lampposts were festooned with buntings sporting the imperial colors—red, white, und black. The imperial flag flew in windows. Spontaneous concerts were held with marches und martial music. Speeches praised the kaiser's courage und steadfastness, praising him as the guardian of all things German. Articles on what a great leader the kaiser was und how beloved he was by his people appeared overnight. Newspapers called the coming conflict a righteous cause against enemies who sought to encircle us und keep us from our rightful place. Glorious accounts of parades also appeared in the newspapers. The radical Socialist newspapers, the fiercest critics of the government, urged their readers to stand united with the nation. Such was the enthusiasm for war that grabbed the people at the outset. I have since learned that practically all European countries that fought reacted similarly; it was not uniquely German."

Mobilization was ordered the next day, setting in motion the soldiers to their posts and depots.

Franz packed, his orders requiring him to leave the following afternoon. His older son sat on his bed and watched, not understanding.

"Why are you packing, Papa?" Herman asked.

"Papa has to go away for a while. I hope it won't be for long."

"Me too; I don't want you to miss my birthday. I'd be sad if you did," Herman answered.

"That'd make two of us. But your birthday isn't for several months, and if I did have to miss it, I know you'd understand, since you're going to be a big boy."

Herman pouted at that remark and then asked, "If you're not going to be here, can you make sure my presents are?"

"I'll make sure you have my presents in plenty of time, even if I'm not here to watch you open them. How does that sound?"

Nodding, Herman answered gleefully, "That sounds good, Papa. Where do you have to go?"

"I don't know," he replied.

"If you don't know where you're going, how do you know what to pack? What if you end up in a jungle? You might need a safari hat."

Franz laughed. "I'll buy one there if I do."

"Make sure you take money, Papa."

"I'll do that. Anything else?" Franz asked.

"Can I come along?" his son asked. Out of the corner of his eye, Herman saw his mother come in carrying Alois in one arm and clothes in the other. "I'd ask for Alois, but he's too small."

"Not this time—maybe another. Perhaps Alois can go along then. How does that sound?" Franz asked.

"I'd rather it just be you and me. Alois should stay home with Momma," Herman declared, folding his arms in front of him and jutting out his chin.

Franz smiled and tousled his hair. He knew that he would miss both boys, particularly Herman.

Hilda, sensing their conversation had come to an end, interjected. "These clothes should get you through for a while.

If you need more, let me know," she commented, dropping the clothing on the bed.

"Momma, do you know where Papa is going?" Herman asked his mother. "You should tell him if you do."

Hilda tousled his hair. "I don't know. What I meant was once Papa gets to where he is going, he should write so we will know. We can look it up on our map if we have to send him things."

"Franzis would march off with his unit," Magdalena explained. "My grandmother hoped that the war would be short und that her husband would return unharmed und unchanged. Her hopes would go unfulfilled."

John cleared his throat. "So let me get this straight, because it just dawned on me—your grandfather *could've* stayed home but instead elected to go before he had to," John stated cynically. "Is that right?"

"Jah," Magdalena answered. "But I should have said that he would have had to go at some point; in the beginning, he did not. Why do you ask?"

"Just curious," John replied, a smirk on his face.

"There must be more to your question than curiosity," Magdalena riposted.

"Well, if you must know. You make it sound like they had a comfortable life together and were happy."

Magdalena translated for her brothers. Both shrugged and looked at the other.

"I believe that they were," she replied. "Is there something that makes you think otherwise?"

John shrugged indifferently. "Do you have any proof they *were*?"

"I do not understand what you are saying. Why would I need proof? From what I know, I have no doubt that they were happy. Do you think that my grandfather und grandmother were not happy?"

"I think that's possible."

Magdalena translated for her brothers. Wilhelm said something in return, an edge in his tone.

"My bruder wants to know why you would say that. He would like to know why you think that they were not happy."

"It's simple. It seems to me people who're happy," John explained, "don't voluntarily risk life or limb if they don't have to. You yourself said he wasn't immediately required to go."

Magdalena translated and then turned her attention back to John.

"It has been more than ninety years. I would say to you that times were different then. People believed then that their families were important but not more important than their God, their country, or their ruler. I have no proof that my grandparents were unhappy with each other, so I believe that they were. Our grandfather's"—Magdalena pointed at her brothers, then John and Steven, and finally their sisters—"behavior was typical. More than today, I think that people then saw themselves less as an individual und more as part of something larger, something greater."

"Maybe superior? That'd be a typical German perspective. Isn't that the reason why Germans let Hitler come to power and stay in power—because Germans believed they were superior and he played to that? And as a consequence, our father"—John pointed at his brother and two sisters—"was almost killed in the next war Germany started. We"—again John motioned toward his siblings—"almost didn't get the chance to be here."

"I am glad that you are here," Magdalena quickly replied, glancing from John to his siblings. "Regarding Herr Hitler, I cannot answer. We were very young at that time, but I can say that it will do no good to argue about the past; there is nothing that we can do about it except try to prevent it from happening again. That can come about by understanding und showing respect for each other. I do not believe that most Germans of my grandparents' generation thought of themselves as superior; I think that they saw themselves as a part of something larger, something greater. Germans today do not think of themselves as superior. I am not saying that we do not have problems in Germany. A diverse population creates diverse problems, just like in your country."

Magdalena leaned toward Johann, who had been tugging at her elbow. She translated. "Johann points out that every society has a history. In your country, you have but to study the history of slavery und the treatment of Native Americans. No matter where it occurs, it is deplorable. That is how Germans of today feel.

"Germany lost two global wars," she added. "After the first, Germany was made to take the blame. After the second, there was no need; Germany was to blame. But I can tell you that having lived through the occupation und having been old enough to comprehend what was happening, because of what Germany had done, we were made to suffer. It would have been easy for Germans to again feel like outcasts, as they had been made to feel between the wars. Yet Germans did not. We survived und came through." Magdalena stopped, gesturing by interlocking her cupped hands.

Mimicking her gesture, John asked cynically, "Is that supposed to mean stronger and more united?"

"Jah. That is what I wish to express," Magdalena responded, nodding in emphasis.

"Phooey!" John gestured with a flick of his hand as if to shoo away a bothersome gnat. "That's just more self-serving twaddle!"

"Stop, John!" Donna barked in an authoritative and annoyed voice. "There is nothing to gain from going down that path. These people are guests in our father's house. Magdalena has already said it'll do no good to argue over the past. I agree. Leave the past in the past, for God's sake."

John replied, "If that's what you're advising—to leave the past in the past—then why in the hell are we gathered around this table rehashing it? Huh? Answer that."

Donna shook her head, a look of disgust on her face, and, in exasperation, remarked to Magdalena, "Please do what we do with my brother at times like this: try to ignore him if you can."

An embarrassed and uncomfortable silence fell upon the group until Donna prompted Magdalena. "Please go on with your story. You were saying your grandmother hoped the war would be short and her husband would come back unharmed and unchanged."

Magdalena glanced in John's direction. "My grandmother would see her husband only a few more times. She could see the changes that war brought in him, herself, und those around her. War changed everything und everyone. Hardships und losses were felt by all. Problems arose not from these but from how people viewed und judged those who did not deal with these as expected. As if there were but one way to grieve! She too grieved—for the life that she had enjoyed und the death of the men und boys who she had once known. She grieved for the hopes that she had once had. After his first leave, she knew that Franz, even if he were to return unharmed, would not be unchanged.

"Franz's unit would march through Belgium und France." She motioned in a great, sweeping arc from right to left with her right arm. "In September 1914, when the advance came to a halt, they had fought almost continuously, suffering terribly. Trenches were dug und then extended all the way to the sea und Switzerland. By late 1914, trench warfare had set in.

"Our grandfather lived in these until his first leave in May 1915. He was lucky; he was still alive und had not suffered any serious wound. Und he was unlucky, for those who had already perished did not have to suffer the trenches or deal with having to return home. When he arrived, Grandma Hilda knew that he had been wounded; his wounds were just not visible. Most of the time he seemed ..." Magdalena gestured with her hands and her eyes.

Monique interjected. "Anxious?"

"Jah," Magdalena replied. "He was thinner; he looked sad. He had dark circles under his eyes, und though he slept very deeply when he slept, he slept very little und only for short periods. Despite these changes, sometimes he could be himself. Our grandmother felt that she knew the man who still shared her bed. By the end, he was ready to return to his world—one in which he felt comfortable und safe und where he knew how to survive. For Grandmother Hilda, he had been a visitor—a rover who had traveled far from a remote land, a land known only to its inhabitants und inaccessible to outsiders."

Magdalena caught her breath, her chin dropping slightly. Johann put his arm around his sister and gently patted her shoulder. She looked up at him and smiled wanly. "It would be almost a year before he would return. Und that man, the one who came back, was a complete stranger."

Donna reached her hand across the table to Magdalena. "This must be very hard. I can't imagine what you're feeling."

Magdalena reached tentatively for Donna's hand and grasped it tightly. A thin smile formed on her face; her eyes softened.

"It is difficult," she replied. "But it will be worth it if we can learn what we came to learn."

"What was it like," Donna asked, "for your grandmother to live alone? Did she mention anything?"

Magdalena nodded almost imperceptibly before answering softly, "She did write about her home life. She und her sons lived alone until just after the first leave. The house became too large for them, so her parents moved in. With the extra people in the house, it was easier to stretch the rations. Plus, either our grandmother or her mother, while she could, would take turns standing in lines for provisions. To conserve heat, rooms were closed off, not to be used. This arrangement worked well during 1915, but in early 1916, our grandmother learned that her only brother had been killed. Und though the family should have been honored that he had died in combat, fighting for his country, no one could find consolation in that honor. Soon after, our grandmother's mother stopped eating und refused to come out of her room. Before long, she fell ill; she died not long after."

Steven cleared his throat; Magdalena looked at him. Donna also glanced in his direction, a cautionary look on her face.

"By this time in the war," Steven began, his attention on Magdalena, "except for the very wealthy or the well connected, everyone was suffering. Germany had essentially taken over command of the Austro-Hungarian armies and had sent military advisers to the Ottoman Empire. Germany was being stretched on all fronts. Whatever resources were available were earmarked first for the war effort. The relatively little left over were available for civilian consumption, and there was a pecking order. I say this only because I'm surprised the hardships you described were only just then being felt."

Magdalena translated and then responded. "Our grandmother's family was wealthy. Her father was an industrialist. He owned a company that supplied uniforms und shoes to the army. His workers had enjoyed extra rations to maintain morale und production. By mid-1916, the extra rations had disappeared. Our great-grandfather could have taken extra. He did not. He believed his family should suffer alongside the others."

Shaking his head, John commented, "Do you expect us to feel sorry for you and your family? I've got to tell you, by 1916, the unfortunate ones who found themselves in the occupied areas of France and Belgium would've gladly traded places. You'll get no sympathy from me; those people had already suffered much more and much longer."

"How do you know those people suffered more?" Magdalena asked testily.

"Because I do," John replied curtly.

Wilhelm leaned toward his sister, whispering something to her. "Wilhelm wants to know what makes you say that."

John glanced to the far end of the table. Francis said, "John, if you have something to share, share it. A story is being told—that's all. What you know might help. They can understand what was happening in different places at the same time during the war."

With a snarl, John looked from Magdalena to Wilhelm. "I know for a fact the French civilians who got caught behind lost much; some lost their lives, most lost most of their possessions, and all suffered." John had gone red in the face. He took a slow, deep breath. "Farm animals were slaughtered by the Germans for the German army. Germans reaped too much of the annual harvest, leaving little for those who'd actually done the work. Let's not forget that in the occupied areas, like in Germany, but even more so, anything essential to the war—chemicals, coal, and metals in particular—was diverted for that use. The result was no chemicals, no fertilizer; no coal, no heat; and no metal, no new plows, scythes, or other implements. This all added up to smaller and poorer harvests. Yet the Germans took what they wanted, caring little about what remained. So yes, I do know something about how the suffering was unequal."

Francis interrupted. "So everyone knows John's comments are triggered by his reading of my mother's journals of that time. Isn't that so?"

"Yes. What I'm sharing comes directly from those."

Francis cast a glance at each person at the table. "She kept journals throughout the war."

"I don't think so, Dad," John interjected. "I don't think she did *throughout* the war."

"Yes, she did, Son. She kept them *throughout* the war," his father replied assuredly.

John shook his head slightly, pursed his lips, and then glared at his father. "If that's so, Dad, then why ..." The rest of the thought went unspoken.

"Don't give me that look. I'm telling you, for a fact, I know. The war didn't stop her."

Magdalena held her hand up to stop the conversation. Finishing her translation, she nodded.

"How do we know the things she told you were right, and not what she told us?" John asked.

"Because a given in the human condition is the more distance—in time, space, and relationship—you can put between yourself and the person who's hearing your story, the easier it is to tell the story as you'd like it to be, not necessarily as it was. What I can tell you is the stories she told were different than the ones she wrote down." Francis sighed. "What's in the journals isn't important at this point." He looked at each person. "But everyone should understand a written account was kept. It's this John alludes to. For a change, to be fair to him, what John is saying is correct. That's all that needs to be said at this time. John, if you have anything else to share—"

"I appreciate that, Dad," John replied insincerely. "I was just getting started when you commandeered the conversation." John looked across the table at the Germans. "I really don't have anything else to add at this point. I do want you," John continued, looking at each German, "to understand I have a lot more to say; I'll wait until it's my turn. What I've said was fresh in my mind from having read last night the journals."

Johann's and Wilhelm's faces perked up. Simultaneously, they asked their sister a question.

She laughed at their timing and then turned to John. "After we left?"

"Yeah, after you left," John replied. "Thanks to you, I was up past one."

"We are sorry for that," Magdalena explained. "But would it be possible for us to read the journals?"

John said, "They're in French. Do you read French?"

The three shook their heads.

"I guess that takes care of that," John added flatly. "Anyway, I volunteer at the museum; there are plenty of photos of destroyed towns and villages in the German-occupied areas."

Magdalena took a moment to translate. Wilhelm whispered to her. "Wilhelm points out that it is possible that some of those villages may have been destroyed by the French or British shelling," Magdalena reported.

"Do you really want to go down that path?" John asked. "Need I remind you which country invaded which?"

"Is it possible for us to agree that the war was terrible for all?" Magdalena asked. "Millions suffered und died; it was not just the soldiers. I tell my story to show that the war had an effect on everyone, including the people left behind. You have also made that same point. Understand that we have not come to argue whether the war, or the peace, was just or not. We have come to learn about what happened to our grandfather."

Glancing around the table, John noticed everyone's eyes were on him. He flushed red, less from embarrassment than from anger. Robotically, he said, "Yes, we can agree that the war was terrible, and millions suffered and died as a result." He took a deep breath. "You all probably think I should apologize for my behavior, and you can think that all you want. But I'm not going to. I'm incensed about what their grandfather"—he pointed at the three Germans—"did to *our* grandmother."

"Oh! So she's now *our* grandmother?" Steven asked facetiously.

"Say whatever you want, but I want you to know it's really shaken me. And though I know in my heart none of us played a part in what happened more than ninety years ago, it doesn't change how I feel. I'm mad also because it's always the little people who suffer the most."

A quick translation followed, prompting a brief and intense conversation among the Germans. Finally, Magdalena turned to John. "It is interesting what you have just said. In the context of the story, our grandfather also suffered like that. During his next leave, Franz complained about the Prussians taking command over the armies. Because of that, the morale of his soldiers suffered."

A look of dismay came to Monique's face. "I don't understand."

Steven interjected. "Let me explain; fighting is done by small, discrete groups of men. The men have typically trained together for extended periods. This allows them to form bonds—bonds that will serve them well when they go into combat. These bonds aren't really about some larger, nobler ideal; they are almost always about the men in their unit. The generals and politicians sell the larger, nobler ideal to the people back home so they will support the war. But for the men in the front lines, who can't see beyond their tiny space, it's not that they don't care about the ideal; it's just that they care more about the men around them. When that cohesiveness and their loyalties are loosened, there's a good chance morale will suffer. When morale suffers, the men don't fight as well."

Magdalena replied, "I could not have explained as well. *Danke*."

"*Bitte*," Steven replied, smiling. "Please go on."

Magdalena yawned, stretching her arms. She glanced at her watch. "Excuse me. I am suddenly very tired. It is almost ten o'clock, und I have talked for a long time. Perhaps we should stop at this point."

Francis asked, "Does anyone have a problem with that? It does seem to be a good place."

All nodded except John, who gave no indication.

"Okay, it's decided. We'll call it a night. Tomorrow at the same time?" Francis asked.

All nodded except John.

"John, you can't tomorrow evening?" his dad inquired.

"I can't tomorrow night. I'm available the next night after work," John replied. Catching Magdalena's gaze, he added, "And I'm not around the house tomorrow, so don't even think about coming over."

"We have learned our lesson. Though I would like to see the journals und try to understand some of what your grandmother wrote, we will not be bothering you at your home," Magdalena replied.

"In that case," Francis added after allowing ample time for John to extend an invitation—one not extended, "how does Monday night work at seven?"

Steven immediately remarked, "I can't that night. I have a date."

"Can't you reschedule?" Francis asked.

Steven raised both hands to shoulder height and made a motion with them as if he were weighing something. "Let's see—go out on a date or hang here and hear the rest of the story." He laughed. "I won't be here Monday night. If that works for everyone else, then that's fine."

"Too bad. Monday then?" Francis asked, glancing around. "Seven o'clock? Should we order something to eat?"

Everyone nodded except Steven.

"That settles it then. I'll order enough for seven and have it delivered around seven," Francis commented.

Steven cleared his throat; all eyes turned to him. Sheepishly grinning, he added, "Make it nine."

"That's too late," John answered. "Who knows? By then, we could've already said what we have to say."

"I doubt that, but that's not what I meant." Steven again laughed. "Not nine p.m.—nine people. My date might enjoy the story."

AUGUST 1

Eighteen

"At the end of his third leave, in late 1916, our grandfather left the house that he had once called home und returned to his home," Magdalena recounted. "There would be one more leave before he would leave our grandmother a widow."

Magdalena sighed deeply and glanced around at the seven other faces settled around the table. Each face outwardly expressed the emotions it was feeling; by her count, five shared her sadness. She spent an extra-long moment considering the face of John, who, in mid-discourse, had shoved his chair back, making a racket, and gone to lean against the kitchen counter. She sensed he knew something. She wanted only to know so that there'd be no gaping holes in the story when they returned home. His eyes remained cold and blank, betraying nothing. She wondered how to reach him and draw him back.

In the little time she had known those around the table, she had come to like each in his or her own way. But she liked one more than the others—John, the least likeable. Her fondness for him had to do with his awareness of family. As her visit was related to family, she respected him for that. In that vein, they were related; they just weren't family—at least not as she defined it.

A wave of melancholy crept over her, and for the first time since her arrival, she felt a pang of longing for home. She raised her right hand to her face, cupping her chin, and leaned heavily forward.

"Are you all right?" Francis asked.

Wearily, she smiled, nodded, and then shifted her glance to Steven, who sat on his father's right. He was the other whose emotions she would not have included with the others. To be fair, his attitude might have been because his companion had opted out of joining them.

Steven slouched in his chair, his head resting on the top of the chair back, his eyes looking up at the ceiling, and his arms folded across his chest. To a casual observer, he might have had an air of being not very bright. Yet Magdalena had a hunch he was anything but; she sensed he might even be too intelligent, grasping things too quickly and becoming bored as the others tried to catch up. The entrance he had made, making a production of it after having acted as though he were not the least bit interested in them or their task, had been, well, she was not sure. He had gone so far as to conspicuously close the front door and tromp heavily down the hallway, making sure to draw everyone's attention. Then he had had the nerve to peek around the corner coquettishly.

She had been surprised to see him alone, for she had not expected him to show without a companion. Perhaps this evening's act was yet another attempt to draw attention and to demonstrate to his family, particularly his father, that he was giving up something—something he would rather be doing than this. It would not have surprised her to learn that this son was the favored one, and that would have been perfectly understandable, considering the options. She shot a glance in John's direction; he still leaned against the kitchen countertop, his arms crossed and his chin tucked sternly into his chest.

She turned her attention again to Steven. Magdalena wondered if he was present in spirit, since he had an air of distraction about him, an air of being elsewhere. Suddenly, his head turned in her direction, and he locked eyes with her. She smiled, checking to see if he had checked in. His expression did not change.

Donna and Monique were sitting next to each other, just as they had two nights ago—that was, before they had been forced to relinquish their spot to the younger son, who had barged in and wedged himself between them. Tonight they were sitting close, arms interlinked. She doubted Steven had thought about trying to pull off the same trick. Three piles of tissues sat in front of them. Magdalena suspected that by the end of the night, there would be but one.

After clearing her throat, Magdalena started up again. "Our grandmother felt relief and worry at her husband's departure. She was relieved that he was still alive. At the same time, she worried that he would be back. Having him around had been particularly difficult. Shortages were the way of life—food, coal, clothing, transportation, und patience. She had set aside some of their daily rations in anticipation, hoping to have enough. The children were the hardest hit. Franz could see that. He had blamed her for not doing enough. 'There is so little und too many after the little,' she had explained. He had not listened. 'Explanations do no good,' he had replied and then walked out."

Magdalena wrung her hands for a brief moment. "Franz had not once shared their bed, choosing to sleep in the same room as the boys or alone. *Sleep* is probably not the correct word; she would hear him come und go in the small hours of the morning. Many times afterward, she would find extra wood or bread for the table. She would not ask from where they had come, grateful for their appearance, yet she was sad for those who would have to suffer more because of their disappearance.

"There was good news also. Franz was soon to be moved from the trenches to the rear. Because of his background, his commander believed that he could train troops to survive the trenches as he had, particularly during that year."

John cleared his throat, causing the others to turn in his direction. “That year? You’re talking about 1916?”

Magdalena nodded. “Jah. That would be the year.”

Again, John cleared his throat. “Do you know where your grandfather had been in 1916?”

Magdalena started to respond. “Verdun und the Somme were—”

Before Magdalena could finish, Monique interrupted. “What’s the big deal about 1916?”

“Are you familiar with the words Magdalena just said—*Verdun* and *the Somme*?” John asked.

She shook her head. “I’ve never heard of them. Should I have?”

“If you were,” John replied, “you’d not need to ask.”

“Well, I’m not,” Monique replied, an edge to her tone. “Tell me what the big deal is.”

Magdalena, who had been following the conversation, glanced at John. He pointed to himself with a thumb, arching his eyebrows. She nodded.

“The big deal,” John said, walking back to the table, pulling his chair out, swinging it around, sitting astride the seat, and crossing his arms atop the chair back, “is the Germans attacked the French at Verdun in February. The battle would continue the rest of the year. For the French, Verdun held a special place and was to be defended no matter what the cost. The German high command had picked Verdun for that reason, hoping to inflict such severe losses that the French would sue for peace. With the French out, the Germans could turn on the British. After the Brits had been dispensed with, the Russians would surely see the folly of continuing and quit the war. If not, the Germans would steamroll them. With luck, the war on the western front could be over in 1916, and by the end of 1917, in Russia, maybe earlier.”

John went on to explain how the Germans had scored initial successes at Verdun, but the French had been able to hold on by pouring in hundreds of thousands of reinforcements from other areas and keeping the only supply route, known as *La Voie Sacrée*—“the Sacred Way”—open.

John tapped the fingers of his right hand on the table. “The French requested Allied attacks along other fronts to relieve the pressure on Verdun. The Russians attacked Austria-Hungary, driving to the southwest. These met with huge early gains, pushing the enemy back hundreds of miles—not yards, as on the western front. It was so successful that Romania, waiting to see who would likely win the war, decided it was now impossible for Russia not to. They cast their lot with the Allies in August. Shortly after, the Russian attack sputtered. The Russians were repulsed, retreating back to where they’d started. The Central Powers then turned on Romania. By Christmas, Romania, battered and beaten, was out of the war.

“In July, the British launched a massive attack against entrenched German defenses along the Somme River. The goal was breakthrough, at which point the cavalry, waiting in the rear, lances with pennants snapping in the breeze and sabers in hand, would ride through, roll up the enemy, and continue on to Berlin. Done! The war would be over!”

John swallowed hard and then rubbed his Adam’s apple. “On July 1, after a weeklong bombardment, the troops went over the top, believing that the barbed wire protecting the enemy had been destroyed and no one could have survived. The soldiers advanced shoulder to shoulder across the shell-pocked no-man’s-land. Moments after the shelling had stopped, ten minutes too soon, the Germans came out of their dugouts practically untouched. They set up their machine guns and sighted them. When the soldiers poured over the top, the Germans opened up with everything. Descriptions of the slaughter compare it to the reaping of ripe wheat. Twenty-five thousand men were killed or wounded in the first hour. The second and third lines could hardly take a step without stepping on the bodies of the fallen—their comrades who, moments before, had been joking with them. By the end of the day, with not a single strategic objective secured, sixty thousand men had become casualties. The German machine gunners would shoot over the attackers' heads, hoping they'd go back to their trenches.

"The year 1916 was a year of failures on a monumental scale. Men were slaughtered—not in the hundreds or thousands, as in previous wars, but in the tens of thousands. The most appalling thing was that by year-end, the armies would essentially be where they'd started. Over one million men were casualties at Verdun, six hundred men fell at the Somme, and untold hundreds of thousands along the eastern front—all for nothing."

Looking at Magdalena, he asked, "He was at Verdun and the Somme?"

"Jah," she replied softly, nodding. "When he was finally pulled from the front in late October 1916, he was sent on leave."

Steven interjected, coming out of his funk. "From what you've described of his behavior at home, it sounds like he was suffering from what we call today post-traumatic stress disorder. These are classic PTSD symptoms."

Magdalena translated before commenting, "That sounds like a modern term."

"That's right," Steven replied. "I believe the term most frequently used at the time was *shell-shocked*."

The grandfather clock struck nine, prompting Steven to look at his watch.

Magdalena, sensing that she was starting to lose her audience, spoke up. "I would like to get to the last facts that we have regarding our grandfather. Franz moved out of the trenches. His duties were to command an area of occupied territory und to train soldiers, new und old, to survive the trenches. He was in command of an area near Beaulieu-en-prés." She turned to Francis. "Do you know that village?"

"Of course," he replied. "I was born there."

Steven scooted his chair in.

Turning to John, Magdalena asked, a coy smile on her face, "Do you know that village?"

"That seems rhetorical at this point," he answered sourly.

"Why?" she continued.

"Obviously, if what you claim is right, your grandfather and our grandmother had to have both been there."

"Do you know more than that?" she pressed.

Steven, staccato-like, tapped the tips of the fingers of his right hand on the table, louder and louder each time, drawing attention. When all eyes had turned on him, he suggested, "Mag, why don't you let this subject go for the time being and get on with your story? Finish your part so the rest can be told, since you only know a portion of the whole. I'm sure Frandad"—he pointed at his father—"has got something to share, and as you remember, my brother said he has more to say. Weren't those your exact words, John Boy?"

Without acknowledging his question, John replied, "Stick with real names. I doubt Magdalena has ever been called Mag before. Show our guests some respect, and while you're at it, the rest of us too."

"Good for you, John. Maybe he'll listen to you," Monique responded, giving a quick thumbs-up. "He's never bothered to when I've asked."

Magdalena translated the exchange for her brothers' benefit. When she pronounced the word *Mag*, they lightly laughed. Magdalena glanced at John. "I know that you know more. We are most anxious to hear what it is. But your brother makes a good suggestion; I will finish. Through letters, we learned that Franz did transfer out of the front lines und had been promoted to *Kapitan*. He was put in command of an area that included Beaulieu-en-prés. The area was to provide for his needs."

Clearing his throat, John waited for Magdalena to turn her attention to him. "Would his command have included the people living there?"

Without much reflection, she nodded in response. "I believe that he had broad powers; he could take what was needed or wanted."

John's face darkened. He coughed, covering his mouth with his left hand while his right balled itself tightly up.

Not understanding why he had reacted in this manner, Magdalena decided to quickly move on, giving John no chance to interrupt. "His outlook was changing; as a result, the tone of the letters also changed. Our grandfather spoke as openly as he could to get his letters through the military censors.

"When Franz came home on leave in late November 1917, our grandmother noticed a change for the better. He had lost his air of resignation that he had had during the last leave; something had changed in him. The conditions at home were bad und getting worse. America had joined the war, though not many American soldiers had arrived in Europe yet. There was optimism in the air. The czar had abdicated, und the Russian armies were retreating, melting away as the soldiers turned their backs on the war und trudged home. Remember that the German people only ever heard accounts of numerous und glorious victories over our enemies und of our enemies' desperate situation und great suffering. Based on these, the only possible conclusion was that our enemies were on the brink of defeat. Once more, the people were implored to sacrifice—if we could only hold out a little longer, if we could only dig deeper und only give a bit more. Hindsight would confirm that the brink had been reached. It was not, however, our enemies who stood there."

Magdalena laughed caustically. "From my readings of the war, I learned that all people, in all countries, were being told the same things. Each side's armies were victorious at every encounter, und each side's enemies were suffering. The enemies' fighting spirit was on the verge of cracking. All were being implored to sacrifice—if only they could hold out a little longer, if only they could dig deeper und only give a bit more. Und like us, they did. But what was given was what could no longer be afforded—more pots und pans for more bullets und shells, more money for more bullets und shells, und, the greatest sacrifice of all, more men for the bullets und shells. Each country wanted to believe that its cause was just und that the war had been forced upon them. Each country wanted to believe that what it was being told was true. Because of this, the war continued und would for another year."

"You said something had changed in him, in your grandfather. What was it?" Donna asked.

Magdalena looked surprised by the question.

"Is that not a good question?" Donna asked in response to Magdalena's reaction.

"*Nein, nein,*" Magdalena replied. "I forget that I know what I know und that you do not. Your question is good."

In reply to Donna's question, she added, "You were wondering what had changed. Part of the change had to do with being out of the trenches und not having to witness the daily slaughter. He did not have to worry whether he was to be killed at any moment. Part of the change had to do with being a teacher again. According to our grandmother, he had been a good teacher. Perhaps the biggest change had to do with him believing that, having survived thus far, he would survive the rest. He could then return to the life that he had once known. Was that not one of the most repeated reasons for going to war und continuing the war—to preserve what had been? Our grandmother had believed that at one time, but she no longer did. She had accepted that their life would never be the same. When Franz returned in November 1917, he returned to her bed. That was a big change. This leave went so well that when he left, he left her pregnant with our father. Don't you think, John, that that must have meant that they were happy?"

"It could mean many things. Just finish up, preferably without any further editorializing," John rejoined.

"Was that necessary? And in that tone?" Donna immediately snapped at her brother, a nasty look on her face. "Especially since, just moments ago, you scolded Steven for his lack of respect."

"Thank you, Donna," Magdalena said. "That would be the last time that Grandmother Hilda would see her husband. It was memories und hopes from this leave that kept her going during that last month of the war. She had written to Franz the news. By return letter, he said that he was very pleased. He was hoping for a girl, but another boy would also please him. Our father would be born in July 1918."

Magdalena described German attacks launched in spring 1918 as the final gamble to win the war before the Americans could bring their numbers to bear. By late May, the German advances had been brought to a halt. The gamble had failed. The German armies would never attack again, only retreat toward their borders. The war was lost, but the German high command could not—or would not—negotiate. The Allies understood that time was on their side; they were in no hurry to parlay. By early August, she explained, the German high command could no longer delude itself. The war had to be brought to a quick conclusion.

Magdalena exhaled, looking from one brother to the other, and then she reached for a hand of each. She leaned first toward Wilhelm and whispered something and then repeated the gesture with Johann. Each gave a barely perceptible nod.

"Please excuse me. I wanted to tell them where I was in the story," Magdalena explained. "Fighting on the western front ended on November 11, but our grandfather would not live to see it. We do not know how he died or why or precisely where. But we think that he died in Beaulieu-en-prés, at your grandmother's farm."

John glanced down at his father, who was watching him like a hawk.

"And how would you come to think that?" John asked.

"Our grandfather did not return from the war. In the chaos that followed, our grandmother did not receive notification; she just knew that he was missing. She waited for weeks before inquiring about what might have happened. Finally, in early January 1919, she received official word that he was missing in action und presumed dead. In the meantime, the aide-de-camp to our grandfather learned of her search. He contacted her. That spring, our grandmother met Heinrich Mueller. This man had been with our grandfather during the last year of the war. Herr Mueller kept his schedule und knew where he was. At times, he accompanied our grandfather, sometimes even out to your grandmother's farm, but had not when our grandfather made his last visit."

"Why?" John inquired.

"Herr Mueller said your grandmother caused trouble. She always wanted more; she was never happy with what she had. To keep her disruptions to a minimum, our grandfather saw her several times a month. With the end in sight, our grandfather made one final visit. He went alone, not wanting to expose anyone else to needless risks. He walked out the door und never walked back in."

Magdalena pulled several times at her right ear. "When he failed to return, Herr Mueller went looking. His first stop was your grandmother's farm. Herr Mueller confronted her. She admitted that he had been there but that she had not seen him since that morning. She invited Herr Mueller to search the property. The search had to be hurried because the Germans were to evacuate the front lines by the next day. No sign of him was found."

Slyly, John smiled. "Sounds like any number of things could've happened to him. Since he was an officer, he could've come across German stragglers who could've killed him and dumped his body somewhere; or on his way back, a random artillery shell could've found him and blown him to bits; or he could've been killed by locals who disposed of his body somewhere where no one would ever find it. From having read my grandmother's journals, the last one might be the most plausible."

"Those are all believable. However, our grandmother sensed something different. Her intuition told her that he had died at your grandmother's farmhouse, since it was the last place that he was seen alive. For years afterwards, she found no peace, not knowing what happened." Magdalena fell silent.

Steven pushed back from the table, catching her attention. He shot a glance at his watch, slapped his hands on his thighs, and loudly proclaimed, "That's a damn fine story. I've got to go so I can get up in the morning. How about tomorrow night for, as Paul Harvey would say, the rest of the story?"

"I do not understand," Magdalena responded. "Who is Paul Harvey?"

Francis placed the palms of his hands on the edge of the table, preparing to get up. "He was a longtime radio announcer here in America. That was his tagline, though it's not important for this. What Steven is saying is shall we continue tomorrow night?" He then added, "By a show of hands, who can't be here tomorrow night?"

Magdalena translated for her brothers and then looked around to see if anyone had raised a hand. No hands were in the air.

"Okay, that settles it. We'll meet here tomorrow night at the same time. You pick up the story, John," Francis commented.

With a callous smile on his face, John had already plotted how to drop his bombshell on the Germans. They would learn about what their grandfather had done—when he was ready for them to learn. Then they would understand why he was so angry—their grandfather had raped his grandmother and been caught in the act. For that, his grandfather had killed their grandfather. He smiled wickedly at the three guests. "I'm ready."

AUGUST 2

Nineteen

John stationed his sisters at the end of the table, where he had been the night before. He consigned Steven to a spot behind them. This allowed him free reign over the side of the table they had occupied the previous night. Also, with the freed-up space, he could more easily lay out the journals he had brought along.

He paced back and forth in that vacated space, his head bent forward in contemplation, his arms behind his back, his right hand clutching his left. At each turn, his eyes darted in the Germans' direction, studying them. He had yet to sit, having moved his chair into a corner of the kitchen.

Other than the soft padding of John's to-and-fro movements and the equally soft breathing of those around the table, the only sound was the grandfather clock's muffled ticking, which had fallen into step.

"Are you going to start?" Steven asked, glancing at his watch. "It's been more than five minutes."

"In a minute," John answered, not bothering to look up and continuing to pace.

"In a minute?" Steven exclaimed. "You said last night you were ready. What's taking so long?"

Not bothering to look in his brother's direction, John responded, his left hand stroking his chin, "Just framing up my opening statement."

"Opening statement? You make this sound like an inquisition," Steven remarked, guffawing when finished.

"It just might turn out to be one," John remarked, his tone ominous.

Sizing up the seating arrangement, Steven remarked, "Obviously, you're the prosecutor; our sisters and I must be the galley. Are we to assume the Germans are in the dock?" he asked, motioning toward Magdalena and her brothers. "Frandad," he continued, "that must make you the judge. That is, unless, John, you're taking that on as well. If so, just pronounce them guilty and let's be done."

"You're all to judge," John snapped.

Raising his eyebrows, Steven added, "Okay. Since there's apparently nothing specific for Frandad, what's expected of him, John?"

"To listen and confirm what I'm about to tell. Maybe a clarification or two, if necessary," John answered. "That's all I expect from you," John remarked, staring into his father's face.

Francis studied his son, neither word nor gesture passing between.

John turned to his brother and stroked his chin pensively. "As for the word *inquisition*, you have no idea how right you might be—without realizing it, of course. As you refuse to learn anything about the family history, you have no idea what happened. Had you bothered to ever read the journals, you might understand."

"Remember, I neither speak nor read French. That honor was strictly reserved for you," Steven replied smartly.

"French was offered in high school," John commented.

"As if I were going to study *that* language! And for what purpose? Grandma Jeanne was long gone by then. And even if she'd still been around, she'd never have deigned to speak French with *me*—or, for that matter, our sisters. As far as I recall, she refused even to speak it with Dad, though it was their mother tongue. French was just for her favorite," Steven replied.

"What's that have to do with anything?" John asked.

"Only that though I can't read the journals, one doesn't need to be a rocket scientist to figure out what happened."

"What does that mean—figure out what happened?"

"You said if I'd bothered to read the journals, I'd understand what happened. I don't need to read the journals to understand what happened."

"Then tell me," John riposted. "Tell me what you understand to have happened."

"Honestly, John, it's not that mysterious."

"Please, brainiac, humor me. What happened?"

Looking from John to Johann, Steven answered, "Do you really need me to spell it out? Is it really that hard? Plain and simple, it's been going on ever since ... forever. It's how Frandad over there"—Steven pointed to the far end of the table—"ended up here. And the rest of us, for that matter."

"Stop being glib; this is serious. It's a question of how and why, not what!" John rebuked. "If you'd let me get started, you may come to appreciate that."

"I'm not the one holding up the proceedings. We've been waiting for"—Steven looked over his right shoulder at the clock on the stove—"now going on ten minutes. What have we heard so far? Squat."

"Well, I'm ready now. Can I start?" John asked.

Steven slouched down in his chair, folded his arms across his chest, tucked his chin to his chest, and closed his eyes. "I'm all ears. Get going, please."

"Are we ready then?" John asked Magdalena. "Have you translated everything so far?"

Magdalena sat between her brothers but behind. Magdalena leaned forward, her chin almost resting on their shoulders. John had suggested this arrangement so that she could keep up a running translation without having to worry about what each was hearing.

Magdalena nodded.

"Remember, once I get started, I'd prefer not to stop, so unless it's really important—"

"I understand," Magdalena remarked curtly with a nod.

"Okay, I'm starting," John said, causing Steven to clap derisively.

John approached the table and, with great care, took a moment to arrange the journals chronologically in a sweeping arc from left to right. He left enough space at the table's edge to open one journal flat. He left a spot between the 1917 and the 1919 journal. As there was no 1918 journal, the spot was just that—a spot.

With a sweep of his left arm, mirroring the array of journals, John commenced. "These are my grandmother's journals from the war."

Steven piped up. "Don't you mean *our* grandmother? Though you were her favorite, she was still *our* grandmother."

John narrowed one eye, arching the opposite eyebrow. "Correction. These are *our*"—John motioned to his siblings—"grandmother's wartime journals."

Turning to his siblings, he added, "For simplicity, could I say 'my grandmother' but mean 'our grandmother'?"

His sisters nodded; Steven smirked.

"Thank you." He reached for the 1914 journal and randomly opened it. "This is my grandmother's handwriting. Study it carefully, and note the particular style she used to make the first letter of the first word in each individual day's entry."

Holding the journal like a kindergarten teacher might while reading to the class, he turned the journal toward the Germans, giving them an unobstructed view.

He set the 1914 journal back in its place and took up the 1915 one. Again, he randomly opened the journal and showed that particular day's entry. He repeated that exercise with each journal, taking care to replace one before picking up the next.

"I show you these so you will feel comfortable that the entries were made by the same person. Any questions?" he asked, his eyes locked on the Germans.

"Yeah, I've got one," Steven asked.

"I wasn't asking *you*," John replied, keeping his eyes on Magdalena as her lips moved slightly while translating.

"I don't care whether you did. So the handwriting is the same—what does that signify? How do they—or, for that matter, we—know the handwriting is Grandma Jeanne's? Just because you say it is, or believe it is, doesn't make it so," Steven sniped. "What if it turned out it wasn't? Where'd that leave you?"

Francis waded in. "That's a good point and a valid question. I think we need to establish that's her handwriting. Otherwise ..." Francis's comment trailed off.

Irritated by the interruption, John fixed his gaze on his father. "You can confirm it," John remarked, hoping that would satisfy all members of the audience.

"I could, but I think it should take more than just me saying it is. I get the sense tonight could get testy, so ..." Francis scratched his left cheek absentmindedly.

"So? What?" John said. "What are you getting at?"

"I've seen you like this before, and each time, the results are—shall we say—not pretty. Voices rise, accusations fly, and emotions explode. We should be certain *your* grandmother was the one keeping the journals. Your siblings included."

John glared at Francis, his hands akimbo. "What do you propose? Do you have some letter or other document you'd like to put into evidence?"

"See? I told you this was an inquisition," Steven said, wearing a self-satisfied look.

Francis pushed back. "Excuse me. I'll be right back." He disappeared around the corner. They could hear a steady, rhythmic, and ponderous tread on the stairs. Moments later, they heard the creaking of those same treads as he descended. Coming back into the kitchen, he had several items in his left hand.

"First, I can confirm the handwriting in the journals"—he pointed at them—"is my mother's. I'd recognize it no matter where or in what language. Second, here are some letters she wrote, both in French and English. Compare these to the handwriting in the journals. You'll find they match."

To his younger son, Francis commented, "Good question, and thank you for asking it."

"Everyone satisfied now?" John asked, having allowed them several minutes to examine the letters and compare them to the journals. Everyone nodded.

John rearranged the journals in their proper order. "The journals are in chronological order, starting with 1914"—he placed his left hand on the far-left journal—"and going to 1919." With his right hand, he quickly touched that one's cover. "You will no doubt note the spot between 1917 and 1919. That's because there's no journal for 1918."

John glanced at Magdalena. Her eyes were locked on his; her lips moved almost imperceptibly. She nodded when caught up.

Steven asked, "Was there one? And if you say yes, how do you know? And where is it? And what happened to it?"

John placed the fingertips of both hands on the table and leaned slightly forward. The top joint of each finger bowed inward, and the crown of his knuckles blanched. His chin dropped slightly, and he breathed slowly in and out, mumbling to himself. All eyes came to rest on him.

Slowly opening his eyes and turning them on his brother, John remarked, "These are questions that could be asked later, between us, once they've"—he pointed across the table—"gone. Why do you insist on disrupting me?"

A roguish smile formed on Steven's face. "First of all, I'm not disrupting you; I'm just asking obvious questions. If they're obvious to me, then they surely must be to others. I only ask perfectly good and germane questions." He tapped his sisters' shoulders, looking for support. His sisters nodded in agreement, as well as the three guests.

"See. Now aren't you glad I asked? Just think what could've happened had someone asked about it later, after you'd made your way to some far-distant point. *That* would've been disruptive."

"Okay. You've made your point. Regarding the 1918 journal, I don't know if there is or ever was one. These are the journals Donna had. I assume she has no others. Is that a good assumption, Donna?"

"I have no others," she replied. "What I gave you is all I ever had."

"Thank you," John responded in a self-satisfied tone. "Second, in spite of that, I believe there is, or was, one. I have no proof, just a hunch." Holding up the pointer finger of his right hand, he continued. "Note that all the journal books themselves are identical: same color, same leather, same size, and same style. Even the one for 1919 is identical. I've tried to reason my way through this. Did she buy all of these before the war started? Could she have bought a journal each year of the occupation? Did she have all but one for 1919?"

John turned to the Germans. "I don't have any answers to my questions and haven't come to any conclusion other than this: during the war, she kept her journals, making entries most days. Sometimes the entry was short, sometimes lengthy. So back to your question, Steven: Is or was there a journal for 1918? I don't have it, and I don't know, but I believe so. Satisfied?"

"For now," he replied, smiling at Magdalena, who had a look of appreciation on her face.

"On a similar tack," John stated, "and so we can be finished with it now versus later, I need to disclose that the entries for the last seven months or so in the 1917 journal are gone." He held up a finger to thwart any effort to interrupt. "Before anyone says anything, let me show you."

He reached for that journal, pulled it to himself, opened it, and flipped to the last page. Holding the book again like a kindergarten teacher, he moved it slowly from his left to his right. "Note the date of last entry is May 28, 1917." His finger moved to the date as he looked over the top. "Notice how clean the edges are where the following pages had been." He ran a finger down the edge, making sure all were looking where he wanted. "No, Steven, I don't know if there were entries after this date, but I suspect there were. I say that in case you're wondering. Assuming there were, whoever removed the pages was meticulous about the task. Whoever it was left behind no telltale tongues or scraps of paper." Before Steven could say anything, John continued. "A reason I suspect this: all the other journals have unused pages, and those pages haven't been removed. I can tell you no more than that."

John picked up the first journal, riffled its remaining pages, and then laid it open to let everyone see for him- or herself. When he had finished, he closed it and returned it to its place before proceeding.

"I can show you each one if you want," John commented, reaching for the next.

"We'll take your word for it," Steven responded for everybody. "That is, unless someone wants to see each one."

John waited and then continued when no one said anything. "That's the end of the mysteries surrounding the journals, except for what happened to the missing portion of the 1917 journal and the 1918 journal. Oh, and also, who took them and why? Don't ask that yet; it'll become evident several people had reason to." Looking at Magdalena, he said, "Do you need a minute to catch up?"

Magdalena shook her head.

"Are there other questions?" he asked, his tone exaggerated, as he cast a guarded glance in his brother's direction. No one said anything, so John pulled the 1914 journal to the table's edge and flipped it open to the first page.

"The entries chronicle what seems to be a typical life for a married woman of that time. The entries speak of life on the farm. To her journal, Grandma Jeanne confided she didn't love her husband and never had. She wrote of his brutality, particularly when he had been drinking, which, according to her, was most nights. She was made to feel less important and less valuable than the horses, pigs, geese, and oxen. She was often reminded they at least contributed. She knew her life was to be this way; she had witnessed how her mother had been treated. It now was her turn. It was this way until she was with child. At that point, Jean-Pierre let her alone. After his son was stillborn in 1913, it got worse again, until she was again pregnant."

He read the entry for the day Alain, his half uncle, was born, in spring 1914, his voice mirroring the elation of his grandmother's entry.

"That he was healthy made her so happy. Alain was small and helpless, but she felt even smaller and more helpless while holding the baby in her arms."

He described the difficulties of daily life, according to the journal. John remarked, "She had no way of knowing that in just a few months, it'd become more difficult." He went on to say that when war came, Jean-Pierre, along with most men his age, left. Within weeks, that area of France would be invaded. "The timing was particularly bad," John said. "Alain had fallen gravely ill, preventing them from fleeing. His illness haunted her. She feared another child wouldn't make it out of infancy.

"Scathingly, she wrote of local officials who had been among the first to escape. Right beforehand, they'd posted official notices explaining that it was necessary to keep the government intact for when the invaders would be tossed out.

"Following entries told of her son's recovery. But for him getting ill, they may very well have escaped south. But he had, to the point she feared he wouldn't survive. But he did survive, and for that, she was grateful. But her gratitude was short-lived, if the tone of her entries of the time was an indication. She semi resigned herself to the German occupation, hoping it would be brief. She, like everyone, had no inkling it would last four years. By late 1914, the German presence developed a sense of permanence. Camps were set up, patrols were sent out, and curfews established."

John described her concerns about the food supply and how they'd survive. People had begun to hoard and hide what they had—from the Germans and from each other. "Jeanne," he explained, "did the same, stashing provisions in various places, noting these in rough, cryptic pencil sketches in the journals." He turned the journal around to show a hand-drawn map.

"Life took on a predictable pulse. The Germans came around to 'requisition'"—John emphatically made air quotation marks—"more cows and pigs, paying for them with worthless scraps of paper redeemable after the war in Berlin. Beasts of burden went away as well. Their disappearance would cause the women and boys to become the beasts of burden.

"At the end of 1914, despair crept into her entries. There was not enough coal, there was not enough bread or beets or turnips, and there was not enough cloth. There were only a few things that there was not not enough of. There was not not enough hay, since the forage-eating animals had been taken, and there were not not enough visits from the village priest."

He leaned in toward the Germans. "She complained about the priest. She didn't like him, for two reasons. First, he was a priest and lorded that over people. Grandma Jeanne wasn't a believer; she barely suffered those who were. She was convinced that the priest became one as an easy way out. The second is more interesting." Glancing at his father, John stated, "You know what it is."

"Yeah, the priest was her husband's younger brother."

"That's right," John said. "Her other reason to not like him. Out of the blue, he'd knock at the door, usually around suppertime, and ask how she and his nephew were getting along. He had nothing to offer other than his concern, real or not. As there was so little for the two of them, she didn't feel bad about not inviting him in. She hoped he'd finally get that he wasn't wanted or welcomed. Either he didn't get it or didn't want to get it; he continued to show up. Plus, she was certain he was keeping an eye on her. If he was going to keep an eye on her, she'd keep one on him.

"He'd ask each time he showed up—two or three times a week—when she planned on having his nephew baptized, insisting she must since God had, as part of his plan, spared the child."

From the journal, John read the following: "What kind of plan would that be? To spare one who has no concept of God? Did his plan call for the Germans to kill my father, a true believer, for protecting what little he owned?

"'Nothing belongs to us; it belongs to God,' the priest replied righteously, pointing to the heavens. 'My child, as to his plan, it will be revealed in due course. In the meantime, it is not our place to question; we must have faith. God spared Alain for a reason. Your son is marked with sin. Baptism will wipe that out,' the priest said, 'and he will become part of the fellowship of Christians.'

"'If soldiers wiping each other out in God's name is part of the fellowship of Christians, I'm not interested,' she replied.

"In spades," John said, "she had faith the priest wasn't to be trusted.

"Later, she recorded another conversation with the priest. 'Occasionally, I'm allowed to pass through the lines. If you'd have your son baptized, I'd have a reason to search out my brother, your faithful and loving husband, and let him know. I could carry a message to him and bring one back from the other side.'

"'First of all, no one but you would use those words to describe my husband, and secondly, how do I know he's not already there?' she cynically responded and then shut the door in his face.

"On occasion, she'd see her brother-in-law along a ridgeline, slipping in and out of the woods or a house or a building in the village. Other times, out retrieving something from a cache, she'd see him snooping around. She'd even caught him rummaging in her grange.

"That year's last entry mentioned that the invaders had not left and the local officials had not returned."

He closed the journal and picked up the next. John recounted that the tone of the 1915 entries mirrored those at the end of 1914. Life continued to get more difficult.

"Spring 1915, before the planting, the Germans rounded up the older boys, the ones who were to work the fields, to prevent them from slipping through the lines to join the fight. They were marched to the rear."

He explained that roundups had occurred in practically every village in the occupied zone. Many of the boys, too young to fight but not too young to die, would not return. John flipped several pages.

"Her suspicions about the war grew darker with the comings and goings of German units. My grandmother could predict when a major battle was about to happen by the tempo of supply and troop movements.

"By mid-1915, her entries focused more and more on growing shortages of everything except the dead and wounded; there was nothing scarce about those. She worried the French might run out of men before the Germans. She understood what that'd mean—the same thing had happened to Alsace and Lorraine after the last war with Germany."

Steven cleared his throat, drawing attention.

"What do you want now?" John asked, not masking his annoyance.

"It might help if everyone knew what happened after the last war between the two countries. That's all," he replied.

"Why don't you tell them, if you think it'll add to the story? I'll sit and listen for a change." As if beseeching him, John extended his right arm in his brother's direction.

"So you know from late-1870 into mid-1871, France and Prussia went to war. France lost. Prussia occupied large parts of northern France and imposed a huge war-reparations bill as part of the peace treaty signed at Versailles. The pact called for the French to cede Alsace and Lorraine, provinces bordering Germany. From that date, France looked for a reason to get the lost provinces back. It became a national obsession and was often referred to as *La Revanche*. That's French for 'revenge.'" Steven fell silent.

John asked, "Can I continue?"

"Sure, unless there are questions."

"There appear to be none." John picked up the 1915 journal. "Grandma Jeanne was worried that the French were going to run out of men. The increasing toll of war losses she'd learned from the priest. Not allowed to bring back newspapers, he could at least report on what he'd read and heard on the other side. The French high command was convinced that the Huns were teetering on the verge. They were starving, short on ammunition, and suffering a shortage of men. She refused to believe this. From what she could tell, the Germans seemed as strong as at the start of the war.

"The priest spoke of rumors about the latest plans for another offensive. The attack, delivered with the élan only the French possessed, would breach the Huns' lines and allow the cavalry to flow through as a flood.

"Similar optimistic assessments had already been made, yet nothing changed except the length of the list of the honored dead," John said. "Her war, fought daily on and around her small farm, was never-ending and had no end in sight. She would need to protect what little she had from the preying and praying."

John told of how the illness du jour swept through the village, further thinning its population. The old and young were the first but not the only to succumb. "Grandma would go to the garrison captain and badger him for food or a bit of medicine for her, her son, and her neighbors," he explained. "If not successful, she'd return. If not successful that time, she'd go back. Eventually, the captain would relent. At his own pace, each captain learned to be done with her quickly—to quickly give her a little less than what she first asked for. In turn, she quickly learned to ask for a bit more."

John reported on two other trips the priest made across the lines, returning both times with news of the war's progress. "As nothing seemed to change in Beaulieu-en-prés, the progress must've been elsewhere, she noted. Both times," John said, "the priest regretted he had no news of Jean-Pierre. That news Jeanne received without regret.

"By mid-October, the harvest was in. Jeanne was pleased with the results, considering there was no fertilizer. What she got would have to be enough to get through next spring, when surely the war would be over and life would return to normal."

John set the 1915 journal down in its place and picked up the next. Opening it as if under a spell, he continued, not worrying whether anyone needed a break.

"The winter of 1916 was colder than normal. Grandma had to break apart furniture to keep warm, leaving only the basics. Threadbare blankets hung from all windows to keep the cold at bay and tame the wind as it blew through. The better blankets hung from her and her son's shoulders for the same purpose.

"Alain was growing in spite of the shortages. He was walking by summer 1915 and already talking. His speech was good and his curiosity without bounds, something that wouldn't have troubled her in another time and place. Here, though ..."

John glanced at Magdalena. Her eyes were riveted on his, her lips moving slightly as she translated. She nodded when she had caught up.

"They were faring relatively well—better than many others. Those who'd barely survived the last year weren't likely to survive this one. The war's casualties would continue to climb.

"Hoping to get a jump on planting before the roundup, the field teams had been reworked. When the Germans realized what was going on, they marched the year's harvest off. The remaining boys, too small, starving, and sickly, were forced to take to the plow."

John flipped many pages. "Ah, yes. Toward the end of April, Jeanne had been working outside on the first warm spring day. That night, she wrote of how, for the first time in a long time, she'd noticed the leafing of the trees, the first green sprouts as they poked through the soil, and heard the birds chirping. After a difficult and dismal winter, the sights and sounds of springtime were welcome. That mood was spoiled later that same day, when the priest came by, the first time in several weeks. She wrote down the news he brought—Verdun."

He turned his attention to Monique. "You remember Magdalena already mentioned Verdun. Her grandfather fought there, and I talked about it at that time, so I won't repeat myself, unless there's a question."

John cast a sideways glance at Steven.

"No need here," Steven responded, holding up his watch and tapping its face. "Move on. This is already taking too long."

"I wonder why," John said.

Everyone turned to Steven. He shrugged as if to say, *I've only tried to help.*

John continued, "The priest had just returned from one of his across-the-lines forays. The Germans had attacked in strength along a wide front. Jean-Pierre, our grandmother's first husband, was in the midst of the fighting. The priest was glad to report that he had no news of Jean-Pierre's death."

Glancing up from the journal, John added, "The journal is silent as to her reaction."

John leafed to about the midpoint of the 1916 journal. "It's now August 1916," John stated. "The priest has again been out to visit. His news this time was of a large-scale, joint British and French attack along the Somme River. High hopes had been pinned on this attack. The British high command was sure this would be the defining campaign of the war. The priest had learned—how he learned, she'd never find out—that Jean-Pierre's unit had been transferred from Verdun to the Somme. His unit was part of the attack. This battle, like many before, ended the same way: another failure and another slaughter. Jean-Pierre somehow survived this one as well."

John flipped back to mid-October. "It's just after the harvest. It was smaller than hoped. The weather had been too wet in the spring and too hot and dry in the summer."

He closed the journal and set it down in front of himself.

Patting the front cover, he intoned, "There wouldn't be enough to get them all through. Slow death by starvation was now staring her, her son, and the rest of the villagers in the face. For two years, she'd been fighting to stay alive, hoping something would happen. Up till then, she'd remained sure they'd make it. Now she wasn't. Many people, including her and her son, might not be around when spring arrived. That'd mean the next year's planting team would be smaller, which would lead to another smaller harvest, no matter how good the weather. The result of that would be yet further thinning of the population. They were caught in a vortex, a result of the war. People eyed one another, gauging their prospects of survival. If the look of death had descended on someone—and everyone learned what that looked like—the others would circle. At the moment, they'd swoop down and scavenge anything remotely useful. Who knew what would be just enough?

"At some point, she'd figured out that if the war lasted much longer, there may very well be no one left. Time was running out."

The grandfather clock in the hallway mournfully gonged out nine times. "So ended 1916." John pushed the journal away from him and grabbed the 1917 one.

Without opening it but, rather, cradling it in the crook of his left elbow, John explained, "A quick read showed the same issues as prior years. But for the first time, names of those who succumbed to illness, hunger, or despair during the winter of 1917 were written down. She wondered how she and her son had made it this far and, at the same time, marveled they had. In case her time came too soon, she, like everyone, had a plan for her son's care.

"She hardly remembered life before the war. She hoped it'd end, hardly caring anymore if France won. In the 1915 journal, she was fearful of what peace would look like if the Germans won—no longer. Suffering from the war's effects, she sensed all sides were going to lose, even the one that'd parade triumphantly through its enemy's capital."

He set the journal down and rested the fingertips of his right hand on the journal cover. "She had little remaining allegiance to

France. The town officials had fled early on, and the army hadn't forced the Huns out. Her son and the farm were the only things that mattered." John opened the journal and read, "So what if I have to learn German if it means living? As surely as the sun will rise tomorrow, there'll be another war. The loser will want to even the score."

John closed the journal and continued. "That spring, the Germans announced there'd be no roundup. She could see why. There were hardly any boys left, and those who were weren't worth the trouble."

He read from the journal: "I have tried to keep everyone together. But some families have opted to go it alone. I explained that only by staying together could more be done. I asked what would happen if their harvests failed and then, before letting them answer, explained that those of us who worked together wouldn't be in a position to give anything to those who didn't."

He closed the journal, a finger marking his place. "It'd gotten to that point. Not only had the war pitted French against Germans; it now pitted French against French."

Steven interjected. "Just so everyone knows, it wasn't just in France. Russia was truly on the verge of collapse. There were bread riots in St. Petersburg and Moscow. In Germany, the winter of 1917–1918 became known as the turnip winter. Turnips were about all that was left. Much of everything in Germany was ersatz."

"Ersatz?" Monique asked immediately. "What's that mean?"

"That's a nice term for fake," Steven responded. "In histories of the period, the authors speak of ersatz coffee, ersatz bread, ersatz this, and ersatz that."

"Okay, but how do you fake bread?" Monique inquired. "Bread is bread after all."

Steven explained, "In Germany and Russia, what was being sold may have looked like bread but was, in fact, more sawdust or plaster. And even then, the bread lines stretched for blocks. People waited in these for hours. Many times, they'd be turned away because that day's ration was gone just as they got to the front."

Monique lowered her eyes, her shoulders softly shaking.

"Anything else you want to say, Steven?" John asked. Then, looking about, he inquired, "Any other comments or questions?"

When no one answered, he reopened the journal and read: "I asked several families how they could risk going it alone when their family was at stake. The answer made me shudder. To the person, the answer was the same: it no longer mattered. As all were going to die anyway, they'd prefer to take their chances as a family."

John let out a sigh. "The village fabric was unraveling. How long before family members turned on one another to survive? What would happen when the war ended? No matter who won, some would be seen as agitators; others would be seen as collaborators. Would the fighting continue long after the shooting had stopped?

"In late April, the priest dropped by. He had news. America had declared war on Germany. His other news was that the latest French offensive had been badly beaten back, again with huge losses."

John leaned in, resting on one hand. "Jean-Pierre's unit had spearheaded the attack; Jean-Pierre had not returned. It wasn't known whether he'd been captured or killed. Unfazed, the priest was going back across to try to find him.

"At this point in her journal, gaps began to appear. Earlier, it was unusual for more than a couple days to pass between entries; from mid-April until late May, only three were made."

Keeping a finger in its spot, John explained, "I've thought about this. Was it possible, with the news of her husband's disappearance, that she was concerned, though she claimed she didn't love him and never had? It's one thing to say you don't until that person is thought to be gone for good. Or could it be she was running out of energy and was conserving what little she had? Or maybe she or Alain had fallen ill, which kept her from writing. Or maybe she had grown tired of writing essentially the same things and decided to record only significant events. Or could it be she just didn't care anymore? Whatever the reason, there's this one last entry in late May." He held open the journal to the page. "It's this last entry *you'll* find interesting," he commented, looking directly at Magdalena, Wilhelm, and Johann.

John read the entry.

> Good news today. Captain Loeb, the latest garrison captain, is gone. He'd been difficult to deal with, not caring whether we lived or maybe just preferring we didn't. The new captain, his replacement, brought the news. I was coming out from the grange, having finished what I'd been doing, and found him at the door to the house. From where I stood, I asked him what he wanted. I must have startled him, because he jumped. He took two or three steps toward me and clicked the heels of his boots together. He introduced himself as the new garrison captain replacing Captain Loeb. I was overjoyed by that. I asked if he had come here only to deliver that news. He smiled. "I'm here because Captain Loeb advised me to be mindful of Madame DuFour and to learn quickly how to deal with her. Intrigued, I decided to come to you on my terms rather than wait for you to come on yours."
>
> I thanked him for the courtesy but then asked if it was a courtesy, since his predecessors had never exhibited any.
>
> "Self-preservation may be a better description," he replied. I wanted to ask if he meant his or mine but was afraid to, so it went unsaid. "Times are very difficult and are soon to get more difficult," he remarked, and then he added, "I hope I can find a way to work with you, at least better than Captain Loeb."

"Why do you say that?" I answered, surprised by his comment.

"Because your face broke into a smile when I said Captain Loeb had been transferred," he answered, and then he added, "You should be careful; your emotions may give you away."

"That's excellent advice," I replied.

A moment later, he added, "At least that's my hope and intent. We are in this together, whether we like it or not, and no one knows how much more time we have left on this good earth."

He had a nice face, soft, but sad eyes and a kind mouth. He had less of a rough edge to him than Captain Loeb, but there was an edge nonetheless. He wanted me to know who was in charge and that the future wouldn't be too easy. Despite that, I felt I was being spoken to as if I were a human, and that hadn't happened in so long a time. He pulled a watch from his pocket. Clicking his heels again, he thanked me for my time and turned to leave. I called out, "Excuse me. You paid me a courtesy; please allow me to repay it. How am I to properly address you?"

He turned back toward me, the same smile on his face. "Madame, perhaps your courtesy, like mine, is driven by self-preservation. My name is Franz Neuberger. Captain Neuberger."

John closed the journal, set it back in its place, and went in search of his chair.

"That brings us to the end of May 1917," Francis said after John had sat down. "We have two of the three players present; my mother's there, as is Franzis Neuberger. Henry Alston is the only one missing. So before we can go any further, I need to get my dad to France."

"Dad, before you do that," Steven interrupted, "you're still referring to Pappi Henry as your dad. Considering what Magdalena is claiming, shouldn't you just call him Henry?"

"You just called him Pappi Henry. I'm not trying to be flippant, but why is that?" Francis asked. He held a hand up, palm outward. "Let me say, first, Henry Alston was not my father. I learned that from my mother just before she died. Second, Henry Alston was my dad. Though not my biological father, he was the only one who was a dad. Unselfishly, he took on the role; for that, he'll always be my dad. Did you call him Pappi Henry for the same reason?"

Steven answered with a nod.

"Now, let me get him where he needs to be," Francis said. "It starts here, in Mapleton Valley, in April 1917, a world away from my mother's farm but not far in time from her last entry."

A larger-than-normal crowd had gathered where Grand Avenue, Carnoustie Boulevard, and Eleventh Street intersected. In front of the Flatiron Building, which dominated the intersection, and where the Mapleton Valley World Journal had its offices, a newsboy stood, waving a fistful of newspapers above his head. "Read all about it; US to war! Read all about it! United States declares war on Germany! President Wilson says US must make world safe for democracy!"

From across the street, Henry Alston watched as the crowd swarmed, arms outstretched in an effort to grab a paper. Voices raised, vying to get the newsboy's attention. "Here! Here! Over here! I want one!"

Henry had been following the buildup to war. Germany had resumed unrestricted submarine warfare and sunk several

American ships without warning. Hundreds of American citizens had gone with them to the bottom. Americans wanted revenge. President Wilson had gone in front of Congress and demanded a declaration of war. When an overwhelming margin voted in favor, Henry would get his chance to become a war hero—provided he could get into the military.

The issue, theoretically, was his age; at nineteen, he was too young to enlist without his parents' consent. Yet being big for his age, he fully expected to talk his way in without parental permission. But if he couldn't, he'd leave the recruiting station with the form and return the next day with it signed, even though both parents were dead. A friend would sign for his dad, and his twenty-one-year-old cousin, who shared his mother's name, would sign on her behalf.

Watching the crowd surrounding the newsboy, Henry was as good as a marine, just as he had daydreamed about. He could envision the Huns, seeing himself and his fellow marines charging across no-man's-land, faces and bayonets fixed on the coming fight, throwing their rifles down and their arms up. By Christmas, the war would be over, thanks to him, the marines, and America—in that order. He'd return home, medals hanging heavily on his uniform, clinking together as he strode through the streets. He'd wear his marine cap to one side at a jaunty angle; women would swoon.

Henry pulled out his loose change. Sifting it like a prospector, he saw the three coins he needed. He strode like a marine across the street, dodging the buggies, trams, and cars. He hollered louder than anyone else to the newsboy, motioning for a paper.

Exchanging the coins for the paper, he called out, "Is there a list of recruiting stations?"

"On the bottom of page three; better hurry, or there may not be a spot for you," the newsboy answered, turning away and continuing to shout. "Extra! Extra! The US goes to war!"

Henry opened the newspaper and scanned the list. Two recruiting stations were within blocks of where he stood. He folded the paper and slid it under his left arm; he took off in the direction of the nearer one.

A line of men a block long wrapped itself almost around the corner of the building. A tall, square-jawed sergeant was walking the line, eyeing the hopefuls. Occasionally, he'd stop and say something. A man, either too young or too old looking, would slip out of line, look over his shoulder, and walk away. Once in a while, a man would argue back, as if he thought that might make a difference. The sergeant moved on, periodically looking back over a shoulder.

Under his breath, with as much confidence as he could muster, Henry practiced replying to the one and only anticipated question: "I'm twenty-one years old, sir." He heavily stressed the last word.

The line inched slowly forward. The sergeant, eyeing some in line and ignoring others, moved closer. Henry pulled the bill of his soft cap down lower on his forehead, kept his gaze forward, and determinedly set his jaw.

The sergeant, who was shorter than Henry, stopped and studied him. With a steely gaze, Henry stared back and then returned his gaze forward. The sergeant, leaning in and almost touching Henry's right ear, said, "You sure are a big fella. We sure could use you over there. Heck, if I was the Boches and saw you coming at me, I'd turn and run, not daring to stop. You just might be the secret weapon we need." He continued, loud enough for those nearby to hear, "Gents, here's the end of the war. This man is going to come back a hero." Turning back to Henry, the soldier added, "There's no reason for me to ask you how old you are, is there, son?"

Henry replied, "No, sir. I'll tell you anyway, sir. I'm twenty-one years old, sir." As practiced, Henry repeatedly stressed the last word of each sentence.

"I figured as much." The sergeant walked away.

Henry smiled to himself as the sergeant distanced himself. The line shuffled forward. Suddenly and unexpectedly, Henry heard the sergeant ask, "What year were you born, son?"

"In 1898, sir," Henry replied too quickly.

Henry immediately realized his mistake. "I meant 1896, sir! My brother was born in 1898, sir," he said, stressing the last words.

"Go home, sonny," the sergeant ordered, grabbing Henry at the elbow and gently pulling him out of line. "I don't care how big you are; this is a man's war."

Those around him laughed as he slunk away. Henry disappeared around the building corner.

Henry didn't go home; he opened the newspaper and found the address for the next-closest recruiting station. He walked the long route there, repeating to himself, "I was born in 1896, 1896, 1896."

The line at the second station was just as long as the first. Here too a sergeant, one looking less soldierly, walked the line. Henry found his place and pulled his cap down over his eyes, muttering to himself his new birth year.

This particular sergeant was talking to practically every man in line. Several walked away after he'd spoken to them. A few wore glasses; others looked too young. Henry was getting edgy as the sergeant approached. *Settle down,* Henry repeated to himself, breathing deeply and exhaling slowly.

The sergeant was now only two men away. Henry kept his eyes locked on the sergeant's face, afraid to avert his gaze. Unexpectedly, the sergeant skipped the man in front of Henry, Henry, and several men behind him.

Once inside, a recruiter finally asked Henry, "Are you twenty-one years of age?"

"Yes, sir," he answered. "Do you want to know what year I was born in?'

"Hell no. I don't give a damn. Are you here to enlist?" the man asked.

"Yes, sir. I want to be a marine."

Ignoring that statement, the recruiter asked, "Are you of German descent?"

"No, sir, I'm not of German descent. I'm of English descent, sir."

"Are you willing to kill Germans?"

"Yes, sir."

"You sure? People say that until—"

"Until what, sir?"

"Until it comes time to pull the trigger, stick a bayonet in, or draw the knife. If you hesitate, you die. You understand?"

"Yes, sir. I understand, sir." Henry stood ramrod straight. "I am ready to go fight for the United States of America, sir."

"Good!" The soldier pointed at a line and instructed Henry, "Sign here."

"Will I be a marine, sir?"

"Just sign," the soldier instructed, pointing to a line on the form. "You won't regret it."

Henry signed his name, stood, and snapped an awkward salute.

"Congratulations, son; you're a proud member of the United States Army. Now move out, soldier."

"B-B-But I want to be a marine," Henry stammered.

"Don't make a fuss, soldier; the army will give you just as good a chance to die for your country."

"That's how my dad got in," Francis explained. "He went through basic training in central Kansas. He shipped out in late spring 1918. He went into the trenches, where he received instruction on how to maintain them; what to expect from the enemy; how to keep an eye peeled for signs of danger, raids, or attacks; and, most importantly, how to improve his chances of staying alive. In late September, he and his unit moved into a sector near St. Mihiel. A major American attack was planned in that area, and his unit would be in the thick of it. After several weeks of heavy fighting, Henry found himself not far from Beaulieu-en-prés. The German lines had stiffened, and headquarters wanted a breakthrough—and fast. The Americans had to show that they could fight and die like the rest of them. A reconnaissance in depth was ordered to find a way through and to get the attack back on track. Henry's unit was picked. Late on the night of November 1, his unit slipped into no-man's-land." Francis stopped and asked, surveying the table, "Any questions?"

No one said anything.

"In that case, this might be a good spot to call it quits for the night. We can take up again tomorrow, if that works for everyone."

All nodded.

Turning to John, he asked, "You didn't happen to bring along the newspaper articles, did you?"

Before John could say no, Magdalena asked, surprised by the question, "Newspaper articles? When were those written?"

"Yes, newspaper articles," Francis replied. "They were written shortly after the armistice by a local reporter who covered the war. There are four. They appeared serially, if you understand that word."

"If you mean that one followed another, then I understand," Magdalena replied.

"That's what it means," Francis confirmed.

Looking first to Wilhelm and then to Johann, Magdalena said something. Each shrugged. Magdalena asked, "What are the articles about?"

"About what happened to my dad," Francis answered.

"Could we read them?" Magdalena asked.

"Sure," John answered. "I'll bring them tomorrow." He added, a cutting smile on his face, "But I'm not sure you'll want to."

"Und vy not?" Johann asked, not waiting for a translation.

"Because you'll learn how your grandfather died at the hands of mine."

AUGUST 3

Twenty

Four plastic baggies sat on the table; John's hands were crossed, resting protectively on top. The fingers of the underneath hand were splayed wide, obscuring all but splotches of the articles within. Magdalena and her brothers locked their eyes on them.

"Dad, I don't care what you think; I think it should be their turn next," John commented, clearing his throat and keeping his eyes on his father. Both had reclaimed their original spots at the table. While pointing an accusing finger to his right, he added, "We've got Pappi Henry almost to the farm. Grandma's already there. We need for them to get their grandfather there. They need to fill in the gap between his first encounter with Grandma and the fateful day."

"That's not a bad suggestion, actually," Francis added, "and makes sense. Do you mind?" he asked Magdalena.

She turned toward Francis and smiled thinly at him. She shook her head. "I am afraid that there are blanks in what we know. I will tell you what we do know, though it is not much."

Her brothers leaned in and spent a moment speaking with her before she would begin. "Our grandfather was scheduled to have gone on leave in early May 1918. But with the setbacks at the front und the slow retreat of German troops, all leaves had been cancelled. Every man was needed. In a letter, he tried to explain; it was his duty to stay und do what he could. He knew that Grandma Hilda would understand."

"How did that go over?" Steven asked.

Magdalena mulled over the question, wanting not to rush an answer. She waved off Wilhelm, who had again leaned in. She arched an eyebrow at him and patted his knee, smiling at him.

"My grandmother was not pleased und was afraid for what might happen with the fighting coming closer. He was behind the lines, but he had written that at night, he could see on the horizon the flashes from the artillery. It made him think of distant lightning. The muffled roar of the cannons made him think of thunder. She was fearful that he would have to fight once again."

She stopped, turned, and spoke with her brothers.

"Johann," she said when they had finished talking among themselves, "used the word *premonition.* Perhaps our grandmother believed that her husband would not make it home alive. I am not sure that I share that opinion. But to be fair, I am not sure that he is not correct.

"She sent letters most days; he would send letters back when he could, even as the battles drew nearer. The tone of their letters became more nostalgic. Maybe *premonition* is a good word, because in their letters, it was as if they had set out to chronicle their life together, almost a recollection."

"A recollection?" Donna asked. "A recollection of what?"

"A recollection of the life that they had known und shared. They wrote about their moments together," she explained. "Then something very strange happened; in a letter sent in late July 1918, for the first time, our grandfather mentioned your grandmother by name."

"Why did he do that?" Monique asked.

Magdalena let out a slight laugh and then smiled. "He wrote of how she was troublesome und that as the difficulties caused by the war mounted, so did her demands. He could not understand how she did not see that the suffering of the German soldiers was equal to hers. Everything was scarce. As John mentioned earlier, the harvest had been much smaller. Everybody was hungry, slowly starving. Our grandfather knew that an army could not fight on an empty stomach—more precisely, would not. He recounted how he had told her that he had little food, supplies, or medicine to spare.

"In early November, he posted his last letter. It was short und appeared to be hastily written; there were many erasures. The war's close was close at hand. Soldiers were surrendering without a fight. Unsure of what might happen, he asked her to forgive him if something did."

Magdalena sighed heavily. "The war ended within days, und the soldiers would return home. But not our grandfather," she remarked. "After living through much, he fell in sight of the end. That is all I can add to my story." Turning to John, she added, "Now it is your turn to finish."

"Before I do, should we rearrange ourselves like we were at the start of last night?" John asked, pushing his chair back and starting to get up. "That way, you could translate what I have to say without worrying if Johann and Wilhelm are following. Shall we move?"

"Sit down," Steven said. "I'm not going through that charade again. I'm sure Magdalena can keep both in the know. Finish up."

Looking down the length of the table, John saw his father nod in agreement, a smile on his face. A glance at his sisters confirmed that no one was interested in changing places.

He pulled his chair back up to the table and refolded his hands on the baggies. Muttering, "Okay, okay, okay," John slid his hands off, reached for the top bag, opened it, and pulled out its content. Laying the paper flat, he, with both hands, pressed out the creases.

"This is the first. It was written a week after the armistice. It's short, more a summary. At the end, the reporter wrote of Henry returning to the American lines like a prodigal son; the big news was the twenty German soldiers he had captured. The story of a local boy becoming a war hero was born at this moment."

John pushed the article along with the plastic baggie across the table toward Magdalena. "Fold it back up the way it was and put it back when you're done. And be careful with it, if you would. It's the only one."

Magdalena nodded. She scanned the article and then spoke with her brothers. Finished, she then carefully refolded it, placed it gently back in its bag, resealed the bag, and slid it back to John.

Setting aside that one, John opened the second baggie and went through the same routine. "This is the first detailed article of what happened the night of November 1, when my grandfather went on patrol. This article was written a week following the first. We're now two weeks beyond the end of the fighting. In this article, Henry Alston recounts, from his perspective, what happened that night in no-man's-land."

Pushing the article and its baggie to his right, he sat back.

Magdalena read it, both brothers leaning in as she translated. At times, a brother interrupted her. Patiently, she answered before picking up where she had left off. At the end, she refolded the article and slipped it back into its baggie, pressed the seal, and pushed it back to John.

"Any questions so far?" John asked.

"Just one," she replied. "What do these two articles have to do with what we have been discussing?"

"Ahh!" John answered energetically. "They're setting the stage for what's to happen and where." John opened the second installment of the three-part series. "Here's where it gets interesting. I'm not going to summarize this one for you; I prefer that you read it on your own. Once done, I'll need to bring my siblings up to speed."

"Up to speed?" Magdalena asked, reaching for the offering.

"Sorry. I mean I need to tell them what has happened. I don't think they've read the articles, or if they have, it's been so long they've probably forgotten."

"Pass the first two articles to Monique, and let her start while our guests read that one," Steven commanded. "Monique can pass the first one on after she's read it and go to the second, and then so forth. That way, we'll all be in the know." Addressing Magdalena, Steven added, "Don't bother giving the article back to John; pass it to Monique."

Magdalena nodded while Steven, at the far end of the siblings and next to his father, motioned with his right hand for John to start the procession of articles.

John slipped the first two baggies to Monique without saying a thing. He stared at her as if saying, *Be careful.*

Monique finished the first article and then pushed it along to Donna. She did the same for the second. As Donna finished, she offered it to Steven, who, sitting on her left, passed them on to his father without bothering with them. Francis also set them aside unread.

Magdalena finished, laid the article down on the table, and sat motionlessly. Her brothers' reactions mirrored hers. Coming out of her daze, she pushed the article in Monique's direction.

"Did you notice anything?" John asked Magdalena, not waiting for his siblings to get through it.

"The date of this article was more than two weeks later than the first," Magdalena responded. "That seems like a long time. Do you know why there was a gap?"

John scrunched up his face. "Before I give you my thoughts, was there anything at the end that could shed some light on it?"

"Should I wait?" Magdalena answered with a question. "Your brother and sisters have not had a chance to finish."

The table fell quiet, everyone waiting for the last person to finish.

Donna cleared her throat and halfheartedly edged the article toward Steven. As with the first two, he slid it unread to his father, who added it to the pile to his left.

John glanced around, satisfied that all had had a chance to read the article. "Anyone who wanted to read this has done so. Would you like now to venture a guess?"

The three Germans huddled before Magdalena answered. "'For the next five days und nights, she shared everything.' That is an interesting statement. It could have so many meanings. Johann believes that it means only that he was given what was needed to keep him hidden und alive. Wilhelm, the cynic, believes that the sharing went beyond basic needs. If Johann is correct, I have only one explanation." She halted for a moment. "However, if the cynic"—she motioned toward Wilhelm with a thumb—"is correct, then I have two."

"And what would that explanation be, if Johann is correct?" Monique asked.

"There was an epidemic of the flu at that time. My explanation would have to be that either Henry became ill, or the reporter did. May I ask a question?" she stated, looking at John.

He nodded.

"Did the same reporter write the last article?" she asked, motioning with her eyes to the only baggie left under John's control.

He nodded.

"Then, in that case, that would be my explanation. Illness had to be the reason for the gap," she remarked assuredly.

Tentatively, Monique asked, "And if Wilhelm?"

Magdalena coughed a few times. "It could be as simple as illness." She cleared her throat twice. "But it may be more complicated."

No one spoke; they all waited for Magdalena to complete her thought.

"Yes, it could be more complicated. If Wilhelm is correct that your grandmother shared more than basic needs," Magdalena reasoned, "it could be that your grandmother realized that she was with child." She continued, "She had to have found a way to get word to your grandfather Henry of her condition. I can imagine that he made his way back to her. That would be the other explanation." Magdalena massaged her brow with her right hand.

"That's a wrinkle you hadn't considered, huh?" John asked, and then he simplified. "You hadn't thought of that."

"I had not considered that possibility. That is true," Magdalena said slowly, a look of puzzlement on her face. Softly, almost as if to herself, she repeated, "I had not considered that possibility."

"Now read the last installment." John pulled open the last baggie, withdrew the article, flattened it with the palms of both hands, and practically thrust it into her hands.

Magdalena looked at John. "Will this provide an answer?"

John replied, "You're about to find out what happened to your grandfather. When you're done, pass it on. They have yet to read it."

He pushed back from the table, a self-satisfied look on his face, and crossed his arms.

When Magdalena finished, she set the article down and looked to Johann and then to Wilhelm. She pushed the article to Monique, who, when finished, passed it on, as instructed. Donna finished up a minute later and slid it on to Steven, who passed it on without reading it.

"Everyone's had a chance to read the newspaper articles," John commented. "Do you have anything you'd like to say?"

"Your grandfather showed great courage to have done what he did. What that German soldier did was not proper," Magdalena commented, having discussed the story with her brothers while the others read. "That man deserved what happened to him. When did this occur? What date?"

"Let me see the article, Steven," John said, motioning with the fingers of his right hand.

Scanning it, he said, "Let's see—the armistice took effect the morning of November 11. Henry said that the last day he was behind enemy lines was when he started corralling his prisoners, so that would've been the eleventh. I'd say it happened on November 10, 1918."

"We came to that same conclusion," Magdalena said, wagging a finger between herself and her brothers. "We are relieved to hear you say that date," she added, smiling.

"Relieved? You've just read of how your grandfather died, confirming your suspicions it was at my grandmother's farm. So why in the world," John asked, "would you be relieved and smiling?"

"We are relieved because that was not our grandfather," Magdalena replied, a tone of confidence in her voice.

"Yes, it was," John countered. "It had to have been."

Magdalena, not backing down, replied assuredly, "I have no idea who that man was, but that man could not have been our grandfather."

"You just read the article," John stated. "It's just as you had suspected; your grandfather was killed at the end of the war *and* at my grandmother's farm. How can you say it's not him?"

Francis cleared his throat.

All eyes turned in his direction.

"John, you asked how they could say that man wasn't their grandfather. The answer is simple: Henry killed that soldier a day before their grandfather died. Franzis wasn't even there when that happened."

Openmouthed, John, whose face had gone a speckled scarlet and white, stared down the length of the table. His hands had a slight tremor; his breathing had become shallow and rapid. Several times, as he leaned toward his father, it appeared that he was on the cusp of saying something; each time, he retreated without a word. His eyes danced from person to person, starting with Steven and then bouncing back and forth across the table and down each side, landing ultimately on Johann's face, where they came to rest.

Finally, he stammered, his voice quivering, "But-but-but ..."

He could not—or chose not to—finish his thoughts, but then he murmured, to no one in particular, "I can't believe that. How's that possible? It had to have been their grandfather; he was in the act of ... That resulted in ... And from that ... There is no other way. Obviously, he hadn't intervened in time to ..."

All eyes remained fixed on John as his rambling came to an end.

"Who hadn't?" Francis asked.

"Pappi Henry! Who else?" John answered brusquely.

"In time for what?" Francis asked, looking straight at his oldest.

John swallowed hard. "To stop him!" John remarked confrontationally. "I'm telling you—you have to be wrong. There can be no mistake about what happened and when. It's right there in the newspaper." John pointed to the far end of the table.

"I'm not wrong, John. And there's no mistake," Francis commented assuredly.

"There's no other way other than ..." John didn't finish his statement.

"Unless," Francis said.

All eyes turned toward Francis.

"Unless what?" John asked cautiously.

All the eyes turned to John.

"Unless it didn't happen as you suppose."

All eyes shot back in the opposite direction.

"That's no answer," John replied.

The eyes turned on John at his reply, but then, in anticipation of a return volley, they quickly shot back again.

"You're right; it's no answer, but it's *the* answer. Think about it," his dad commented. "While you're doing that, I need to retrieve something from upstairs."

Francis pushed back with both hands and then pushed himself up from his chair. Using both hands, he steadied himself before walking from the kitchen. They could hear him climbing the stairs, and moments later, he returned with a folder and a leather-bound book in one hand. He sat back down and set the items in front of himself. Protectively, he placed both his hands on top, the fingers of the underneath hand splayed wide, partially covering the items.

"Have you come to a different conclusion?" Francis asked.

"What did you go get?" John questioned.

"Don't worry about it," his dad replied, patting the book and file folder with his left hand. "Have you come to a different conclusion?"

"I am going to worry. Are those what I think they are?" John responded.

"I told you; never mind these. We'll get to them in good time. Have you come to a different conclusion?" his dad questioned, annoyance in his voice.

Steven leaned forward, looked around his two sisters, and said to John, "Let it go for now and answer Dad's question."

"Okay, I will. I have come to a different conclusion."

"Care to share?" Francis questioned.

"The only conclusion," John reasoned painfully, "would have to be that conception had to have taken place before Henry came on the scene," John muttered.

"Agreed," Francis answered.

Magdalena, Wilhelm, and Johann shot darting glances at one another. Magdalena looked in Francis's direction and hesitantly stated, "From your answer, it sounds like you know about our grandfather und how he died."

Before Francis could reply, John interrupted. "Hold on! I've got it! If it happened before Henry came, that'd mean ..."

Everybody's attention had turned back in his direction.

He stopped and then sat back in his chair, his hands drumming the tabletop and his lips moving as if he were speaking to himself. He leaned forward and crossed his arms on the table, and his head bounded rhythmically up and down as if he were building up the courage to finish. "The rape occurred beforehand. She was raped before by him. That'd explain the resemblance," John exclaimed, smugly nodding in the direction of the guests. "Dad, now explain to them what happened to their grandfather."

"He died on November 11, the last day of fighting. My mother killed him at her farm."

"There you go!" John exclaimed, a look of relief spreading across his face. "Payback for what he'd done! She killed him, and for good reason!" He leaned in menacingly toward the Germans. "You said earlier his area was to provide everything he'd need. You said he could take what he needed or *wanted*. Obviously, he took what he wanted, not worrying about retribution. But retribution found him. So no matter when, when all's said and done, your grandfather got his due."

"It wasn't like that," Francis remarked softly.

"What do you mean?" John asked, trepidation oozing from his voice.

"Just what I said—it wasn't like that."

John took a moment to frame his next comment. "To me, it sounds like there's more to what you said."

"There is."

John studied his father's face. "I believe you."

"Good. You need to," Francis intoned.

"Are you going to expound?"

"I'd prefer not to. But I will, in a minute. John, do you remember your last conversation with your grandmother?"

"The last conversation I had with her? That's been more than forty years ago."

"You remember; you told me about it the other day," Francis prompted. "The one on her deathbed?"

John's right cheek began to twitch; he bit his lip. He sucked in a breath, and his eyes grew suddenly big. It was all he could do to barely nod.

"What did your grandmother tell you?" Magdalena asked.

Without hesitating, John blurted out, "She told me she killed my grandfather. She called out a name right before she passed."

Magdalena translated.

Francis asked, a hint of sympathy in his voice, "And what name did she call out? Was it Henry?"

Openmouthed, John, whose face had again gone a speckled scarlet and white and wore a look of total disbelief, leaned slightly forward and stared down the length of the table. His hands had a noticeable tremor; his breathing had once more become shallow and rapid.

"No, Henry wasn't the name she called out," he murmured, zombielike. A heartbeat later, he stammered, his gaze still fixed on his father, "Sh-she called out the name Francis. I-I-I thought—I thought she was calling for you."

John fell silent and closed his eyes, the deathbed scene playing out in his mind's eye. "When I told her I'd go get you, she told me she wasn't talking about you." John's eyes remained closed. "She said you were angry—something about how you'd come into the world. I thought at the time—because she was old, because she was sick—she had to be confused. But she wasn't, was she?"

Francis shook his head.

John told his father, his voice washed out, "Just tell the real story, if you would."

Francis pushed the retrieved items to one side and then laid his hands, one on top of the other, on the tabletop. Glancing about, he started. "I wish I didn't feel compelled to. If I had it my way, it'd be best for all if it could go to the grave with me." He swallowed hard. "But I don't get to have it my way." He studied the guests to his left. "Now that you've shown up, are you sure you want to hear it? It might not be what you expect."

"We have no idea what to expect. Whatever it is, can it be worse than what your son thought?" Magdalena asked.

"I'll let you judge," Francis replied.

"Thank you. What can you tell us?"

"I can tell you, first, my mother killed your grandfather the morning of November 11, 1918," he stated, his tone unequivocal. "Shot him and buried him in the grange. It was near where Henry had buried the other German. Second, also for the record, she had to kill him."

"See?" John interjected energetically. "I knew there was more to it."

"Not so fast," Francis replied. "Once again, it's not what you think."

"Huh?" John muttered. "You just said she had to kill him."

"I know what I said, and I stand behind it," Francis replied. "John, you want only to see the world as you see it. It's one of your many failings."

"This is neither the time nor the place," John said.

Francis held up both hands as if he were a third-base coach stopping a runner hell-bent for home.

"What?" John asked testily.

"You want to believe she had to kill him because he'd forced himself on her, right?" Francis asked. "Even if it was before Henry happened along."

Magdalena quickly translated.

"Why else would she?"

"She didn't kill him because he had forced himself on her. In fact, other than the one time, she'd never been forced." Francis dropped his eyes to the table, a soft and melancholic smile breaking across his face.

"What is it, Dad?" Donna asked softly.

"She did have to kill him. But it wasn't for what you think he'd done, John. What he'd done was to love her. And she loved him back. Two ordinary people falling in love is not unusual; it happens all the time. But two ordinary people, one French and one German, whose countries are sworn enemies and are at war, falling in love during those times and under those circumstances is extraordinary on many levels. And from that extraordinary love, I would come about."

"If what you say is true," John commented warily, "then why would she have had to kill him?"

"It's simple; she was forced to," Francis reported.

John sat back in his chair, a darkness descending upon his face. "She was forced to?"

"Or else."

"Or else?"

Francis nodded once. "Yes. Or else. Does that prompt anything? Anything else you heard from your grandmother on her deathbed?"

Wide-eyed, John nodded a moment later.

"Part of my last conversation with Grandma Jeanne—she said she had had to kill my grandfather or else. I told her she must be mistaken. I told her she couldn't have killed Pappi Henry. I reminded her he'd died two years before from cancer. He'd died in the very room where she lay dying. So there was no way she could've killed him."

"And you were right. She didn't kill Pappi Henry; cancer did. But as you now realize, it wasn't Henry she was referring to, was it?" Francis asked.

"No, but I couldn't have known that then."

"Do you remember what the 'or else' was if she didn't kill your grandfather?"

"Yeah, I remember," John commented. His face had a faraway look on it.

His dad prompted, "What did she say would happen if she didn't?"

"She said someone would take away her baby," John responded robotically.

"That's right. And what baby did you think she was talking about?"

"Alain, the only one she had," John replied.

"But he wasn't a baby, was he?" Francis probed.

"No. Not really. He would've been almost four and a half. Too old to be considered a baby," John countered.

"That's right," said Francis. "And if Alain was too old to be a baby, she could only have meant the baby she was carrying—me."

"So Grandma Jeanne *was* pregnant at the time Pappi Henry showed up," John said.

"Yes. Having been pregnant twice before, she knew what she was feeling wasn't an illness; she knew she was pregnant."

Magdalena asked, "Und she knew it was our grandfather's child?"

Slowly turning his eyes toward her, Francis responded, "There was no other."

Magdalena continued, "She had fallen in love with an enemy officer, und worse, she had become pregnant by him?"

"Yes," Francis answered simply.

"Is that why she had to kill him?" Magdalena asked.

"Yes," Francis answered.

"But who would make her?" John queried.

"Don't you know?"

John shook his head cautiously. "How would I?"

"You know," his dad replied. "You've known for almost four decades. Remember, I told you a few days back that though we think the truth is invisible, it's usually staring us straight in the face. Want to venture a guess?"

John nodded. "Sure, though I'm not positive."

"How before who," Francis remarked. "Tell us how you think you know before you tell who."

"It was something else Grandma Jeanne muttered that day. She was burning up with fever and was slipping in and out of consciousness. She was pleading in French with someone," John said. "I haven't given this any thought for the longest time." John pursed his lips. "She said her father would take her baby away."

Magdalena leaned in and cleared her throat. "But it was said earlier that her father had been killed in the first year of the war. Is my memory correct?"

Francis answered, "It is; you're right. My mother's father was killed shortly after the occupation began; he was trying to protect what was his. So it couldn't have been her father."

John looked baffled at that clarification. "I'm sure she said 'father,'" he commented.

"She did," Francis countered, lightly patting the pile of articles with his left hand. "So if she said 'father' and if it couldn't have been her father, who would it have been?"

John followed the up-and-down motion of his father's hand. "It could've only been ... *père. Père*—father." John hesitated and then finished. "The priest."

"That's right. The priest," Francis confirmed.

"But why?" John asked.

"*La revanche*," Francis said softly, and then he translated for everyone else. "Revenge."

"Revenge?" John asked. "For what?"

"His brother."

John sat back in his chair. "What did you just say?"

"He wanted revenge for his brother."

"Because he had died fighting the Germans?" John asked uneasily.

"No," Francis replied. "His brother didn't die fighting the Germans; the priest knew, at a minimum, he had not died in battle. He wanted revenge because he believed his brother had been killed in cold blood."

"I'm not sure I understand."

"He wanted revenge on the person who killed his brother."

"The priest thought Captain Neuberger killed him?" John asked.

"Yes and no," Francis stated.

John exclaimed, "Can't you just tell it straight? Do you have to peel this thing back layer by layer?"

"To believe it, it has to be peeled back layer by layer."

"Is the rest of the story in there?" John pointed at the pile to his father's left.

"Yes." Francis placed his left hand on the retrieved materials and held the file up. "These are the missing pages from the 1917 journal, and," putting them down and picking up the book, he continued, "this is the 1918 journal. Take a careful look; it's just like the others. So as you can see, they both exist."

Magdalena translated.

"You've had those the whole time?" John asked. "Where did you get them?"

Ruefully, Francis smiled at his son. "I've had them since right after your grandmother passed away. Later, when Donna wanted the journals, I kept these. The rest of the story—the part we're now talking about—is in here." Possessively, he patted the journal and file. "So you know—I'm the one who tore the pages from the 1917 journal and confiscated the 1918 one."

"You? Why you? What did you have to hide?" Donna asked.

Surprised by who asked the question, Francis turned to his older daughter. "You might think I did it to hide what's now obvious—that my dad wasn't my father. And I suppose that was partly my reasoning then, but—"

"But?" Donna pushed.

"But not completely; ultimately, I did it to keep you and"—he nodded to his right—"the others from learning the rest of the story," Francis replied.

"Why? What's the story, Dad?" Donna questioned.

"Let me take you back to the day in 1917 when their grandfather"—Francis nodded to the Germans—"showed up at my mother's farm. John read that my mother had just finished what she'd been doing in the grange and had come out. There at the door to her house stood Captain Neuberger. Seeing him, she was stunned, fearful he must know what she'd been up to. Instead, he'd come to inform her of Captain Loeb's transfer and that he was now in charge."

"I remember that," Donna replied.

"What you don't know is what she'd been doing in the grange. What I'm about to tell you is one reason I tore the last half of the pages out of the 1917 journal and kept the 1918 one. She recorded it all," Francis said, patting the pages.

"Why didn't you just destroy them?" John asked. "That would've taken care that no one would've found out."

"True, that would've," Francis replied. "But I knew someone was out there, and I couldn't be sure *they'd* not want to know. I kept these just in case they showed up on my doorstep." He turned his attention onto the Germans. "And here they are."

"But still—" John started.

Francis stopped him with a gesture of his left hand. "Imagine—they'd have shown up to learn the story, and I'd have no proof other than what I could tell them. Having heard so far what I've had to tell, who'd have believed me? You, John? How about you, Steven? Particularly you, since you've already started worrying about my mental state. No, I don't think so. The story, with no proof, would get me committed."

With nodding heads and shrugging shoulders, they silently acknowledged his reasoning.

"Remember, the priest," he continued, "had told my mother that her husband had disappeared during the Chemin des Dames offensive. He'd told her he was going back through the lines in hopes of finding out what happened. The night before Captain Neuberger made his first appearance, Jean-Pierre, my mother's first husband, showed up at her door, dressed in his brother's cassock." Francis glanced around to gauge the reactions to that revelation.

"But how did—" Donna began.

Francis held up a finger to stop her. "Long story short, the priest had learned that his brother, fed up with the army and the war, had deserted and gone to ground. Before returning to Beaulieu-en-prés, the priest learned where his brother was in hiding. He went to him. Together they came up with a plan. The priest would return with an extra set of garments. Disguised as a priest, Jean-Pierre would try to cross the lines, hopefully unsuspected and unchecked. And before anyone asks, I can't tell you why the priest said nothing about this to my mother. Maybe he couldn't trust her. And that's what happened."

"Whoa!" John exclaimed, holding his hand up. "In the newspaper article, Henry mentioned that the priest came out several different times while he was there. Was that the priest or his brother?"

"The priest," Francis answered.

"The priest? So where was his brother?"

"Killed."

"Killed?" John answered in an exasperated voice. "You just said he showed up at Grandma's door. So he made it through the lines?"

"Yes. He made it through the lines and back to the farm."

"What happened to him then?" Donna and John asked simultaneously, and then they glanced apprehensively at one another.

"What did happen to him?" Francis asked in response. "He made it through the lines and made it to the farm and then vanished. What do you think happened?"

Donna said, "You pointed out the entry in which Captain Neuberger showed up for the first time. You did that on purpose, didn't you?"

Francis nodded.

Donna screwed an eye upward and flicked her tongue out. "She'd just finished in the grange. As she came out, she found Captain Neuberger on her doorstep. You said she was stunned. That's the key, isn't it?"

Francis nodded.

Donna got up from the table and stood behind her chair, both hands firmly gripping the top. Tentatively, she spoke. "There can be only one answer, right? Unless, somewhere later, her husband shows up again, like after the war."

"He doesn't. Never shows up again."

"In that case, that could only mean ..." Donna sat back down before blurting out, "Grandma killed him and buried the body in the grange. That's what she was doing, wasn't it?"

No one made a sound around the table; all eyes had turned to Francis. He nodded slowly, his lips pursed.

"Why?" Magdalena asked moments later. "Why would she kill her husband?"

"I'll get to that. First, let me set the table," Francis stated. "Keep in mind that hers had been an arranged marriage. She didn't love her husband; plus, he had been abusive. When mobilization came and Jean-Pierre left, she was anything but sad. By late May 1917, she'd survived almost three years of occupation. She'd found ways to keep herself and her son alive. She'd also found in herself the courage and strength to stand up and look out for herself, her son, and those around her. Though life was full of hardships and deprivations during the war, so had life been before. Wartime hardships were just different, and more acute."

He cleared his throat. "There was a knock late that night. With a lantern in her hand, she answered; outside stood the priest. *What could this man want at this hour?* she must've thought to herself. What do you think her reaction to his being there would've been?"

No one answered.

"Annoyance. How about irritation? Would it have bordered on exasperation?" Francis asked.

Wilhelm interjected in his heavily accented English, "Fury?"

"Bingo!" Francis exclaimed, snapping the fingers of his left hand and then stabbing that hand's pointer finger at him. "She was furious. He, the priest, showed up unannounced far too often, and she was fed up with it. I can hear her asking, all the while barring the door, 'What do you want?'

"The priest spoke. Imagine her shock when, seeing a familiar face in familiar garments, she realized that the priest at the door was not the priest, because the familiar voice wasn't the expected voice. She knew only at that split second it wasn't the priest; it took her a split second longer to realize who it was."

Turning to Magdalena, Francis continued. "To answer your question as to why she'd kill her husband, I'm afraid the answer is simple: the opportunity presented itself. She never loved him and, having lived without him, had no intention of living with him again. Standing there at the door, in the darkness of the night, with a war going on three years raging through her country, and her long-absent husband dressed up as a priest, she immediately decided what she'd do. It was the perfect opportunity. She stepped out of the house, gave him a hug, laughed to herself at the notion of hugging a priest, and told him to follow her into the grange.

"'Why can't we go inside?' he'd have probably asked.

"'Because if someone's out and about, a priest shouldn't be seen going into the house of a married woman whose husband isn't at home. You'd be disappointed to learn I'd let that happen. Besides, if Alain should wake up, he'd be frightened with a strange man in the house,' she explained.

"'I'm no stranger; I'm his father,' Jean-Pierre answered.

"'I know that, but he doesn't. He won't remember you; he was but an infant when you left, and he hasn't seen you since. I'm going to put you in the grange,' she answered, tugging at his elbow. 'We'll start anew tomorrow.'

"He'd have seen the logic of her argument," Francis commented, "and let himself be led to the grange. Inside, she told him to disrobe while she went to get a change of clothing. He turned his back, and at that moment, she picked up a spade and struck him hard."

Francis stopped and looked at his children, watching their reactions to this news.

"What happened next, Dad?" Donna asked sheepishly.

"Without going into detail," Francis said, his eyes still on Magdalena, "she made sure he was dead. She dug a hole under the hayloft, laid him in, filled it, and arranged things on top. She'd just finished when their grandfather"—Francis jutted a thumb toward his guests—"showed up."

"Grandma Jeanne killed him on purpose and buried him? By herself? Without anyone ever finding out?" Monique asked in disbelief. "My grandma Jeanne?"

"Yes, your grandmother and my mother," her dad replied. "She worried about getting caught."

"What would've happened if she had?" Monique asked.

"She would've been tried by the German authorities or the French, as the case may have been. If found guilty, she probably would've been executed for ..." Francis left the rest of the phrase unsaid before finishing. "It's only a guess on my part. In any case, it didn't get to that."

"So if Jean-Pierre came across the lines dressed as the priest, how did the real priest make it back?" John asked, suspicion dripping from his question.

"She never asked after he'd returned—probably afraid of tipping her hand," Francis responded. "You probably wouldn't be surprised to learn it took weeks for him to make a reappearance. That's what I think since there was no mention of him again until mid-October."

"What happened between the priest and Grandma Jeanne once he was back?" Monique asked.

"If anything happened, she didn't write about it," Francis commented. "And now that all this is out in the open, anyone is free to flip through the pages to make sure I'm telling the truth. It's in French, though."

"No one doubts you," John quickly replied.

"Thanks. That's reassuring," Francis curtly replied. "What's bothering you, John?"

"What's bothering me is her not noting what transpired once the priest returned," John commented after a momentary silence.

"Why's that?"

"He, the priest, had to have known his brother would head home; they'd probably planned it, believing his wife would shelter him. The priest would've come back expecting to find his brother. Maybe not out in the open, but at least alive. Yet the priest gets back, and no Jean-Pierre. What gives?" John asked.

"Can't answer that, and don't know what to say," Francis added. "And if I did, it'd probably be wrong. I'm with you, though, in thinking he would've been surprised, maybe even dumbfounded, to learn his brother wasn't around. To top it off, he couldn't even be sure his brother ever was."

"Do you think Grandma Jeanne considered that when she decided to kill him?" John asked. "Looking at her husband in the priest's vestments, she had to instantly know the priest was in cahoots."

Magdalena stopped in midsentence of her translation and asked, "What does *cahoots* mean?"

"Cahoots? It means he'd been part of the plan," John answered.

"John, to answer your question," his father added, "I wouldn't put it past her. Could my mother have simply said, when asked, that her husband had never shown up? You bet. I can see her acting astonished to learn he'd tried to cross the lines in hopes of getting back home." He paused for effect before adding emphatically, "And I can hear her saying to the priest, if what he was saying was right, that her husband had, in all probability, been captured or killed en route. That'd be totally believable." Francis paused. "Plus, it'd have been impossible for the priest to go to the authorities, even if he could've fingered her. What exactly would he have said? He'd helped an enemy soldier infiltrate the rear area? To raise her story above suspicion, she needed only to invite the priest to search the place or to talk to others in the village as to whether they'd seen him. Knowing damned well no one had, it would've been safe. I'm guessing the priest probably took her up on the first but not the second, afraid the German authorities would hear of what he'd done. Relying solely on his own limited resources and having been away for too long, he'd have learned nothing, as his brother's trail—and his brother—had grown cold. And that's where the story probably would've ended, if the war had ended. It didn't. Magdalena, are you staying up with me?"

Distractedly, Magdalena held up a finger as she translated. When she had caught up, she nodded.

"My mother believed the priest, unable to prove anything or find anything or anyone who knew anything about his brother's whereabouts, came to accept that his brother must've been killed en route and would never be heard from again. In the absence of any other explanation, it had to have been the Germans, in the priest's mind, who'd killed his brother." Francis took a deep breath. "Yet"—his delivery and voice hinted at something darker—"we need to accept that some degree of suspicion regarding her story lingered within the priest. Her version would've nagged at him. Because of that, the priest would've kept after her, baying like a hound dog each time he showed up. Remember, in the newspaper article, Henry mentioned the priest's almost daily appearances during his stay. The last visit, I believe, was the last day Henry was there."

"I remember that," Magdalena said in English, and then she repeated the words to her brothers in German. "I wonder to myself if the priest had changed his mind about what may have caused his brother's disappearance."

"I'm not following," John commented.

"Your grandmother thought that the priest had accepted that his brother had been killed while trying to get back. As time passed und no word came of his brother's fate, I wonder if the priest suspected that your grandmother's story did not hold up to scrutiny."

"We'll get to that, but first, by late summer, my mother and your grandfather"—Francis nodded in the Germans' direction—"had become lovers. I'd be the result. I was born on Bastille Day of the following year. That'd be July 14. Subtract nine months, more or less, and you see she was pregnant by the time my dad came along." Francis paused.

Johann spoke to Magdalena as she finished translating. She nodded and then turned to Wilhelm, speaking to him. He did not answer at first, lowering his eyes and pursing his lips instead. A moment later, almost imperceptibly, he nodded.

"We are not surprised," Magdalena remarked, looking at Francis. "Our grandfather, in his last letter home, asked our grandmother to forgive him. I believe that she would have forgiven him und would have gladly welcomed him home in spite of that relationship, if only he had returned. There are worse things. Having lived through the hell of postwar Germany, we have experienced some of those. As for us, we are hardly surprised by much where people are concerned, und what they are capable of doing. At least what happened between them was—what word am I looking for?"

"Consensual?" Donna interjected. "It means by mutual agreement. That's to say, no one forced himself or herself on the other. I guess that'd mean my father was a love child." She laughed lightly. "Would that be right, Dad?"

"That'd be right." He nodded.

"Jah, *consensual* is the word," Magdalena commented. She then turned her attention on John. "So you see that what you thought had happened did not."

He sputtered a "But" and a "Hold it a second" before falling silent and staring at her. A moment later, he added, "I guess you're right about the soldier not being your grandfather." Turning his attention to the far end of the table, he asked pointedly, "But something did happen. What was it?"

"First, Franzis knew she was pregnant; she told him as soon as she was sure," Francis recounted. "He was disturbed by the news. If she stayed, he was concerned about what might happen to her when the pregnancy became obvious. If she went, he was concerned what might happen to him when the pregnancy became obvious. My mother told him she was going nowhere, he was going home, and he wasn't to worry. Besides, she'd survived almost four years of war; she'd figure something out."

Francis rubbed his chin, half smiling. "My mother thrived under pressure. Her mind worked very quickly in such situations. Today you'd say she was quick on her feet. I've related how, on the spur of the moment, she decided what to do with her husband. So I suppose she felt confident something would come to her."

Francis stopped to let Magdalena catch up.

"In early November 1918," he continued, "something came to her. My mother found herself pregnant with a German officer's child, the war was clearly coming to an end, and she was unsure of what the villagers might do at war's end in light of her delicate condition. Some, she thought, on learning the news, would see her as a collaborator, even though it'd been her efforts that'd helped many of those around her keep access to food and medicine. She didn't think anyone in the village knew, but she wasn't positive. Nonetheless, she wasn't taking any chances if she didn't have to. Worse, the priest still was coming out almost every day. Though she'd be able to hide her condition for some time, there'd come a day when she couldn't. What would she do then—pregnant and no husband? Then, magically, Henry Alston came to her." He laughed. "According to her, this was the one time she considered lighting a votive candle; it was as though providence had sent him her way. She knew what had to be done; she'd take him in."

Francis glanced at each of his children. "He'd be no wiser and would never need to know. She'd get what she needed—a plausible story—and assumed he'd not complain. Sure, she'd have a child out of wedlock, but at least it would be a child supposedly by an ally she'd sheltered. There were worse things, and she had no intention of finding out what those could be. No one would have to know the truth, especially the American. Unwittingly, he'd play his part, slipping in and out and then moving on. That was her plan.

"We know from the newspaper articles that my dad, Henry, appeared as if on cue, snuck into the grange, climbed the ladder, and burrowed into the straw. Hardly did he know what he'd walked into. The next morning, he was awakened by the prick of a pitchfork. He opened his eyes and," Francis recounted, his eyes seemingly gazing into the distance, "listening to him tell the story, he beheld an angel."

John laughed explosively and slapped a knee with an open hand. "That's a good one! An angel? Boy, was he wrong!"

"Not from his perspective. My mother was a physically attractive woman when younger. Who knows how long it'd been since Henry had seen a woman, let alone been this close to one and alone? I imagine that my dad, like most guys in that situation, had no problems doing what was expected. And despite the risks she'd run, she took him in. Of course, he had no idea what he was to be a part of.

"My mother insisted that she never planned on letting Henry know she was pregnant. He'd come and go, and that'd be that. She simply needed to prove she'd provided haven." Francis fell silent.

"But she did tell him. Was that why there was a gap in the newspaper articles?" asked Donna.

"No. The gap had nothing to do with that; Henry came down with the flu," said Francis.

"Then did her deciding to tell him have something to do with what happened with that German soldier?" asked Donna.

"It had nothing to do with that," Francis remarked. "She felt no more affection for him as a result of his 'saving' her." Francis punctuated the air with quotation marks. "By that time, she was ready for him to move on. The story could've ended there; in fact, it should've. However—"

"However what?" Donna prompted.

"However, it didn't. She'd end up getting word to him in late December. I suppose you want to know why."

"Yes," Donna replied.

Shifting his eyes back and forth from one side of the table to the other, he mulled over his response. "This is going to make my mother sound coldhearted."

Cynically, Steven remarked, "Too late for that."

A slight *hmmm* escaped Francis's mouth. "I suppose you're right—she killed her husband, used Henry as she needed and then discarded him as quickly as possible afterwards, and killed Franzis Neuberger." Distractedly, he repeated, "I suppose you're right."

"Well?" Donna asked. "Why did she?"

"Someone in the village had found out."

"Who had found out?" Donna asked.

Swallowing hard, Francis murmured, "The priest."

"How?" Donna shot back.

"From the confessional."

"From the confessional? But Grandma—" Donna stopped, not finishing her thought.

In anticipation, Francis replied, "That's right."

"If not her," Donna stated, not surprised by the answer, "then that could only mean ..."

She looked hastily across the table and then shifted her gaze to her father and once more back across the table. A moment later, her gaze drifted back to her father. She arched an eyebrow at him in silent question.

Francis had followed her gaze across the table and had met it as it came to rest on him. "That's right," he murmured in response to her unasked question, adding an almost-imperceptible nod in case she failed to hear.

Magdalena looked from Donna to Francis and back again. "I do not understand. If it was not your grandmother, then who would it have been?" she dared ask.

Francis motioned to Donna to let him answer. She nodded, relief washing over her face.

Turning to Magdalena, who was speaking to her brothers, Francis replied, "It'd have been your grandfather."

"My grandfather? What do you mean my grandfather?"

Francis studied her face and then glanced from Johann to Wilhelm. "I mean your grandfather was the one who confessed."

Magdalena's hand shot up to her mouth, her eyes growing large. Her hands then dropped back into her lap. Barely audibly, she repeated, "*Nein, nein, nein. Sagen Sie, dass es nicht wahr ist.*"

"What's she saying—anyone?" John asked.

"I think," Steven replied for Magdalena, "she's saying, though I'm not sure, 'No, no, no; say it's not true.'"

"I'm afraid so," Francis answered sympathetically, reaching his left arm out toward her.

She reached for his, clutched it, and gave it a squeeze. "*Es tut mir leid. Ich bin so traurig. Er wußte nicht.*"

Steven translated haltingly. "I'm sorry. I'm so sorry. He didn't know."

Rapid-fire, she continued. "*Wenn er das gewusst hätte, hätte er das nicht gemacht.*"

"If he'd known, he wouldn't have," Steven translated.

Steven's siblings looked quizzically at him. He smiled sheepishly back. "I know more German than I let on originally."

Turning her attention to Francis, she asked with her pleading eyes, "*Warum hätte er das gemacht*?"

"I think she just asked, 'Why would he have done that?'" Steven translated.

In a consoling tone, Francis said, "I don't know why; I wish I did. But if I were to guess, I'd say his humanity got to him."

"I do not understand." Magdalena looked first at Johann and then at Wilhelm. They shrugged.

"What I mean is, despite the brutality of the past four years and the daily uncertainty of continued existence, he'd been able to resummon who he'd been. He had to think he was about to return home against all odds." Francis let his response sink in. "Remember, you told us your grandfather, in his last letter, asked for forgiveness."

She nodded in acknowledgment.

Giving Magdalena's hand a squeeze before releasing it, Francis continued. "He had two lives: one in front of him and one at the front. The former, he didn't know at all, and the latter, he knew too well. When he realized he couldn't have both, the conflict between the two had to have suddenly reared up. Facing the prospect of returning to one and ending the other, he'd have begun to make the emotional transition. I assume he went in search of spiritual guidance. The problem was, your grandfather didn't know of the priest's relationship to my mother. He'd only done what he felt he had to. I find no fault with him for following his convictions. That he confessed makes me admire him more."

"*Danke. Aber es hätte anders sein können,*" she said, and then she switched to English. "But what might have been different ..." She fell silent, her eyes sweeping the faces across from her.

"We'll never know," Francis replied comfortingly to Magdalena, who wore a tortured half smile on her face. "It could very well be nothing. Events, once set in motion, tend to move at their own speed and follow their own course. As if we control anything? You want to think his confession set the events in motion; I believe otherwise. I'm of the opinion that well before your grandfather showed up, events had already burst from the starting gate."

Donna said, "So the priest found out. What was the big deal, Dad?"

"He was looking for someone to blame. He'd been stuck on the other side of the lines after he'd helped his brother. When he returned, his brother wasn't around, but your grandfather was," Francis recounted, addressing that statement to Magdalena and her brothers. "Being suspicious of my mother's account, he probably spied on her, maybe even saw Captain Neuberger coming and going from her place. Could that have piqued his suspicions? I think so. And then, in early November, he learned that a local woman had become pregnant by the captain. It didn't take much for him to figure out who that was. At that point, is it a stretch for him to have believed they'd been involved all along in his brother's disappearance, their now-revealed affair being the reason? With the husband out of the way, nothing would've prevented them from carrying on."

He looked at the faces to his left one by one. "My mother was in love with your grandfather; there's no doubt of that. The priest had to have suddenly seen it also. Is it too much of a leap, with this information and the absence of any other, that the scales fell from his eyes and it became clear who was involved and why?" he asked.

"It's certainly believable," Donna replied, looking for confirmation. Most of the others nodded in agreement.

"Then?" she asked.

"Then Henry turned up and did what was expected of him," Francis stated, his eyes taking on a distant look. "No one should fault him for this. Here was a young man—too young to have seen what he'd seen and too young to have done what he'd done—on his own, behind enemy lines, and trying to stay alive, just like everyone else. He killed those German soldiers, disposing of the first in the brush and burying the second in the grange. Once Henry left, he had no illusions of ever seeing the *madame veuve* again, in spite of what they'd shared. My father was sure she'd never want to ever see him again; after all, she was some mysterious French lady, and he was just some run-of-the-mill guy from some small town in the center of the United States. He became a chance war hero—more a product of the times and circumstances than anything else, particularly since the soldiers he'd rounded up had no intentions of being heroes themselves. Henry returned safely to the Allied lines with his POWs but lost them before they could be interned. Then he came down with the flu."

Francis massaged his brow. "But he got over it and recuperated. In late December, he received a message from the *madame veuve*; she was pregnant. He had no doubt it was his, knowing what had happened between them and having no reason to believe otherwise. To hear the joyful amazement in his voice as he described what he was feeling at that moment. His angel." Francis looked down the length of the table. "Don't say a word!"

Solemnly, John nodded.

"Henry got a pass to return to Beaulieu-en-prés—being a war hero probably helped. Once there, he let her know how happy he was and how he planned on making her his bride. As soon as he could, he'd get the necessary papers for her and their child; they'd live in the United States. While there, he was paraded through the village, my mother hanging on his arm, for everyone to see.

"He started the paperwork before he shipped out. It took longer than he'd hoped or planned. I was born after he'd left. He wouldn't see me for the first time for several years. Finally, he was able to come back and get us. Back in the States, they married, and my sister, Mary, was born about a year later. They stayed married the rest of his life. Up to the day he died, about two years before my mother, he was in love. My mother felt the same way. Unfortunately, though, it was for another man—your grandfather."

Francis looked directly at the Germans, his face taking on a wistful look as he muttered, "My dad died never knowing the truth. I can honestly say I'm glad for that." Francis cleared his throat. "When my mom got sick, she told my sister, Mary, and me everything. She told us it'd all been written down in the journals. My sister, being the fruit of my mom and my dad, had no interest in the journals; they barely related to her. Whereas I, on the other hand, ended up with them."

"That explains what happened after the war, Dad. But they've"—Donna pointed across the table—"come so far. You need to tell the rest for their sake."

Francis exhaled, letting his head drop slightly.

Softly, Donna prompted, "I know you've told us what happened to their grandfather, but what exactly happened that last day at the farm, Dad?"

"The priest had come out every day since learning about them," Francis began. "He questioned my mother. She stuck with her story, telling it over and over and over again." Francis massaged his brow. "Then came the threat, delivered the day Henry departed. John, you know what it was; she told you right before she passed away."

"I don't remember a threat," John responded.

"S'il vous plait. Je ne peux pas. Ne me commandiez pas ça," Francis recited.

"Oh my. I remember that, but there wasn't any threat."

"Maybe not directly, but she told you what she'd done," his dad said.

"She said she killed my grandfather. Is that it?" John asked.

"Exactly. Why did she do it?" Francis questioned. "What did she say?"

"She said she had to—or else," John said in a hollow voice.

"Precisely!" Francis exclaimed, stabbing a finger at his older son. "The priest, who believed my mother had killed his brother, couldn't prove anything. The captain's confession had to have caused a change of mind—the captain must've had something to do with it. He was in a position to, had the power to, and had a reason to. As the captain had to be guilty, all that remained was to carry out judgment—life for a life. But the priest wouldn't do it himself; he couldn't. He was a priest. He would need to find someone else. Armed with the knowledge of the pregnancy, he found that someone—someone who couldn't refuse."

Francis pursed his lips and looked down the table at John.

"The priest threatened to expose my mother's pregnancy and who the father was. The village would turn on her. All she had to do to prevent this was to do what he asked—kill her lover. If she refused, bad things could happen; she'd be ostracized, and her son might be taken away from her. He explained that if she didn't do as he asked, he'd find someone else. Then he'd make sure she'd not keep her baby, who could end up in a faraway orphanage. And she'd never know where. She stood to lose everything, and for what? The captain was going home; he couldn't stay if he wanted to. She was going to lose him no matter what. Here at least was a chance for her to keep what she had. The captain would end up just another casualty of the war. They'd concoct a story for what she'd done. With a good enough story, there'd be no serious consequences.

"My mother asked, 'Why should I believe you, even if I were to agree?'

"'I'm a priest.' He smiled devilishly at her."

Francis smiled to himself. "No worse reason existed as far as she was concerned. Remember, he'd already betrayed the sanctity of the confessional. She sensed time was working against her, so she was resigned to do what was asked of her. She'd kill him. That night, she made her plans and then, after taking Alain to a neighbor's, went into the grange to prepare.

BEAULIEU-EN-PRÉS

NOVEMBER 11, 1918

Twenty-One

The morning was gray and dreary. A stiff breeze out of the northeast brought with it the promise of more rain. Pewter-colored clouds had been piling up to the point that Jeanne's house and grange, both long neglected and in need of paint, blended harmoniously into them.

Jeanne, standing just inside the doors to the grange, kept watch.

"Is there any sign of him?" the priest asked. He was in the shadows, dimly lit by the light coming in through the thin slits between the slats. "You told him ten o'clock, right?"

"Don't worry; he'll be here," she replied.

The priest had arrived earlier than planned. He'd wanted to make sure that she understood what he expected of her and what she could expect if she failed to do it.

Jeanne was thinking of all that needed to be done around her place once the Germans marched off. She could do little of it; she was pregnant, and her son wasn't old enough to help out. Even if he had been, they had no animals with which to plow. Plus, her neighbors weren't likely to help until they'd done what was needed around their places.

Franz Neuberger came into sight. She whispered over her shoulder, "Here he comes."

"He's alone?"

Jeanne nodded and then walked out to meet Franz.

"There is much I have to do today. What is this about?" he asked.

"It's about us," she answered. She pulled him by the elbow into the grange and shut the door behind them.

The priest stepped out of the shadows.

Franz asked, startled. "What is he doing here?"

"I'll explain everything in just a moment, but first …" As if to give Franz a hug, she reached around his waist. When she stepped away, his service pistol was in her hand. "Stand next to the priest," she instructed, motioning with the barrel.

Franz balked.

Jeanne stated in no uncertain terms, again waving the pistol at her lover, "Do as I say."

Cautiously, Franz moved away and sidled up to the priest.

"You should know he"—Jeanne gestured with a nod of her chin at the priest—"has threatened to expose me, to make sure the truth about my pregnancy is known. To buy his silence, I'm to kill you."

A slight laugh escaped Franz's lips, sounding more like a cough.

"I'm serious," she said.

Looking at the priest, Franz asked, "Could that be right?"

The priest nodded, barely able to hide his delight.

"Why?" Franz asked.

"You murdered my brother," the priest answered.

"I've murdered no one."

"I don't believe you. I don't know exactly when or how, but I know you murdered him."

"When would I have murdered him? In battle? That's not murder."

"My brother didn't die in battle. He died somewhere around here, and I think you know where."

"I know nothing about your brother. I don't even know who he is," Franz commented.

The priest turned his gaze upon Jeanne. "Ask her who he was."

Franz asked, "Who's his brother?"

"My husband—his brother was my husband."

Franz continued, "I didn't know. You never mentioned him or talked of him. I assumed your husband was dead."

The priest answered, "Her husband is. I just don't know how or where. That's what I want to know."

"What do you know?" Franz asked.

"He deserted in the first days of the Le Chemin des Dames battle. I learned of it while I was across the lines; I also learned where he'd gone. I went to him. Together we plotted to get him across the lines. He'd dress in my clothing, passing himself off as a priest. Since we looked alike, we hoped a sentry would hardly glance at his papers and then let him pass. He was to come straight here. As planned, I met him, and we made the switch. I expected to find him here when I returned."

"And?" Franz asked.

"When I returned, there was no sign of him. She claims," the priest continued, pointing a bony finger in Jeanne's direction, "he never made it. She claims he was probably killed en route."

"That makes the most sense," the captain affirmed. "Some guard probably figured out that he was not who his papers said he was. Your brother likely panicked, thinking he'd be taken as a spy. He probably ran and was shot."

"That's why I don't believe it; it's too neat, too tidy. I figured she was trying to protect someone; I just didn't know who—that is, until the other day in the confessional, when my suspicions about you two were confirmed. It all fell into place then. I think you know something," the priest stated.

"Why would you think I'd know something?" Franzis asked in bewilderment.

"You two have been having an affair. She's pregnant with your child," the priest responded. "For that to have happened, my brother would've had to have been out of the way."

Jeanne interrupted, bewilderment in her voice. "So you think he's responsible? What if you're wrong? What if you were to find out he wasn't—would you let him go?"

The priest smiled, emphatically shaking his head. "No. He has to die now no matter what."

"Why? He didn't have anything to do with it," Jeanne replied, implicating herself.

"Even if he didn't, he has to die for what he's done."

"What has he done?" she asked angrily.

"Let me rephrase that," the priest said. "He needs to die for what he's not done. And before you ask, I'll tell you; he didn't do enough to make sure those in this area had enough to eat or clothing enough to stay warm when there wasn't enough coal to burn. He didn't do enough to keep them from dying from illness and disease; he didn't do enough to protect them from his own soldiers. He's guilty of these and more."

"He was following orders. He had no choice."

Franz held up a hand. "I had nothing to do with your brother's disappearance and have no idea what might've happened to him. But I'm guilty as accused of the other charges; I won't hide behind orders. I could've done more and didn't."

Stunned by his admission, Jeanne took a moment to catch her breath. With her next, she followed suit. She looked straight into the eyes of the priest. "*I* killed your brother. He got what he had coming for the way he'd treated me. Ever since he went off to war, I could only hope he'd die a glorious death for *la patrie*. With that, he'd become a hero and be out of my life. But somehow a shell, a bullet, or a bayonet failed to find him."

The priest and Captain Neuberger stared at her, shocked by what she'd just said.

"Now you know." Turning her attention to Franz, Jeanne asked, "Why did you have to tell him about us?"

"I didn't know you knew him," Franz said, looking in the priest's direction. "How would I have known you were related? You're not religious. I just figured ... If I had known ... I was only confessing." Turning to the priest, Franzis said, "You've betrayed your oath as a priest. For that, you will burn in hell."

"Maybe, but so will you," the priest replied smugly.

Captain Neuberger turned to Jeanne. "I'm sorry; I never thought going to confession would be anything but good. I felt I had to make amends to God. Though I love you, what we had was wrong."

"Wrong? What we had was wrong? How could you think that what we had was wrong? How could you say your child I'm carrying is wrong? How could you say our child, conceived through love, could be wrong?" Jeanne caught her breath, shaken by what she'd just heard.

"Why did you have to say that?" Her voice quivered in anger. "You should've stayed quiet and ought to have gone home! You could've easily left and left us alone," she remarked, rubbing her abdomen. "We're going to be fine. I've made it this far with very little help. Believe it or not, I would've been fine." Her voice took on a harsher tone. "I never wanted anything from you other than what you'd already given me. With you, I felt love for the first time. When I got pregnant, I wanted nothing more than this child, your child. This child means everything. Did you not know I would never come looking for you? That I never could? Never would I have interfered with your life in Germany. We'd been thrown together; under other circumstances, what we had would never have been. I knew you couldn't stay, knew you wouldn't. You were always going back to your family if you survived. I knew that. You had history with your wife and children by her. I also knew you really loved her more than me. I was fine with that. You were always going to honor her and your family; I accepted that. It's one of the things I love about you. That and you are a good and decent man. I could never say that about my late husband." Tears ran down her cheeks.

The priest made a move to leave. Jeanne turned the pistol on him. "What do you think you're doing?" she asked, sniffling.

"I'm leaving. I'll expose you for what you are—a murderer and a whore," the priest hissed, and then he looked contemptuously at Franzis. He pulled a watch from his pocket. "The fighting will be over in minutes. Nothing now can be done to keep Captain Neuberger from leaving, unless, of course, you kill him. But if you don't, I no longer care. I can, however, destroy you."

"No, I don't think you can," she replied threateningly. She raised the pistol, took a step in his direction, and aimed it at the priest's head.

He asked her, "What are you going to do?"

"If I do what you demand, tell me you're going to keep your word."

He shook his head, snickering. "I would've if it were only your condition. But it's more than that now."

Without warning, she turned the pistol on Franz. "As I said, I knew you were always going back—if you survived. I'm sorry, but you won't. You shouldn't have gone to confession. You shouldn't have said what you said about what we had. You shouldn't have allowed me to fall in love with you. Our child," she said, caressing her stomach, "deserves a chance. For that to happen, you'll not leave here; you'll remain here forever."

"What are you going to do?"

"I'm going to kill you both. One I don't want to"—she glanced at the priest—"and the other I can't wait to."

"You don't have to; you have a choice."

"I have no choice; I don't. We," she'd replied, rubbing her abdomen, "have no choice. If I let him go"—she pointed the pistol at the priest—"I'll be ruined. If I let you go, I'll be destroyed." She again caressed her stomach. "We'll be okay." She squeezed the trigger.

Franz dropped his eyes to the wound and then sunk to the ground, blood pooling around his body.

She then turned the pistol on the priest. "I'll bet you never believed I'd do it. Now it's your turn."

The priest, shocked that she'd done what he'd demanded, trembled like a leaf in a strong breeze, his eyes the size of goose eggs, his face gray.

Motioning with a flick of the pistol to the far side of the grange, Jeanne said, "I want you to know where your brother is. He's over there, under the hayloft and that pile. He's been there since the night he dared show his face again. I hit that *salaud* as hard as I could with a spade and then finished him off. If only the war would've killed him off. As for my child," she continued, rubbing her lower abdomen with her left hand, "you'll never get your hands on him."

Regaining a bit of his composure, the priest said, "I knew it was you; I knew it all along. You won't get away with what you've done. There's nothing I can do now. Truth is, there never was; I only ever promised to keep my mouth shut. You should know I was never going to. You're going to lose what you want most to keep; you're going to lose that Boche baby." He spat at the feet of the dead German. "You'll get exactly what you deserve."

"No, I won't—but you will." She aimed the pistol and squeezed the trigger. The priest slumped to the ground, his life flowing out of him.

MAPLETON VALLEY

AUGUST 3

Twenty-Two

"In the grange, on top of each other, she buried them in a hole she'd dug the night before. With them into the grave went her secrets," Francis said.

Deathly still, lost in thought, the other seven stared at Francis. The pulsing ticktock of the grandfather clock was the only sound other than Donna's and Monique's occasional sniffling.

"By the time someone came looking, any sign of the captain or the priest having been there had been wiped clean. With their disappearances, they joined the list of the thousands who simply up and vanished."

Francis leaned in. "It took years for me to come to grips with what my mother had done. All the emotions—astonishment, disbelief, anger, resignation, and, finally, acceptance—worked their way through me. But for what she'd risked, I'd not be here, and neither would you." He cast his gaze on each of his children, finishing with John at the far end of the table. "No one here can or should judge her, not even you." Francis directed his last remark at the Germans. "She did what everybody was doing—what was needed to survive. That's the end of the story." He sat back in his chair.

Magdalena cleared her throat. Smiling thinly, she kept her gaze on Francis. "Thank you for sharing with us. We have learned what we came to learn; for that, we are grateful. I am not sure that we can say that we are grateful for *what* we have learned. But before we can say that, we need time to reflect."

She shot a glance at her brothers and smiled weakly. "*Wir sollten gehen. Wir haben genug von Ihrer Zeit in Anspruch genommen.*" Turning to her host, she translated. "I told them that we should be going. We have taken enough of your time."

She made a halfhearted effort to get up but then settled back into her chair. She pointed a finger at Francis. "In my mind, I know that I should not judge. But in my heart"—she placed an open hand on her left breast—"my first reaction is to hate you for what happened. Your mother"—she shifted her gaze to the four siblings—"und grandmother killed our grandfather und stole any chance for us to know him. Under most circumstances, my feelings would be justified. But then I ask myself, *What would I have done?* Since I cannot know, I cannot judge. If I were to hate, I would be like those who started the war und made sure that the killing continued to the very end. With the millions who perished, there must have been a great deal of hatred in the world. I ask myself, *For what did they die? Peace?*" She shook her head and screwed up her face. "The next war only brought more hatred, death, und destruction. We"—she motioned toward her brothers—"lived through that, und when that one ended, there was still no peace." She swallowed hard, rubbed the back of her left hand with her right, and remained quiet for a long moment. "I am sorry. I should not have said what I said." She looked contritely at those sitting apart from her and her brothers and softly remarked, "Please accept my apology."

Francis reached for her hand. "You don't need to apologize. I said the first night we met that when all was said and done, it'd be you who'd be owed the apology."

Magdalena gave Francis's hand a light squeeze before surveying the table a final time. "To think our grandfather came so close, only to die as the war came to an end." Wistfully, she added, "He had to be one of the last casualties of the Great War."

Looking from side to side, Francis studied each face around the table, ending on John's. "One of the last but not *the* last." He said no more.

MAPLETON VALLEY

DECEMBER 26

Twenty-Three

John sat at a table in his favorite coffee shop, his chair facing the front door. His coffee—in a ceramic cup, not the usual paper one—sat untouched. At this time of afternoon, the place was quiet. Several nearby tables sat unoccupied. For that, he was thankful, as he had no idea what to expect of what was to come. He lifted his eyes to the wall clock to his left.

They were late; his sons were supposed to have already been there. He hoped they were still coming. He also hoped he'd recognize them.

He'd been surprised they'd accepted his e-mail invitation. Maybe he shouldn't have been; after all, his e-mail had hinted at the story. Plus, he'd played the pity card by strongly suggesting they should show up—if not for his sake, then for their grandfather's.

He squirmed in his chair, inadvertently elbowing the top journal. It fell off the table and onto a small, scrawny artificial Christmas tree at his feet.

The idea of a tree had come to him that morning as he got ready. He'd stopped and bought it on the way. He'd have preferred a real one—one that still had a hint of pine scent—but the one he'd ended up with had been the only one left. He could understand why, glancing down his nose at it; it was one of the saddest-looking trees he'd ever seen.

He reached down and retrieved the journal, put it back on top of the others, and pushed the pile to the far right-hand corner of the table. He then picked up the tree, straightened out the bent branches, and set it where the journals had been.

His glance drifted to the journals; all were there. The 1918 journal was in its chronological place, and the top part of the folder containing the ripped-out pages protruded from the 1917 journal. John had read and reread the recently restored portions to the point he knew them as well as the others. As his father had claimed, Grandma Jeanne had faithfully recorded what she'd done: the doing-in of her first husband, her affair with Captain Neuberger, the resulting pregnancy, Henry Alston and his role, and, of course, the events of the morning of November 11, 1918.

As his sons had never met Grandma Jeanne—she'd died long before either was a glimmer in his eye—he'd struggled with what part of the story to start with. He'd ultimately decided to start with Pappi Henry's appearance at the farm and go from there. If his sons wanted to know more of what had happened before, he'd move backward. This would give him the chance to spend more time with them. Perhaps, he hoped, this could be the start of something better between them. If it was, he'd know where to give credit.

Up until a couple of weeks before, John wouldn't have felt that way. The Germans had obliterated his long-cherished perceptions of his grandparents' story. That had been the last casualty of the Great War. To be fair, though, only a portion of his grandfather's story had been obliterated, since the part about his being captured, escaping, evading recapture, returning safely to the American lines with his prisoners of war, and ultimately returning to France to retrieve Jeanne and his dad remained true and intact. His grandmother's story, on the other hand ...

John swallowed hard. For several months after, he'd tried hard not to think of his grandmother as a murderer—three times over, to boot. But the facts were there in the journals and in her hand. This information had come to light only because of the sudden and unexpected appearance of Magdalena, Wilhelm, and Johann. What his grandma had done, and why, had just begun to sit better with him. Like his father, he was experiencing the full range of emotions working their way through him Though short of acceptance, he was resigned to what she'd done. It was obvious there had been extenuating circumstances, and he found solace in these.

On their last night together—with the Germans, his father, his siblings, and him sitting around the dining table—Magdalena had recognized Grandma Jeanne's plight. She'd summed it up perfectly. Hadn't she essentially said she shouldn't judge Grandma Jeanne since she couldn't know what she herself would've done in her place?

With the passing of time, and reflection, his appreciation for what the Germans had brought about was changing for the better. Plus, Magdalena had sent a couple of letters. In the first, she'd conveyed her and her brothers' thanks. In the second, she'd expressed—after much thought, she'd said—her admiration and respect for what Jeanne had done, considering the situation.

Sounding a bell above, the front door opened. A rush of cold air hit John. He looked up and caught his breath. Two young men stood in the doorway. John had no problem recognizing them. With a smile on his face, he pushed himself up and took a step toward them.

His sons headed in his direction and came to a stop a few feet away.

"Hi, boys," John said. "Thanks for coming."

"Hi, Dad," his sons said flatly, almost in unison.

"Come and sit down." John gestured welcomingly, a smile on his face. "I have a story to tell."

Sean shot a glance at the table and, with a toss of his head, asked, "What's with the tree?"

John's eyes slowly brimmed with tears. "Like in the Great War, a Christmas truce isn't a Christmas truce without a Christmas tree." With the backs of his hands, he wiped his eyes, and then, his voice cracking, he murmured loudly enough that his sons heard, "If not for the Germans ..." He swallowed hard, unable to finish.

"Germans? What do Germans have to do with this?" Brian asked.

John took a second to compose himself and then reached out and pulled his sons to him. "Everything, boys—everything."